AEGEAN FATE

AEGEAN FATE

JUELLE CHRISTIE

CHAPTER 1

The air was balmy, and the light was gradually fading from the sky. The heavens were a soft shade of yellow, perfectly highlighted by a vibrant hue of orange, covering the island of Santorini like a celestial dome. In a few minutes, the island would be covered in darkness, only to be illuminated by artificial lights.

Her lungs burned as she ran through the narrow streets of Fira, but she had to keep going. She had to keep running, despite the intense soreness of her muscles and push through the pain. She screamed to her friend, who was running at full speed ahead of her, "Kate! Slow down! It's me—Giselle. Slow down! Wait! It's me!"

Why was Kate running from her? It was confusing; she could not make sense of it. She had seen only the back of Kate, but undeniably, it was her friend. The woman running ahead of her had on the same white shirt and faded, fitted jeans that she'd worn on the night she'd disappeared. The satin blue and white scarf, knotted around her neck, appeared to be the same scarf that Kate had bought in Athens. The shape of the woman running ahead of her was a carbon copy of her friend. The woman's hair was swept up in a ponytail, and it swung from side to side like a horse's tail as she ran down the narrow path.

"Kate, wait! It's me—Giselle! Please stop running!" Her words got choppier as her body drained of energy. Her nose and throat felt dry. Why was Kate doing this? After all, it was only a misunderstanding. Sure, tempers had flared and words were exchanged in anger, but it was nothing that they couldn't get through as friends. She, Kate, and Valerie just needed to sit together and work through the pain, listening to each other and accepting responsibility for their words and actions. Essentially, the root of the anger was hurt. Their friendship had weathered many challenges, and they had come through on the other side stronger than ever. This was no different, at least she hoped.

Kate took a sharp left turn and ran down the narrow path. She bumped into an elderly man and almost knocked him to the ground. Surprisingly, there was no one else around, almost as though it were a ghost town. Giselle found the last bit of strength left in her and accelerated toward Kate, closing the gap between them. The remaining light in the sky rapidly disappeared.

Kate suddenly slowed and came to a halt, her back still turned to her friend. Giselle slowed then stopped a couple feet behind Kate. She bent over momentarily, trying to catch her breath. "Kate, why were you running from me? Val and I have been looking all over for you. We've even gone to the police."

Kate's back was still to her. She continued, "Thank goodness you're alive and safe."

Giselle placed her right hand on Kate's right shoulder. "Kate, look at me."

Kate slowly turned. Giselle instantly screamed, the high pitch of her voice piercing through the still air. Her worst fear had come true. Her screams ricocheted off the buildings. Who would have imagined that their eagerly anticipated girls' trip would have led to this moment?

CHAPTER 2

"Hurry up! We're going to miss our flight," Kate shouted as she motioned to her friends to walk faster. Kate briskly walked toward the check-in counter, with her luggage in tow, as she maneuvered through the crowd. Kate's friends, Giselle and Valerie, caught up with her and joined her in line. There were several travelers ahead of them, and it was obvious that Kate was getting anxious.

"Relax, Kate," Giselle said calmly. "We'll make it to the gate on time. We're not going to miss the flight."

"I hope not," Kate replied. "If we do, we can both thank Valerie."

"Hey. When you have kids, you'll understand," Valerie defended herself. "It's not easy with a two-year-old. Bridget was crying her eyes out this morning and throwing a tantrum. I feel sorry for Donald, who has to handle Bridget alone for ten days. In fact, I should not even be going on a girls' trip. I don't know why I let you two talk me into it."

"Oh my goodness, Valerie. Are we going to have to listen to you complain during this entire trip?" Kate rhetorically asked with annoyance.

"Am I complaining?" Valerie asked, as she focused on Kate. The tension built, and it was palpable.

"Okay, ladies. Let's not start this trip off on the wrong foot," Giselle interjected. "We're going to Greece for crying out loud. This is going to be an amazing trip, so please let's not ruin it." Giselle wheeled her luggage forward as the line got shorter, and her two friends did the same.

After a few seconds, Kate's expression softened, and her body relaxed. "Look, Val. I'm sorry that I raised my tone, and I apologize for my sarcastic words. I've been looking forward to this trip, and I was worried that we would miss the flight, but it's no excuse. I'm sorry."

Valerie smiled at her friend, but the strain was still evident on her face. "I'm sorry too. I've never left Bridget before. I also don't want Donald to feel overwhelmed. Bridget has become a handful these days. Donald encouraged me to go on the trip, but I can't help but feel a little guilty. But I don't want to ruin the trip for you both." Valerie forced another smile. "We're going to have an amazing time in Greece," Valerie continued, and it appeared as though she were trying to convince herself of this.

Giselle placed her arm around Valerie and assured her that everything was going to be fine. "Donald is an amazing and fully capable father, and you don't give him enough credit. He'll be fine. You can check up on them as often as you need to when we're in Greece, and Kate and I will understand." The friends steadily moved toward the check-in counter, and they were almost at the head of the line. Giselle looked at her watch as the hands of the clock face approached the check-in deadline.

They checked in with a few minutes to spare. Then they hurriedly made their way through New York City's bustling JFK airport. The friends emerged through the security line unhindered, and they made it to the gate about fifteen minutes before boarding was scheduled to begin. The area surrounding the gate was crowded with travelers. Most of the seats were occupied, and some were selfishly occupied with bags. There were some travelers seated on the carpeted floor as they awaited the boarding call. Giselle had enough time to use the restroom, and she maneuvered her way in the direction of the ladies' bathroom. The line there was a little longer than she'd hoped for, but she took the chance.

After washing her hands, she observed her reflection in the mirror. Her long, dark curls framed her face and fell onto her back. She focused her attention on her hazel eyes. Life had returned, and her eyes were no longer dead. They were no longer filled with discouragement and despair. She was ready to start a new chapter in her life. There was no way she would have considered going on a girls' trip one year ago or maybe even three months ago. She had come a long way, and now she was ready to have fun and enjoy life again. She smiled at her reflection then exited the bathroom.

Boarding was announced, and after about forty-five minutes, all of the passengers had taken their seats. Valerie occupied the aisle seat, Kate the window, and Giselle was stuck in the middle. It was a full flight.

A few minutes later, the flight attendants had taken their places, and the attendants gestured with their hands as a male voice delivered safety instructions through the intercom. The plane glided down the tarmac. Giselle's attention waned, and the voice through the intercom faded into the background. She lay her head on the headrest and closed her eyes. A few minutes later, she felt her body tilt backward as the plane ascended toward the heavens.

Giselle's thoughts shifted to that terrifying night last year when she was kidnapped and held hostage in a dilapidated motel. She did not think she would make it out alive. Her attacker, Jerry Frye, had been someone she was romantically involved with, and fortunately, the police arrived before he could slit her neck. He'd caused tremendous heartache and pain for the other victims' families. Jerry had framed an innocent person, and his actions resulted in the death of three people. In an effort to escape his past, Jerry was able to change his identity and integrate back into society. Valerie, the infamous matchmaker, had set him and Giselle up. Slowly, cracks started to appear in the relationship, and Giselle's intuition told her something was wrong. Her curiosity and determination to find the truth had threatened to tear down his façade, ultimately placing her life in danger. The trial had taken a toll on her body. In the end, Jerry was put on death row for his heinous crimes.

Giselle had received a letter from Jerry after he was placed behind bars, and she felt conflicted. In her mind, she knew he deserved to be punished. But there was good in Jerry. He was shaped by his unfortunate environment, and he was riddled with pain. She knew he was remorseful and capable of change. The letter shocked Giselle. She'd read it at least fifty times and had memorized it to the point that she could see the words clearly etched in her mind.

"Dear Giselle, I hope that you are doing well despite all that I have put you through. I want you to know how truly sorry I am, and I hope you can find it in your heart to forgive me. I want you to know that the good moments that we spent together were not a lie. I loved you, and I still love you. You are a beautiful person inside and out. You deserve only the best in life. I pray that you find someone who will love you and treat you the way that you deserve to be treated. Please do not let me ruin your hope for love. There are good people in this world, and there is someone out there designed for you. Keep smiling, and continue to be the good person that you are. God bless. —Jerry."

Giselle wondered how Jerry was coping in prison. She wondered about his mental and emotional state. It had been a tough road for her, and she wondered where she would have been if not for the help of her therapist and her family and friends. After the terrifying ordeal, she'd had vivid nightmares. Sometimes she would wake up in a cold sweat, and her heart would feel as though it were beating out of her chest. Sometimes, she would experience debilitating flashbacks throughout the day. She constantly tried to keep herself occupied because it kept her mind off of her kidnapping and her near-death experience. Her idle mind tended to wander, and her work was a blessing in disguise.

At first, Giselle did not want to let on to others that she was experiencing these crippling thoughts and nightmares. She would constantly put on a brave face, and she would walk with self-assurance, but inside, she wanted to cry. She wanted to scream at the top of her lungs. Her repressed emotions were bubbling up inside of her like hot lava, and they needed to escape. After a long day at work, upon entering her apartment, her body collapsed from all the emotional weight it was carrying. She'd sat on the hard laminated floor and cried for hours. She found herself constantly on guard with strangers. Dating was the last thing on her mind, and she would quickly turn down any admirers or potential suitors. She could no longer put up a façade, and her loved ones were able to see through her masquerade. Her parents and friends urged her to seek counseling, and she'd finally heeded their advice. Giselle went through intense cognitive behavioral therapy, and she'd experienced positive results. She no longer felt incapacitated when her thoughts revisited her experience. She'd started to go out with her friends more and enjoy life again. She was not going to let that experience define the rest of her life.

Giselle looked at Valerie, who was fast asleep. Valerie was one of her closest friends, and they'd first become acquainted about four years ago, when Giselle had moved to New York City from Shreveport, Louisiana. She'd met Valerie Brooks at a book club, and there was almost an instant connection. They spoke, what seemed endlessly, about the book selected by the club for the month of April. Their personalities meshed well, and Valerie became her first friend after her move to the Big Apple.

Valerie worked as an associate at a firm on Wall Street. Her goal was to one day be vice president or maybe even president of the firm. She did her undergraduate studies at Howard University and received her bachelor's degree in business administration. Valerie excelled in her studies, and she was also the head of the African American Business Club. She met her husband, Donald Brooks, toward the end of her sophomore year in college. Donald was Valerie's first serious boyfriend, and by the end of her last year in college, they had tied the knot. Valerie got into the prestigious MBA program at Columbia University, which precipitated the move to New York City. Bridget was born about a year after Valerie began working on Wall Street. Valerie had met Jerry Frye when she was a second-year associate. She was the catalyst who brought Jerry and Giselle together. Valerie was an infamous matchmaker, and she had struck once again. She truly believed that Giselle and Jerry were a great match, and she was shocked to find out the crimes Jerry had committed, especially toward her dear friend. Valerie blamed herself for putting her friend in harm's way, and Giselle constantly had to remind her that she was not at fault.

Giselle again looked at Valerie, who was deep in sleep. It was almost as though her friend desperately needed the vacation. It was a wonder that Valerie's brown skin was flawless. Bridget was cute as a button, but her tantrums and outbursts often overshadowed her cuteness. The word "no" was the predominant word in Bridget's vocabulary, and it often echoed within the walls of the Brooks' residence. Bridget was constantly getting into mischief, which led Valerie to often ask herself where she had gone wrong. Giselle had to remind her that Bridget was going through a stage and would grow out of it. Valerie had abandoned the selections recommended by the book club and was consumed with reading parenting books. One full day in the presence of Bridget was exhausting, and the experience made Giselle question whether she wanted kids. Frankly, she did feel sorry for Donald, who had to take care of Bridget alone for ten days.

Kate was fully engrossed in a romance novel. The front cover had an image of a shirtless Fabio sensuously embracing a brunette, and the woman appeared to be in a trance. Kate's blonde hair was brushed up into a loose ponytail, and she adjusted her reading glasses as she focused her attention on the words on the page.

Giselle met Kate Davenport approximately three years ago, when their paths crossed at work. Kate worked in the forensic department, and she specialized in forensic DNA. Giselle was in another department working with forensic trace evidence. They were on a case involving a woman who was found mysteriously dead in her apartment. They worked tirelessly on the case, which ultimately led to the capture of the perpetrator, who was the victim's stepson.

Giselle had introduced Kate to Valerie one evening, when she'd invited both of them to her apartment for dinner. It was a wonderful night filled with talk and laughter, leading to a new friendship between Kate and Valerie. Since that time, the three friends engaged in a monthly girls' get-together. It usually involved dinner at one of their apartments, but occasionally, they would have a night out on the town.

The flight attendants wheeled carts of drinks down the narrow aisles. Kate ordered a Bloody Mary and Giselle ordered a Coke. Valerie was temporarily awoken with enough time to order a Diet Coke before falling back asleep.

Kate was looking forward to igniting a romance in Greece. She had an on-and-off boyfriend, and currently, they were off. Kate had made it clear to her friends that she had no interest in settling down any time soon. She viewed her twenties as a time to explore and have fun. She worked hard and she played hard.

Giselle, on the other hand, was still not ready to date. Although she had come a long way in her recovery, she still was distrustful of the opposite sex. She realized that her thoughts were unhealthy, but she could not help how she felt. Maybe she needed a little more time, or maybe it would take the right person to change her mind.

Giselle reclined her seat and closed her eyes. There were still ten hours of flight time remaining.

CHAPTER 3

The plane touched down at Athens International Airport at 4:35 pm, local time. Giselle was exhausted from the long trip, and the muscles of her back felt tense. It was 9:35 am in New York City. The plane taxied to the gate, and a male voice coming through the intercom welcomed the passengers to Athens. The weather was described as sunny, and the temperature was 76 degrees Fahrenheit. The moment the seatbelt lights went off, passengers stood from their seats and congested the aisles.

Valerie stretched her arms out and yawned. She'd slept the majority of the flight, and she'd awoken only to consume the meal and snacks. Kate had dozed off a couple of times, but she'd spent most of the travel time reading her novel. Kate placed a bookmark between the pages and closed the book. She had only a few pages remaining.

After exiting the plane, the friends followed the directed path through customs then toward baggage claim.

"This is so exciting," Kate said with a wide grin.

"It is exciting," Giselle concurred. It was the first time she'd traveled outside of the United States. Kate had been to Mexico and a few of the Caribbean islands. Valerie had spent a summer in Paris as part of an exchange program when she was in college. She and her friend, who was also in the program, had taken a train to London, where they'd spent a few days taking in the sights.

The travelers surrounded the baggage carousel, and some hovered over the belt in anticipation of their belongings.

"I should call Donald to let him know that I arrived safely," Valerie stated. "I don't want him to worry."

"The only one worrying is you, Val," Kate commented. "Can we at least make it to the hotel first?"

"Kate, if Valerie wants to call her husband to let him know that she arrived safely, then please allow her," Giselle interjected.

Kate raised her arms with her palms out to indicate that she was backing off. "Okay. Okay. I'm sorry. I will not get in between you and Donald. I just want you to let your hair down. Enjoy yourself. Live a little. At least for the next ten days. Think about it," Kate paused. "When you get back to New York, it will be all work. Work responsibilities, wife responsibilities, mother responsibilities. This is your chance to be free of responsibilities."

Valerie pondered Kate's words. "You're right. This is my time to relax. I'll call Donald when we get to the hotel. Maybe we can–"

"There's my bag," Giselle interrupted. She grabbed her navy blue luggage and pulled it off the carousel. Kate and Valerie both retrieved their luggage, and the three friends made their way outside of the airport through the automated double doors. Giselle observed the Greek flag high above on a pole. It was a beautiful day, and a light breeze brushed against her skin. A row of taxicabs was parked awaiting prospective passengers. A lanky man exited the driver's side of a yellow taxi and waved in their direction.

"Ladies, do you need a taxi?" he shouted in a heavy Greek accent. He was a tall, middle-aged man with a full head of dark, thick hair.

"Yes, we do," Kate replied in a raised tone.

The taxi driver hurriedly made his way toward them and grabbed a couple of the bags. He opened the trunk and placed the luggage inside. He retrieved the other bags and placed them in the trunk.

The women sat in the back of the taxicab. "Why am I always in the middle?" Giselle joked. "Next time, one of you will have to take the middle seat."

"Where to?" the driver asked as he buckled his seatbelt. Kate gave the driver the address to the hotel, and the taxi made its way toward the airport exit.

Giselle observed the vast expanse of scenery. She was looking forward to sightseeing, but first, she needed a warm shower, a nice dinner, and a good night's sleep. Valerie had dozed off. Her head nodded, which briefly jerked her out of her sleep.

"So where are you ladies from?" the driver asked, interrupting the silence.

"I'm from New York," Kate readily shared. Kate was always one to engage in conversation.

"Ah. New York. One day, I must visit New York. Huge skyscrapers. Times Square. Broadway. It would be a dream come true."

"It's a great city," Kate said with pride. "Born and raised."

"What about you? Are you from New York?" the man asked as he looked at Giselle in the rearview mirror.

"Not originally," Giselle responded hesitantly. She was tired and would rather forgo the conversation.

"Where are you from? Don't be shy," the man continued.

"I'm from Louisiana."

"New Orleans?"

"Baton Rouge. I grew up in New Orleans," Giselle answered. She hoped the driver would end the questioning.

"Ah. New Orleans. One day, I must visit." The man paused then continued. "Mardi Gras. Is that where the women lift up their tops for beads?" The man briefly released his hands from the steering wheel and pretended to lift his shirt up. "Have you ever gotten beads?"

Kate was amused and laughed. Giselle, frankly, did not see the humor, and she did not think that his question warranted a response.

"What did I miss?" Valerie asked. She was awoken, likely from Kate's piercing laughter.

"Mardi Gras is a Carnival celebration. The celebrations typically go on for two weeks and end the day before Ash Wednesday." Giselle observed the driver through the rearview mirror as she spoke. "The biggest and most exciting parades occur during the last five days of the Mardi Gras season, and some of them are family and kid friendly."

"Ah, I see. But some of the parades, the women lift up their tops for beads, right?" The man again released his hands from the steering wheel and pretended to lift up his shirt before putting them back in place. Kate again erupted in laughter.

Please let us get to our hotel in one piece, Giselle thought. Kate inquired about fun and exciting things to do in the city, and the driver was happy to share his knowledge. Giselle looked at Valerie, who was fast asleep again. It always amazed her how Valerie was able to fall asleep at the drop of a hat. It did not matter where or when. In fact, Valerie could probably fall asleep in a standing position.

"There's the Acropolis of Athens," the man stated, as he pointed his index finger forward. Giselle observed the citadel located high on an elevated rock formation. The Parthenon was visible in the distance. Giselle woke Valerie, who became excited at the sight of one of the world's greatest and most well-known monuments. Valerie took out her camera from her bag and took some pictures.

The taxi made its way in the direction of their hotel, and they encountered some traffic. Another twenty minutes elapsed before the taxi driver pulled into the front of the hotel. Two bellmen instinctively made their way to the taxi. They each opened a back passenger door and welcomed the guests.

Kate paid the taxi driver, and he thanked her. "I hope you enjoy Greece, my new set of friends. Maybe I'll see you all one day in New York." The man hopped into the driver's seat of the taxi, and he was on his way.

The bellmen placed the luggage on a cart, and one wheeled the cart through the hotel's automatic sliding doors. The friends followed and made their way to the check-in counter. A petite woman greeted them with a welcoming smile. After checking in, they took the elevator to the fourth floor. The door opened, and there was a large, ornate mirror in front of them. Giselle caught a glimpse of herself, and she definitely needed a brush for her unruly hair. She fingered though it as she tried to tame her curls. The halls were covered with blue carpet, and they followed the number directions on the walls to room 413.

Valerie used her card key to open the door, which revealed a simple room that appeared clean with two full-size beds. The bellman removed the luggage from the cart and placed the bags against the wall. Valerie gave him a tip to which he was appreciative. He wished them a fun time in Greece and waved them goodbye before closing the door behind him.

Valerie fell face forward onto one of the full-size beds. "I'm so exhausted," she grumbled almost incoherently through the sheets.

"I don't know how," Giselle joked. "You've been sleeping since we left New York."

"I'll drop Bridget at your apartment for a weekend, and we'll see if it's still a joke. You would try to catch up on sleep at any possible opportunity too. I feel like I've barely slept since I gave birth."

Giselle and Kate laughed at Valerie's misery. "It's not funny guys," Valerie complained. "One day, you'll both have children, and you'll hopefully be walking in my shoes. In fact, I hope that you have a Bridget to the tenth power."

Giselle and Kate laughed again at their friend.

"So, how are we going to do this sleeping situation?" Giselle asked, as she switched the subject.

"Val will have her own bed in Athens, and we'll share," Kate answered. "Then in Mykonos, I'll have my own bed, and you two will share. Then in Santorini, Giselle, you'll have your own bed, and we'll share."

"Sounds fair," Valerie responded, which was again barely audible with her face buried into the sheets.

Giselle zipped open her navy blue suitcase and pulled out a short, pink and white striped pajama set. "That sounds great. Now let's order room service. I'm starving. Then, I want to take a warm shower and retire early to bed. Tomorrow will be a fun-filled day of sightseeing."

CHAPTER 4

Giselle and her friends had an early start the following morning. By 8 am, they were downstairs in the lobby, and they went to the dining area for a complimentary breakfast that was part of the hotel package.

The concierge had provided information on several tours, and the friends had decided on a walking tour of the Acropolis and a bus tour that would take them around the city of Athens and Ancient Corinth.

They boarded the tour bus, which stopped within walking distance of their hotel. The third stop was Syntagma Square, where they would get off and meet up with their tour guide. Most of the seats were occupied with tourists of different races and ethnicities. Giselle and her friends walked down the narrow aisle of the air-conditioned bus toward the last row that had five unoccupied seats. A flashy middle-aged couple sat in front of them and spoke rather loudly. They were evidently Americans judging from their thick New Jersey accent.

"Say cheese," Valerie instructed as she pointed her camera toward Giselle and Kate. It was almost as though Valerie was infused with new energy that she was devoid of before. Giselle and Kate huddled toward each other and smiled into the camera. "One more picture," Valerie said as she clicked the button again. She then handed her camera to Giselle and posed for a solo picture.

The Acropolis stood high above on the sacred rock, and it was the true symbol of Greece. The Parthenon was visible, and it was indeed a sight to behold. Giselle peered through the window, and the view from the bus was mesmerizing. She experienced an exhilarating feeling, and she was anxious to walk on the soil that was filled with history dating back centuries. The bus stopped at Syntagma Square, and a male tour guide welcomed the tourists as they exited the bus.

"Good morning. Good morning," the tour guide stated repeatedly in a Greek accent, as each tourist stepped off the bus. The passengers gathered closely around the tour guide, who was now the main focus of attention. "Good morning, again, and welcome to Syntagma Square. My name is Nikolas Konstantopoulos, and I will be your tour guide." Nikolas was about five foot ten, give or take an inch, and he looked to be in his early to mid-fifties. He had dark, curly hair that was thinning in the front, and his skin was bronze colored and almost leathery, likely from many years of exposure to the rays of the sun. "Today, you will experience a monumental part of Greek history. I will give you an informative history lesson, and I am open to questions. There's no such thing as a stupid question. Please, I want this tour to not only be informative but also enjoyable. This is a walking tour, and it will last approximately three hours."

Nikolas scanned the group gathered, almost as if he were counting them one by one, then he offered a smile. "So, we are standing at the most important square in Athens. The name *Syntagma* means *Constitution*. The square was constructed in the early nineteenth century after King Otto, the first king of Greece, moved the capital from Nafplio to Athens in 1834." Nikolas described the military uprising that took place in the Greek capital on September 3, 1843, leading to the first Constitution of Greece, and the square being renamed Syntagma Square from its original name, Palace Square. Nikolas then spoke about Hellenic Parliament, which was the parliament of Greece that overlooked Syntagma Square. Nikolas pointed out the Tomb of the Unknown Soldier, below the Hellenic Parliament, which was a memorial dedicated to the Greek soldiers who were killed during war.

Giselle observed the guards, also known as Evzones, who stood erect. They did not appear to move a muscle. Nikolas described the attire worn by the Evzones who guarded the Tomb of the Unknown Soldier, the Presidential Mansion, and the gate of Evzones camp. The attire included a cotton kilt, known as a Foustanella, and a scarlet fez with a long, black, silk tassel. They wore red clogs with black pompoms and held a bayonet-fixed weapon. Nikolas encouraged the group to return, if possible, to witness the changing of the guard. Behind the Parliament was the National Gardens. Nikolas allowed the group an opportunity to take pictures.

"Now, please follow me," Nikolas said with a smile. He turned and walked in the direction of Plaka, the old historic neighborhood of Athens. The group followed Nikolas as their leader, and they turned down Ermou street. "For all of you shopaholics, this is the place to be," Nikolas noted with a grin, as he faced the group. "This is the main shopping street in Athens. It contains all of the big international-name shopping stores." Nikolas turned and guided the group down the street.

"I can't believe you're wearing a fanny pack," Valerie whispered into Giselle's ear. Kate evidently overheard, and she and Valerie started to snicker.

"What's wrong with a fanny pack?" Giselle asked. "My hands are free, and my belongings are secured around my waist. Also, I don't have to worry about my handbag being snatched off of my shoulder."

"Okay. My hands are free too," Valerie stated as she switched her brown leather purse to her other shoulder. "And we're in Greece. No one is going to snatch your purse off of your shoulder." Valerie had teamed her purse with navy blue shorts, a white T-shirt, and brown sandals. Her brown skin was smooth, but her face was slightly oily around the T-zone. Her dark hair was combed back and secured with a jaw clip.

Kate wore a white cap, and her blonde ponytail fell slightly below her shoulders. She wore jeans shorts, a gray T-shirt, and black sandals that exposed perfectly French-pedicured toenails. She carried a small, black purse that she wore crisscrossed over her shoulders. "We definitely have to come back and indulge in some retail therapy," Kate commented before stopping momentarily to gaze through one of the store windows. The group continued down Ermou street, which was crowded with locals and tourists.

"I can't believe you two decided to wear sandals. It would have been better to have worn sneakers," Giselle remarked. She wore khaki shorts with her sneakers and a white T-shirt. Her dark curls were secured in a loose ponytail with tendrils framing her face. Nikolas stopped, and the group did the same.

"This is the Church of Panagia Kapnikarea," he informed the group. "It is an Orthodox church, and it is one of the oldest churches in Athens. It was built in the eleventh century." Nikolas noted that the Orthodox church was the predominant church in Greece. He talked for several minutes about the history and the architecture of the church. "Are we ready to move on?" Nikolas asked.

Giselle zipped open her fanny pack and pulled out a small tube of sunscreen hidden in one of the pockets. She squeezed out a quarter-size amount of lotion onto her palm and placed the tube back into the pocket. She rubbed her hands together and distributed the sunscreen over her olive-toned skin. The high was predicted to be 86 degrees Fahrenheit.

After walking a few more minutes, Nikolas stopped again. "Now, we're in Plaka," Nikolas announced. "Plaka is the oldest section of Athens. It is also known as the Neighborhood of the Gods, given its relation to the Acropolis. Adrianou is the largest and most central street in Plaka." Nikolas led the group though the picturesque neighborhood intersected by stone-paved narrow streets. There were numerous shops, cafés, and restaurants lining the streets. The Plaka neighborhood was nestled in the arms of the Acropolis, lying at its northern and eastern slopes.

The group passed a café, and the aroma emanating from that direction activated Giselle's salivary glands. She'd had a relatively large breakfast, but she was looking forward to an authentic Greek dish for lunch.

"Now it is time to climb the steps of the Acropolis," Nikolas said with excitement. "Is everyone ready?"

"Yes!" the group responded almost simultaneously.

"Are you ready for the hike up?" Giselle asked, as she turned toward Valerie.

"Yep, but I wish I'd worn sneakers," Valerie stated with regret.

Giselle and her friends followed the tourists in front of them and made the ascent. Roughly thirty minutes elapsed before they made it to the top of the Acropolis. They went into the Acropolis through the Propylaea, which was the opulent entranceway into the temple complex.

Nikolas stopped, and the group gathered around him. "Behold the Acropolis of Athens standing 490 feet above sea level. This citadel was inhabited as far back as the fourth millennium BC. The Acropolis was a military fortress during the Neolithic period. Look out as far as the eye can see." Nikolas extended his right arm, and the group looked outward. "Look at the view of Athens, and look outward at the sea. You can see why this would be a great military fortress. In 480 BC, the Persians destroyed the Acropolis during the battle of Salamis. Pericles was a Greek statesman, and he was the founder of Athenian democracy. Pericles made the Acropolis into a city of temples during the Golden Age, with the most famous being...", Nikolas paused.

"The Parthenon," a few of the tourists said, almost in unison.

"Ah, the Parthenon. A symbol of Ancient Greece and democracy." Nikolas gave a detailed history lesson about the Parthenon. He then paused. "Does anyone know the goddess that the Parthenon was dedicated to?"

"Athena," an enthusiastic tourist responded.

"That's right," Nikolas acknowledged. "Athena is the virgin goddess of wisdom, reason, intellect, literature, and war. She was heroic and fought only for a purpose." Nikolas paused again. "Does anyone know who was the father of Athena?"

"Zeus," the same enthusiastic tourist responded quickly. The man smiled and was clearly proud of his knowledge of Greek mythology.

"That's right again," Nikolas acknowledged. "Zeus was the god of the sky. He was the ruler of the Olympian gods." Nikolas observed his followers. "Now let's make our way to the Temple of Athena Nike." Nikolas turned, and the group followed closely behind on the rocky terrain. There were other tours going on simultaneously, and some individuals explored the sights on their own. Nikolas stopped again, and so did his followers. He educated the group about the history and the architecture of the temple.

Nikolas then led the group to the Parthenon. "Behold the Parthenon," Nikolas stated with excitement.

Giselle looked in awe at the sight of the Parthenon. At that moment, she felt as though she were a part of history. She allowed her imagination to take her to that period in time when this great monument was erected. *What was it like in the fourth millennium BC?* she thought.

The enthusiastic tourist raised his hand and asked a question about the Ottoman Empire. Nikolas readily answered, and he also spoke about the wars that were carried out on Greece's soil. "So, let's move on, shall we," Nikolas stated. "The Parthenon is a Doric order of architecture. It is erected on a platform of three steps. There are eight columns facing the front and eight in the back. There are seventeen columns on each side. The columns carry an entablature. The foundations are made of limestone, and the columns are made of Pentelic marble. Each piece of the Parthenon is unique." Nikolas paused again. "Now, I will allow you the opportunity to explore the Parthenon on your own and take pictures. If you have any questions, please don't hesitate to ask."

Nikolas then led the group toward the Erechtheion, situated on the north side of the Acropolis. Nikolas stopped, and the group did the same. He informed them that the ancient temple was dedicated to Athena and Poseidon. Nikolas spoke extensively of the architecture of the temple. He noted the religious functions carried out in the temple. He spoke enthusiastically of the contest involving Athena and Poseidon over who would become the Patron of the City. Poseidon, the god of the seas, struck a rock powerfully with his trident, and streaming water burst forth, but the water was salty and not beneficial to the people. Athena struck the ground with her spear, and an olive tree grew. An olive tree was considered a symbol of peace and prosperity. Athena was declared the winner, and the city of Athens was named after her.

The group was then allowed to roam freely for thirty minutes before reconvening at a designated point. The tour ended after a visit to the Acropolis museum.

Giselle and her friends had worked up an appetite. They decided to return to the Plaka neighborhood and try out the café that had given off that mouth-watering aroma. They requested to sit outside, and the waiter directed them to a round table shaded by an umbrella.

"I'm starving," Giselle commented, as she opened the menu.

"Me too," Valerie chimed in. The friends looked over the menu.

The waiter introduced himself as Elias, and he placed a plate of bread and black olives in the center of the table. "May I start you ladies off with some drinks aside from water?"

The friends each ordered a soft drink. Elias left the table, then he returned with the drinks.

"Are you ready to order?"

"What do you recommend?" Kate asked.

"I must say, you can't go wrong with anything on the menu. But, if you haven't tried fried Greek cheese, it's an absolute must."

"Fried cheese?" Valerie said with a quizzical look.

"Yes. It's absolutely delicious. You take a large slice of cheese, and you flour it, then you pan sear it at a high temperature until it is golden brown on both sides."

"That sounds delicious. Should we get it as an appetizer?" Giselle asked, directing the question to her friends. Kate and Valerie agreed.

"Great choice. Are you ready to order your meal, or should I give you a few minutes?"

"Yes, we are," Kate responded. "I'll have the moussaka."

"Excellent choice. And for you?"

"I'll have the lamb and beef gyro," Giselle stated.

"Superb choice. Our gyros are one of a kind."

Valerie ordered the chicken gyro. Elias collected the menus and promised to be back shortly with the fried cheese.

The Plaka neighborhood had a lively atmosphere. The friends engaged in conversation, and they observed the people walking by, which were a mixture of locals and tourists. Elias returned with the fried cheese, and he recommended that they top the dish off with a squeeze of lemon. The famous Greek appetizer did not disappoint, and the friends debated for a few seconds whether they should order another serving. The consensus was to forgo a second order of the appetizer and save room for the main dish.

Elias returned to their table. "What do you think, ladies?"

"One word. Delicious," Kate answered.

"I'm glad you ladies enjoyed it. Your meals will be out shortly." Elias took the empty plates and walked inside. A few minutes later, he returned with a tray that held up their meals, which each came with a Greek salad, then he placed the dishes on the table accordingly in front of them. "Ladies, I hope you enjoy." Elias retreated inside the café.

Giselle took a bite of her gyro, and it was delicious. Kate and Valerie also enjoyed their meals. Elias checked on them periodically, and after about thirty minutes of them receiving their meals, each of their plates was cleaned.

"I see that you ladies did not enjoy your meals," Elias joked, to which the friends laughed. "May I interest you in dessert?"

Giselle and Kate declined dessert, but as always, Valerie found room, even if it sometimes meant not finishing the main course.

"I'd like to see the dessert menu," Valerie stated.

"May I suggest the galaktoboureko. It is made with custard in a crispy pastry shell."

Valerie replied, "I think I'll have the baklava. I can't come to Greece and not have baklava."

"Still an excellent choice," Elias acknowledged. He took the menu from Valerie. "I'll be back shortly."

Elias returned with a small plate of baklava. Valerie indulged in the dessert and shared it with her friends. The friends thanked Elias for his wonderful service, and they paid for their meal.

They walked down the narrow streets of Plaka, visiting a few shops and picking up some souvenirs. Kate bought a satin blue and white scarf that had an image representing Athena.

The friends enjoyed their leisurely walk through the historic neighborhood, which had a lot of character and charm. They boarded the tour bus at one of its many stops and spent the rest of the afternoon visiting other historical sites, such as Panathenaic Stadium, the Arch of Hadrian, the Temple of Olympian Zeus, and the Olympic Stadium of Athens. The following day, they were booked on a tour to Ancient Corinth.

CHAPTER 5

The next morning started similarly to the previous day. Giselle and her friends were in the lobby of their hotel shortly after 7 am. They walked into the dining area, where they were seated for the complimentary breakfast. The selection offered a delectable variety, from pastries and breads to tasty cuts of meats, such as ham, salami, and pastrami. Fresh tomatoes, black and green olives, and a selection of cheeses were decoratively laid out on a wide platter. An assortment of fresh fruits was colorfully displayed on another platter. A large bowl contained cartons of a variety of cereals. There was a hot bar with a grill, and the enthusiastic chef was willing to prepare eggs as requested. A separate table, towards the wall, held up containers of caffeinated and decaffeinated coffee, cartons of milk on ice, hot water, and bottles of juices, such as orange, apple, pineapple, and cranberry. There was a rectangular wooden container that housed a wide variety of neatly organized, individually wrapped tea bags.

Giselle joined the modest line at the hot bar. There were three people in front of her, and they had already provided the chef their orders. She watched as the chef multitasked on the grill. He whipped up some scrambled eggs on one corner and fried another egg in the same corner. He effortlessly flipped over two pancakes, then he dipped some bread in batter before placing it on the grill.

"What may I get for you?" the chef asked Giselle, with a warm smile. The chef on duty the previous morning had prepared her a mean omelet, and she was hoping that this chef would do the same.

"I'll have an omelet with provolone cheese, spinach, mushrooms, tomatoes, and a little bit of feta cheese, please."

The chef diligently went to work on her order. When he was finished, he slid a perfectly folded omelet onto a plate. Giselle thanked the waiter then made her way to the table with the assortment of breads and pastries. She placed two slices of sourdough bread on her plate and filled a small bowl with fruit. She then maneuvered her way to the table, where Valerie and Kate were already seated with their plates.

"The waiter over there brought us a pot of coffee," Kate said with a wide grin. "He's kinda cute too."

"Kate, I swear. You are boy crazy," Valerie stated, as she shook her head. "I don't even want to know what you were like in high school."

"Valerie, you're jealous because you're trapped during the prime time of your life, and you wish that you could be as free spirited as me."

"Being married with a child is not being trapped. Many women would love to be in my shoes with a loving husband and a family."

Kate ignored Valerie's comment. "So, Giselle, what do you think of him?"

"Which one?"

"Three o'clock position. Tall, dark brown hair."

"Oh, him. He's cute. I think he looked over here."

"I think you're right," Kate responded. Her grin widened, and her eyes lit up. "Look, I think he's coming over."

"Hello, again, ladies," the waiter said in a Greek accent. "I see your friend has joined you." The waiter smiled, which revealed a perfect set of white teeth. "Is there anything else that I can bring for you lovely ladies? Some pastries? Some more coffee? Some–"

"We're fine," Valerie interrupted.

"Okay. But please do not hesitate to ask if you need anything. My name is Maximilian." The waiter flashed another heart-dropping smile that accentuated his deep dimples.

"So tell me, Maximilian, do you bring all of the guests coffee pots?" Kate asked with her face beaming. "As I look around, I do not see coffee pots in front of the other guests."

"Well, to answer your question, no I don't." Maximilian grinned broadly at Kate, again revealing his perfect teeth that almost did not seem real. It was quite evident to her friends that Kate was basking in the attention, and she was sapping it up like a sponge.

"My name is Kate, by the way."

"It's a pleasure to meet you, Kate. And who are your lovely friends?"

"I'm Giselle."

"It's a pleasure to meet you, Giselle." Maximilian looked in Valerie's direction, waiting for a response. Several seconds of silence elapsed.

"I'm Valerie."

"Well, it's an absolute pleasure to meet you too, Valerie. So again, if there's anything I can do for any of you, please let me know." Maximilian smiled again, then he walked away.

"He is scrumptious," Kate stated, as she bit her bottom lip. Giselle looked at Kate, who seemed mesmerized, as she watched Maximilian walk away.

"Snap out of it, Kate," Valerie abruptly stated, as she simultaneously snapped her fingers. "We need to hurry up. The shuttle will be at the hotel in fifteen minutes."

The friends finished their breakfast, then they hurriedly walked outside. A white shuttle pulled up in front of the hotel, which was scheduled to drive them to a location to board a coach bus to Corinth. The shuttle stopped at three other hotels to collect passengers for the tour.

About twenty minutes later, the shuttle pulled up to a station that had several parked coach buses destined for different locations in Greece. Shuttles unloaded passengers booked for the tours. Giselle and her friends made their way to the bus that had a large sign with the city "Corinth" inscribed with bold letters, parked between a bus headed for Thessaloniki and a bus headed for Delphi. The friends presented their tickets and boarded the air-conditioned bus. Valerie led the way, and she decided on a pair of seats that was midway down the aisle. She sat at the window seat, and Giselle sat on the aisle seat next to her. Kate sat on the aisle seat across from her friends.

The tourists filed one by one down the aisles, selecting their seats for the half-day trip. A few had a camera hanging down their neck, like a pendant, ready to capture a piece of history.

"How's Donald coping with Bridget?" Giselle asked her friend, as she tried to hide her smirk. She was torn between feeling compassion for Donald and being thoroughly amused. The thought of Donald running around like a headless chicken was entertaining.

"He's fine. At least I hope he is," Valerie responded with a loud sigh. "Actually, he's in over his head. I called Donald last night, and Bridget was screaming at the top of her lungs. I can picture Bridget's mouth forming a wide 'O' taking up half of her face and her uvula vibrating at rapid speed—not to mention the flood of tears streaming down her cheeks. Donald tried to assure me that he had everything under control and that Bridget was tired, but I could hear the distress in his voice."

Giselle could not hold her laughter in any longer, and it force-fully escaped her mouth like a carbonated drink from an opened can that had been shaken. She immediately looked around, almost embarrassed at the scene she had caused. "I'm sorry Val. I'm so sorry. I didn't mean to laugh," Giselle responded in a low tone.

"What are you two cackling about?" Kate asked as she leaned her body sideward into the aisle.

Giselle noticed a handsome male, of apparent Spanish background, seated by Kate in the window seat. The man reminded her of Antonio

Banderas in the movie *Desperado*, and she knew at that moment that Kate would be preoccupied during the remainder of the trip.

"Welcome," a man at the front of the bus said enthusiastically through a microphone. "If you're not headed to Corinth, then you're on the wrong bus."

The man paused briefly as he eyed the group with a smile. "Good. I take it that we all are on the right bus." The man was muscular with barely any body fat. His face, however, did not match his body, and the years were evident, judging from the wrinkles. He wore a white T-shirt that clung to his chest, accentuating his pectoral muscles. His khaki pants terminated at his knees, revealing large, muscular calves.

"My name is Alexander Stavros. I will be your guide for this tour to Ancient Corinth." Alexander indicated that the tour would last approximately six hours. The portly bus driver placed the bus in motion, and he turned right on a side street before making another right onto a main street. Alexander provided safety instructions, and he warned the passengers not to stand up or walk the aisles while the bus was in motion. He did note an exception to the rule. Alexander pointed out the lavatory that was located at the rear of the bus. He emphasized that it was available for those who needed to do "number one." It was available for "number two" only if absolutely and emergently necessary.

Alexander held the group's attention by filling the time with Greek history and mythology. He somehow managed to insert humor into his verbiage so it did not seem as though he were teaching a history class to his pupils. Alexander was lively and animated, and he almost lost his balance on the moving bus as he tried to reenact a fighting scene. He instinctively held onto a steel bar, which generated a wave of snickers throughout the bus. "And this is why we do not stand when the bus is moving, my friends."

The bus glided down the scenic shore of the Saronic Gulf. It was a beautiful day with barely a cloud in the sky. There were sailboats with billowing white sails that dotted the blue waters. Alexander explained to the group that the Isthmus of Corinth connected the Peloponnese peninsula to mainland Greece, and he noted that the Corinth canal ran through the isthmus. The bus stopped briefly, giving the tourists an opportunity to view the canal and take pictures.

The group boarded the bus again, which headed in the direction of Corinth. The drive was relatively short, under an hour and a half. The majority of the tour was spent visiting the archaeological sites of Ancient Corinth. Alexander noted that the piece of land that they stood on was where St. Paul preached to the people of Corinth in AD 51 to 52, which motivated him to write First Corinthians and Second Corinthians.

Giselle looked over at Valerie, who appeared to be in complete awe of the rocky terrain. "This is the soil where St. Paul walked," Valerie muttered under her breath. "I can't believe I'm here."

Valerie had been born into a staunch Catholic family, and she'd grown up in the Church. As a child, she and her siblings attended children's Bible school, and she'd been an acolyte. Donald, in contrast, could have counted on one hand the number of times that he'd stepped foot in a church before meeting Valerie. After much convincing on Valerie's part, Donald accepted an invitation to church. The priest had preached a fervent and inspiring sermon that had broken down the walls that Donald had erected up until that point. A flood of tears and emotions had escaped his body that had been bottled up for so long, and he'd felt as if a heavy weight had been lifted off of his shoulders. From that moment onward, Donald had dedicated his life to God, and he'd been an active member in the Church.

The group visited the Temple of Apollo and the archaeological museum of Corinth. The tour took them close to Acrocorinth, the acropolis of Ancient Corinth. The tour then took them through Modern Corinth, which consisted of modern concrete buildings, restaurants, and cafés. The group was allowed to freely disperse for lunch, and the instructions were to meet back at the bus in forty-five minutes.

Most of the individuals in the group arrived at the designated spot in the allotted time, but there were a few stragglers who delayed their departure. The bus left to return to Athens almost twenty minutes past schedule. Alexander took an aisle seat behind the driver, and the group was left to themselves.

Kate was engrossed in conversation with the raven-haired man, with dark mysterious eyes, who sat next to her. The man wore his hair combed back and banded in a short ponytail at the nape of his neck. Every once in a while, a patch of loose strands would fall like a tassel over his face, and he would use the fingers of his right hand to rake through them and secure the loose strands behind his right ear.

The bus rolled into the station at almost half past three. The friends found their shuttle, and they were transported back to their hotel after the driver made two stops. They decided to spend the rest of the day leisurely walking through the city.

They approached the Church of Panagia Kapnikarea, and Valerie insisted on seeing the interior of one of the oldest churches in Athens dating back to the eleventh century. The ancient Byzantine church was situated in the bustling shopping district on Ermou street, and the church was a stark contrast to its modern-day surroundings. A sign displayed the visiting hours, and a camera symbol encircled with a red line through it indicated that photography was not permitted. They walked through the entrance into the church. There were several tourists roaming, and some were closely examining the architectural details.

Several minutes had elapsed when a man approached them and introduced himself as Deacon Kastellanos. The friends introduced themselves, and it was immediately apparent to the deacon that they were Americans. The deacon appeared to be in his early to mid-fifties, and his skin was pale, almost as though he had never seen the light of day. A pink, raised scar approximately two inches marred his right cheek. The deacon stated that he had a few minutes to spare, and he would gladly give them a tour of the church, to which the friends obliged. He specified his role in the church, and he informed them that he had been a deacon for twenty-two years.

Valerie was enthralled with the architecture, and she marveled at the paintings on the walls and on the ceiling. The deacon led them around the periphery of the church. He was soft spoken but still managed a commanding presence. Giselle had a keen ear for accents. There were some words that seemed a little bit off as the deacon spoke, but she could not quite pick up the origin of his accent. She was almost certain that he was not Greek. It seemed intrusive of her to ask while the deacon was detailing the history of the church.

Deacon Kastellanos invited the friends to a Bible study the following evening. The study would be in English, and it would be a great opportunity for tourists to interact with Greeks and have a full spiritual experience. He also indicated that there was a pick-up service, driven by a member of the congregation, that could pick them up at their hotel and drop them back off.

Valerie was apologetic. She conveyed to the deacon that she wished she could attend, but she and her friends were heading off to Mykonos the following morning. The deacon seemed disappointed, which was evident on his face. He stated that he had to leave, and he left almost as quickly as he had come.

Giselle stared at the door that the deacon had disappeared through, and the entire encounter seemed odd. Valerie voiced her regret. She wished that they had one more day in Athens so she could attend the Bible study.

Kate had had enough of the church, and she wanted to spend the remainder of the day engaged in retail therapy. They exited the church, and walked along Ermou street, visiting shops along the way. By the time they were ready to head back to the hotel, they each had shopping bags in both hands.

They walked into the elevator and ascended to the fourth floor. They made their way to room 413, and Valerie nose-dived forward onto the bed.

"Can we just order in?" Valerie mumbled.

"No. I made dinner reservations for the three of us for 8 pm, and you are not going to allow Kate and I to eat alone."

Reluctantly, Valerie detached herself from the bed and shuffled into the bathroom to take a shower.

The restaurant offered balcony seating with an amazing view of the Acropolis. They each wore maxi dresses with sandals. The friends were immediately seated at a table draped in a white tablecloth. A candle hidden in a holder flickered through the top opening.

The night was warm with a light breeze, and the ambience was calm and inviting. The view of the Acropolis was breathtaking, which shone like an ethereal light upward in the distance.

The waitress welcomed them, and she detailed the chef's special of the evening, which consisted of rosemary grilled lamb chops with mint jelly, a quinoa salad tossed with diced cucumbers, lemon, and dill, and a side of roasted butternut squash. The waitress filled their glasses with ice-cold water from a steel jug. She offered to bring a bottle of wine for the table, but Valerie declined. Kate ordered a glass of white wine. Giselle ordered a Coke, and Valerie ordered a Diet Coke. The waitress allowed them the opportunity to view the menu and indicated that she would be back shortly.

The waitress returned with their drinks. Giselle ordered the filet mignon, prepared medium well, with the truffle mashed potatoes. She ordered a small spinach salad coated in a light raspberry vinaigrette dressing and topped with almonds and cranberries. Valerie ordered the lemon garlic roasted chicken breast with rosemary parmesan red potatoes and buttery garlic green beans with toasted almonds. Kate ordered the sweet glazed salmon with garlic mashed potatoes and oven-roasted asparagus.

"Kate. Valerie. I want to tell you both that I'm so happy to be on this trip with you." Giselle looked at her friends and smiled. "You are more than friends to me. You are my family, and I don't know where I would be if it were not for the both of you. A year ago, I was living in an emotional state of hell that I thought I would never escape. Your love, support, and encouragement have gotten me through those difficult times, and I want to thank you."

"Giselle, you're going to make me cry," Kate replied. She reached over and gave her friend a hug.

"You're going to make me cry too." Valerie concurred. She stood and gave Giselle a hug from behind for several seconds before taking her seat again.

"It's something I had to tell you both. Many times, people don't take the opportunity to let their loved ones know that they are appreciated or simply tell them 'I love you,' and then it is too late. That near-death experience I had a year ago has made me realize that you can't take life for granted. Every breath is a gift. The individuals we hold dear to our hearts are gifts. We could be taken away from each other at any moment."

"Now that's making me sad," Kate commented. "I love you dearly, Giselle, but please let's not ruin the mood. We're here in Greece to have fun. What could possibly go wrong?"

CHAPTER 6

The friends boarded the ferry at the port of Piraeus bound for Mykonos, scheduled to leave at 8 am. They walked up the narrow stairway to the top level, and fortunately, there were three seats together, as most of the seats on that level were already occupied.

On schedule, the engine came to life, and the ferry started its departure from the shores of mainland Greece. The Greek flag flew high above on a pole. The temperature was 75 degrees Fahrenheit with a gentle breeze, and the high was predicted to be 88 degrees. About an hour into the ferry ride, Giselle stood and walked around on the open-air deck. She left Kate reading another romance novel, and Valerie was fast asleep. She rested her arms on the white railing and looked out at the boundless expanse of blue waters. The sea air was clean and refreshing.

Giselle thought about her life over the past year. Her thoughts often revisited those dark moments, and she often wondered if it was unhealthy. Thankfully, she was now able to cope with those memories, and she considered herself fortunate. She thought about Jerry Frye, who was on death row in Louisiana. The trial made the national news, and it was covered by every renowned newspaper and news network. Jerry's moment on the stand was bewildering and unexpected. His hard outer shell had cracked, and it peeled away in front of her eyes. The shame and deep remorse were evident, and she knew it was not a brazen act. He was a lost and misguided soul who had found the path of light in his darkest hours.

An officer at the Louisiana State penitentiary, whom Giselle considered more than an acquaintance, had informed her that Jerry was a counselor to many of the inmates. An hour a day, he conducted a support group that he called "Positive Men Not Anonymous" or "PMNA." The group started with three members but gradually increased to fourteen. It was imperative that the members first accept responsibility for their wrongdoings and remove the blame from everyone else so that they could move forward. They had to repeat the mantra "I am responsible for my thoughts and actions." Jerry led discussions about love, forgiveness, and spiritual healing. He often read and dissected verses from the Bible. He gave hope to those who were willing to repent but would never be granted the opportunity to leave the confines of the prison. He recited the story of the thief on the cross at the crucifixion of Jesus in Luke 23: 39-43. "One of the criminals who hung there hurled insults at him: 'Aren't you the Messiah? Save yourself and us!' But the other criminal rebuked him. 'Don't you fear God,' he said, 'since you are under the same sentence? We are punished justly for we are getting what our deeds deserve. But this man has done nothing wrong.' Then he said, 'Jesus, remember me when you come into your kingdom.' Jesus answered him, 'Truly I tell you, today you will be with me in paradise'."

It was 12:15 pm when the ferry docked at the port in Mykonos. It was an idyllic scene out of a dreamlike painting. The white buildings were captivating and charming. The friends exited the vessel and walked onto the soil of the Greek island. Kate was particularly excited about experiencing the "party island", and she frequently referred to it with that name. They caught a taxi that brought them to their hotel on a hilltop, and the location offered an amazing view of the Aegean Sea. The room was modest with two full-size beds and an outdated television. The rectangular infinity pool appeared to be one with the expanse of the sea.

Valerie suggested eating lunch at the hotel, but Kate was insistent on going to the hot spots where the young tourists hung out. The taxi dropped them off in the heart of Mykonos, which was swarming with tourists moving in every direction. The stark white buildings and cobblestone-paved pathways added to the charm of the picturesque island. Trendy stores and boutiques lined the narrow paths, and there were no shortages of places to eat.

Kate led the way into a restaurant that came highly recommended by the taxi driver. At their request, they were seated at an outside table that overlooked the water. The surrounding beauty was magical and almost unreal. The young brunette waitress, who could not be more than eighteen or nineteen, handed them a menu as she recited the special of the day.

Valerie ordered the fried Greek cheese as an appetizer, which she was dying to try again since their meal in the Plaka neighborhood of Athens. Kate threw in the zucchini fritters, served with tzatziki and a slice of lemon.

The waitress disappeared, and within minutes, she materialized with a basket of bread, black olives, a glass cruet filled halfway with olive oil, and three glasses of water. After going back and forth in her mind between two entrees, Valerie decided on the shrimp with tomatoes and feta served on a bed of angel hair pasta. Giselle and Kate opted for the special, Greek-style baked cod, served with spinach and rice known as spanakorizo.

The atmosphere of the restaurant was fairly lively but still generated a relaxed feel. A soft flow of music came through the door onto the outside dining area. The friends were in no rush to leave. They savored each bite and enjoyed the moment, thousands of miles away from their problems back home. The meal was absolutely delicious, which would describe every meal they'd had so far.

As usual, Valerie made room for dessert. A Greek custard pie baked to crispy perfection coated with syrup was the absolute way to top off a delicious meal. She consumed what seemed like every crumb from the appetizer to the dessert plate. Valerie knew that she had overdone it when she stood to leave with her friends. Her maxi dress clung to her midsection, giving the impression that she was at least three months pregnant. The thought of having another child briefly entered her mind and sent shivers down her spine. As much as she loved her daughter and would lay down her life for her, she could not bear the thought of having two Bridgets. In fact, Bridget more than likely would be an only child.

The friends roamed the town and adventurously went down some of the narrow side streets and alleyways. They encountered hidden corners conveniently tucked away from the hustle and bustle. They leisurely walked through the town for over an hour, which was enough time for Valerie to get rid of her baby bump.

The distance to the beach was relatively short, and they walked the sun-kissed streets in that direction. The beach was crowded with tourists and filled with sun beds and umbrellas embedded in the golden sand. From afar, two jet skis zipped across the surface of the water, leaving behind a trail of thick mist.

Unprepared to go for a swim, the friends found seating at a table next to the bar. The spot allowed a satisfactory view of the activities on the beach. The waiter took their drink orders. They were still content from their recent meal and had no desire to order anything else to eat.

The bar was seated to its capacity, and the occupants were putting away one alcoholic beverage after the next. Loud talk and laughter flowed heavily.

"My goodness. Do they not have any decency?" Valerie expressed in disgust. She shook her head as she observed two young women prancing along the beach wearing bikinis that left little to the imagination. The blonde wore a bikini top that barely could contain her enhanced assets. "They are literally wearing dental floss."

Kate laughed at her friend. "I love you Val, but sometimes you can be such a prude. We're in Mykonos. It's the place to be free and uninhibited. So relax. Let your hair down. Meet new people."

Kate turned her attention to the bar. "Speaking of meeting new people. Hello."

Giselle and Valerie immediately turned in the direction that Kate was gawking. "Not again," Valerie stated as she rolled her eyes. "Why can't we just enjoy each other's company? Why do we have to meet new people?"

Kate ignored her friend's questions. "I think he looked over here."

Kate was certain that the mystery man was making eye contact with her. About ten minutes elapsed before he walked a direct path to their table.

"Ladies, may I buy you a drink?" the mystery man asked. He was Caucasian with tanned skin and a full head of dark brown hair. He was about six-foot-tall and shirtless with well-defined ripples in his abdominal muscles. He was certainly no stranger to the gym. The man appeared to be in his early to mid-thirties.

"I'm Austin, by the way." Austin was evidently American based on his accent.

"I would love a drink," Kate responded without the least bit of hesitation. Giselle and Valerie declined the offer.

"May I sit down?" Austin asked. He sat in the seat next to Kate before obtaining an answer to his question. He snapped his fingers in the direction of the waiter, who obediently made his way to the table. Kate ordered a glass of white wine, and Austin ordered himself another beer. "So where are you all from?"

"We're from New York," Kate answered. She angled her body toward Austin, and she was fully engaged.

"Fellow New Yorkers."

"You're from New York too?" Kate asked. She had become even more intrigued.

"I'm originally from Boston. I've lived in Manhattan for almost four years. I also spend time out in LA. I have a pad out in the Hollywood Hills."

"Wow. What is it that you do?" Kate asked.

"I'm a real estate broker for multimillion-dollar properties. The commission on some of these properties would set you up for life. I'm very good at what I do." Austin leaned back into his chair and placed both hands behind his head. "So what do you ladies do?"

"My friend Giselle and I are both in forensics. Valerie works on Wall Street."

"Wall Street. Impressive. What do you do on Wall Street?"

Valerie reluctantly answered Austin's question, which was followed up by a series of other questions.

"My buddies and I are here in Greece to have fun, but I'm also here on business. I'm looking at properties on these Greek islands to build a luxury, state-of-the art hotel with breathtaking views overlooking the Aegean Sea." Austin went on about his plans before the conversation switched to a lighter discussion.

Kate and Austin seemed to have hit it off. Austin was obviously keen on telling stories, and she laughed at almost every word that came out of his mouth.

"So ladies. My buddies and I are going to the hottest club in town tonight. What do you say?"

"I don't think so," Valerie interjected.

"Come on. It'll be fun. You have to experience the nightlife in Mykonos. There's absolutely nothing like it."

"Come on, Val. It'll be fun." Kate brought out her puppy dog eyes, but Valerie did not budge.

"We'll talk about it," Giselle added. She was definitely on a continuum between her two friends. On a scale, Valerie would tip toward the prude end, and Kate would fall on the wild side. Giselle fell somewhere in the middle, which she considered a healthy balance.

"I hope to see you ladies tonight."

Austin placed some money on the table to cover the drinks and tip, then he stood. He gave them details of the club and indicated that he and his buddies would plan to be there between 10 and 11 pm. Valerie thought to herself, *That's already past my bedtime.*

CHAPTER 7

"Thank you, thank you, thank you so much for agreeing to go to the club," Kate said with excitement as she gave Valerie a tight hug.

"I would not say I agreed. More like I was forced."

"Agreed. Forced. Whatever you want to call it. Thanks for coming."

"So, what do you think?" Giselle asked as she exited the bathroom. She made a 360-degree turn, modeling her one-shoulder red dress.

"I love it. It hugs your curves in all of the right places," Kate said with excitement in her eyes. She removed a short black dress out of her suitcase. "What do you think? By that, I mean, Giselle, what do you think?"

"It's a cute dress." Giselle reached for the black dress and held it up. "Very cute. So what are you wearing, Val?"

"I'm between this dress or a pair of slacks with a blouse."

"Please tell me there's a third option in that suitcase," Kate pleaded.

"There is no third option. I only have maxi dresses, shorts, and shirts. So which one is it? Dress or slacks?"

Kate held up the dress. "Well, the dress is nice, if you're heading to church."

"Kate. Stop it. Please don't give Val a hard time."

"Okay. Okay. Go with the slacks. Or you can borrow one of my dresses."

"I will look like a cased sausage in one of your dresses. Thanks, but no thanks."

Kate laughed at her friend. "You're an absolute prude, but I love you." She reached over and gave her friend another hug.

"It's almost ten o'clock," Giselle stated, as she looked at her watch. "We need to hurry up. I'll call the front desk so they can call us a taxi."

Giselle hurried into the bathroom to finish applying her makeup. She wore her hair down, allowing her curls to fall freely down her back. She applied a light spray of perfume to both wrists and on both sides of her neck. It was a fragrance that she had worn for years, and it always generated complements.

"Whoa, Kate. You give a little black dress a new meaning. Can you even breathe?" Giselle teased.

"Yes, I can breathe. Maybe not cough or sneeze, but I can breathe." Kate finished her look with six-inch black heels. "You look nice, Val."

"Is that sarcasm?"

"No, it's not. I mean it. You look nice and classy."

"Well, thank you. That means a lot coming from you, Kate."

"You're welcome."

The phone on the side table rang three times before Giselle was able to get a hold of it. It was the front desk notifying them that the taxi had arrived. The friends grabbed their purses and hurried through the door.

The taxi was parked outside of the hotel. The driver held the door open as the friends filed into the back seat.

"I'm in the middle again," Giselle groaned.

The taxi made its way downtown. It was a full moon, and the light gave off an inauspicious vibe.

The town was effervescent and lively, and the nightlife was indeed one of a kind. The friends weaved their way through the crowd as they made their way to the club. They joined the long line for entry into the popular club.

They were in line for almost twenty minutes before gaining entry. Valerie felt as if she had stepped into another world, and she immediately felt like a fish out of water.

The DJ, who reportedly was a high-profile entertainer in the nightlife scene, had already gotten the crowd going. The strobe lights pierced the air with flashes of color from blue to green to purple to red and back to blue again. The DJ mixed a well-known dance hit, and the crowd went wild. The mainly young adult crowd energetically jumped up and down with their hands in the air to the loud, almost deafening music. A man leaped backward off of the stage and was luckily caught by several pairs of hands before being passed overhead from person to person. A stream of smoke ejected from the corners of the room.

"What am I doing here?" Valerie screamed into Giselle's ear.

"What did you say?" Giselle screamed back.

"I said, what am I doing here?"

Kate was evidently entertained, and she followed the crowd by putting her hands in the air. She swayed her hips, but her movements were limited by her close-fitting and unyielding black dress. Valerie was clearly not entertained, and she had her arms crossed with a look of boredom written all over her face.

"Loosen up," Kate shouted as she shook Valerie, hoping that she would knock her friend out of a dismal mood. Valerie's arms fell to her side. Kate grabbed her friend's waist and playfully moved it from side to side. "Let's get something to drink," Kate shouted.

"What?" Valerie shouted back.

Kate pointed in the direction of the bar. "Let's get a drink!" Kate interlocked her arms between her friends' arms, and she led them to the bar.

The power of the music was not as intense next to the bar, and the words spoken among the friends were more audible.

"Val, what would you like to drink? My treat," Kate offered with a wide grin.

"I'll have a Diet Coke."

"No you're not. I'm buying, and I'm not buying you a Diet Coke in the craziest, most happening nightclub in Mykonos. How about a Sex on the Beach?"

"A what?" Valerie replied, almost in horror.

Kate laughed at her friend. "Sex on the Beach. It's a cocktail with vodka."

"No, thank you. You know I don't drink."

"The Valerie who lives in New York with her husband and kid does not drink. But the Valerie in Mykonos, thousands of miles away from her life in New York, will have a drink."

Valerie did not budge.

"Oh, come on. Don't you drink wine in church? Didn't Jesus turn water into wine?"

"Kate, you know that's different."

"Everything in moderation. That's the key. I want you to loosen up and have some fun tonight." Kate offered to buy Giselle a drink, and her friend took her up on the offer. "Two Sex on the Beach and one strawberry daiquiri," Kate shouted to the bartender.

The bartender was busy, and he multitasked, knocking out one order after the next. He placed the three drinks on the counter in front of them. Kate passed the daiquiri to Giselle, and she handed Valerie the orange-colored cocktail. She lifted her glass. "Cheers to wonderful friends, and cheers to a night in Mykonos that we'll never forget!"

Valerie took a cautious sip of her alcoholic beverage. She immediately winced, and her tongue fell out of her mouth as though she were poisoned. "This is too strong."

Giselle looked up; Austin had materialized out of thin air. It was a miracle that he was able to locate them among the thick crowd. "Hello, ladies. Are you all having fun?"

"We're having the time of our lives," Kate responded, although she was clearly speaking for herself.

"Ladies. Let's get out on the dance floor and have some fun."

"You two go," Giselle suggested. "Val and I will sit here for a moment."

Kate was whisked off onto the dance floor. Austin stood behind her and secured his arms around her waist as they danced to the music.

Giselle observed three female partygoers who embarrassingly danced offbeat to the music. A shirtless man, who was undoubtedly intoxicated, held up an opened can of beer and poured it over his face before screaming to the top of his lungs. It was going to be a long night.

Giselle slurped up the remains of her strawberry daiquiri, and she realized that Valerie's beverage had not moved too much further down from where it started. A look of boredom had returned to Valerie's face, and she looked as though she would fall asleep at any moment.

A man sat next to Valerie. "You don't look like you're having much fun," he said.

Valerie turned her attention to the man who had invaded her personal space. He was a well-built black male who appeared to be in his early thirties. He was dark skinned with a shaved head, and he was impeccably dressed.

"This is not your cup of tea, is it?" the stranger continued. His accent revealed that he was British.

"No, it's not," Valerie answered.

"Well, it's not for everyone." A few seconds elapsed. "I'm Maxwell, by the way."

"Valerie."

"Is this your friend?"

"Yes, it is."

"I'm Giselle."

"It's indeed a pleasure to meet you both. So, where are you from?"

"We're from New York," Valerie answered.

"That's amazing. I absolutely love New York. I live in the UK, but if I lived in America, it would definitely be New York."

Valerie sipped her drink, but the burning sensation again hit her esophagus on the way down. She'd had enough, and Kate's money was going to go down the drain.

"I don't mean to be forward, Valerie, but you're quite lovely. Really, you are."

"Thank you."

"Would you care for a dance?"

"Look, Maxwell. I don't mean to be rude. You seem like a nice guy, but I'm not interested. I'm married."

"My apologies. Where is your husband, might I ask?"

"He's in New York."

"So, he let you come to a place like Mykonos without him?"

"What's wrong with that? I'm here on a trip with my best friends."

"I'm saying if I were married, there is no way in bloody hell my wife would be in a place like Mykonos without me."

"Well, my husband and I have a trusting and monogamous relationship."

Maxwell stood. "I hope you ladies enjoy the rest of your night." He disappeared into the crowd.

"Where is Kate?" Valerie asked. Kate and Austin were no longer visible. She looked at her watch; it was almost 1 am. "I'm actually ready to go."

"There's no way we are going to find her in that crowd. We'll have to wait for her to come to us."

"That could be hours."

Valerie looked again at her watch, and only fourteen minutes had gone by since she last checked the time. It felt like an hour.

Kate and Austin emerged from the crowd. "Oh my goodness. You don't know what you two are missing," Kate said excitedly.

"I'm ready to go," Valerie stated with an expressionless look.

"Come on, Val. Don't be a party pooper. It's only 1 am," Kate pleaded.

"I don't want to ruin your fun, but I'm getting tired."

"How about this? Why don't you two take a taxi back to the hotel, and I'll make sure Kate gets back safely."

Giselle looked at Austin and thought he was out of his mind. "No. We came together, and we're going to leave together."

"Austin, don't take this the wrong way, but we just met you." Valerie sided with her friend. "We came together, and we're going to leave together."

"I'm having so much fun. This party is just getting started." Kate was infused with energy and excitement. "I'll be okay. Austin's a nice guy. He'll get me home safely."

"I give you two my word. I will make sure Kate is back at the hotel in one piece."

"How much have you had to drink, Kate?" Giselle asked.

"Only one. The Sex on the Beach." Kate realized what she'd said and broke out in laughter. Her friends did not see the humor.

"Let that be your last drink. And, no sex on the beach," Valerie warned.

"I promise."

"Kate, are you sure about this?" Giselle asked.

"I'll be okay."

"She'll be okay," Austin added.

"Okay. If you insist." Giselle gave Kate a hug. "Enjoy yourself, and get back safely."

Valerie gave Kate a hug. "I love you, Kate."

"Don't get sentimental. I'll see you two back at the hotel in a few hours."

Giselle and Valerie caught a taxi that brought them back to their hotel. Valerie collapsed onto the bed, and within minutes, she was fast asleep. Giselle changed out of her clothes and removed her makeup. She curled into the bed and fell asleep. The peacefulness of the night passed by.

The light shone through the curtains, and the room was sunny and bright. Giselle looked at the clock on the nightstand, and the time read 8:13 am. Valerie was still in the outfit that she wore to the club, and she was in the same position that she was in when she collapsed onto the bed.

"Val. Where's Kate?"

"What?" Valerie mumbled, still in a state of sleep.

"Valerie, wake up." Giselle jumped out of the bed and shook her friend. "Kate's not here."

Valerie sat up immediately and wiped the sleep out of her eyes. "Did she not come back to the hotel? I knew we should not have left without her. I can't believe we left our friend with some stranger."

"Okay, this is not the time to panic. What do we do next? Maybe she has her phone on." Giselle took her cell phone out of her bag. "What if she doesn't have her phone set to receive international calls?" She dialed Kate's number, and it immediately went to voicemail. Giselle felt her heart racing, and she panicked. "Valerie, suppose something bad has happened to Kate."

"You just told me not to panic."

"I know, but some people are not who they say they are."

"Giselle, we have to focus."

"You're right. What do we do next? Should we go to the nightclub and ask around? Should we go to the front desk and have them call the police?"

The door opened, and Kate dragged herself into the room. "Oh my goodness. Last night was the most amazing night of my life."

"Kate!" Valerie called out. "You had us scared out of our minds."

Giselle hugged her friend. "Kate, we're so happy you're okay. You had us worried."

"I'm sorry. I didn't mean to make you worry."

Kate sat on the edge of the bed and took off her six-inch heels. She crossed her right leg over her left and rubbed her right foot. "Austin is the most amazing man I have ever met. After we left the club, we walked on the beach and talked all night. He is smart and funny, and he gets me. I feel like I've known him all my life. Maybe he's the one."

"You feel that way after knowing him for only a few hours?" Valerie asked dubiously.

"I know. Who would have thought that I would be open to settling down now? And he lives in New York. This must be a sign."

Valerie smiled at her friend. "That's good to hear that you're open to settling down. Who knows? Marriage might be in your near future."

"There's only one problem. His last name is Bate."

"So?" Giselle asked, puzzled.

"So, if we get married, my name would be Kate Bate."

Giselle and Valerie erupted in laughter. "Well, you could always go by Katherine," Giselle suggested.

"Katherine Bate," Kate thought out loud. "It does have a nice ring to it."

CHAPTER 8

Giselle and Valerie took a taxi to old Mykonos town and walked to Little Venice. They left Kate at the hotel to catch up on some sleep after a wild and fun-filled night.

They decided to eat breakfast at a waterfront café, and the waitress led them to a table right on the water's edge. It was a beautiful morning, and the air was fresh and clean. The water reflected different shades of blue, and the gentle waves splashed onto the rocks below them.

The waitress introduced herself as Helen, and she poured them ice-cold water from a jug then took their orders. They both ordered a cup of coffee, which was served almost immediately, with a basket of bread and a side of orange marmalade. The ambience was peaceful, and the windmills in the distance created the perfect backdrop. The waitress returned about fifteen minutes later with their orders. She placed a plate with three stacks of Greek yogurt pancakes on the table in front of Valerie, and next to it, she placed a bowl of fresh fruit. The waitress then placed a plate with a large slice of spinach quiche and two strips of turkey sausage in front of Giselle.

Giselle took a sip of the coffee, and the pleasant aroma awoke her senses. The warm liquid energized every muscle in her body. She looked around at the beautiful scenery, and she could not think of a better place to be at that moment. The serenity and peacefulness was almost indescribable. She felt a sense of calmness and freedom that she had not felt in a long time.

"This is the most beautiful place I've ever seen," Valerie commented, interrupting Giselle's thoughts. "I can't wait to see Santorini."

"Me too. I heard the pictures do not do it any justice."

"I would love to bring Donald here one day so that he can experience the beauty of this place. Maybe, when Bridget is a little bit older, and more behaved, we can come to Greece as a family."

"That would be nice."

"So, when will you start dating again?"

Giselle took a sip of her coffee. "I'm in no rush to date, but it would be nice to meet someone, when it's the right time. It has been difficult for me to trust, given my history with men, but I can't live that way. I can't live in fear." Giselle took another sip of her coffee. "It would be nice to get married one day."

"What about kids?"

"Ummm…"

"Why the hesitation?"

"Let's say I'll take it one step at a time."

"It's a wonderful thing to be married and have a child. Donald is the love of my life, and I would not trade my family for anything in the world. Sure, all relationships have their challenges, but it's a give and take. It's about compromise and treating your partner how you would want to be treated. Yes, I complain about the difficulties of motherhood, but it is still a joy. Don't get me wrong. Bridget still may be an only child unless she quickly gets out of this phase."

The waitress came to check up on them. The friends agreed to more coffee, and Helen poured them two piping hot cups. She took time to share the history of Little Venice with her customers. Helen pointed out the buildings lining the water's edge and informed her guests that the structures were eighteenth-century fishing houses that were converted to cafés, bars, restaurants and shops. She encouraged them to return to watch the sunset but warned about the crowds. The waitress suggested that they visit the windmills, which she pointed to in the distance.

They indulged in their coffee for almost fifteen more minutes, then they paid the bill and left. There was no rush to get back to the hotel, as they expected Kate to be out like a light for several more hours.

The town had not fully come to life yet, and they sauntered through the narrow streets and took in the culture. The friends meandered aimlessly down the cobblestone paths with no itinerary or agenda, and they allowed their curiosity to direct their footsteps.

It was almost 2 pm when they decided to grab a bite to eat before heading back to the hotel. They stopped by a café, and Giselle ordered a lamb gyro and Valerie ordered a chicken gyro. They placed a to-go order for a chicken gyro to bring back to Kate. The café was small and quaint. A young, affectionate couple dined in the corner. The man caressed his partner's hand, which rested on the table, as she looked adoringly into his eyes.

Giselle and Valerie sat at a table at the other corner of the small room. They quickly consumed their tasty meal and agreed that the food in Greece was one of the most enjoyable parts of the trip.

They caught a taxi that brought them back to the hotel. Unsurprisingly, Kate was still fast asleep with a black sleeping mask secured over her eyes. She was awoken by the sound of the door when it closed, and she removed the mask, unveiling heavy eyelids.

"We're back," Valerie announced. "We brought you something to eat."

"Thanks," Kate mumbled. "I'm still exhausted." Kate yawned loudly and rubbed her eyes.

"Maybe if you take a shower, it will wake you up," Giselle remarked. "We don't want you sleeping all day and up all night."

"You're right. I'll get up and take a shower."

"I was thinking we could go out to dinner at a restaurant in Little Venice on the waterfront," Giselle suggested. "We were told that that's the place to be to witness the most beautiful sunsets."

"Oh, I'm sorry. I meant to tell you. Austin wants to take me out to dinner tonight."

"Are you kidding me?" Valerie said with annoyance.

"I'm so sorry. Please don't be upset with me. Austin wants to spend some time with me, and I like him a lot."

Giselle let out a sigh. "We're not upset. We're disappointed."

"Speak for yourself. I am upset! This is supposed to be a girls' trip, but you would rather spend time with some guy instead of us."

"I'm sorry, Val. You and Giselle will have me all to yourself in Santorini. I promise. I want to get to know Austin a little more. This may get serious. Didn't you tell me that you would like to see me settle down?"

Valerie's annoyed expression did not change, and her arms crossed in front of her chest.

"But if you don't want me to go, I won't. I'll cancel plans with him."

Almost a minute passed before Giselle broke the silence. "It's okay. You enjoy yourself with Austin. Just be careful. We're in a foreign country."

Kate turned to Valerie and brought out the puppy dog eyes. "Val?"

"Fine. Giselle and I will eat dinner by ourselves."

"Val, please, don't be upset."

Valerie released her arms and allowed them to fall to her side. "I'm okay. I don't want to go through this in Santorini. The point of us coming here is to spend time with each other."

"This won't happen in Santorini. I promise. I give you my word."

"Okay," Valerie said with a smile. "Have fun and be safe. Here's something to eat. It's a chicken gyro."

"Thanks."

The friends spent the rest of the afternoon lounging at the pool. A cruise ship was visible in the distance, drifting on the waters of the Aegean Sea.

Later that evening, Giselle and Valerie got themselves ready for dinner. They called a taxicab that brought them to Old Town

Mykonos. Kate lagged behind for an hour after her friends left. She expected Austin to pick her up at the hotel.

The phone on the nightstand rang, and Kate picked the receiver up after the third ring. The front desk informed her that a man by the name of Austin Bate was waiting for her in the lobby.

Kate took one more look in the bathroom mirror and was pleased with the reflection. She had loosely curled her blonde locks, and her hair terminated below her shoulders. She thought to herself that the royal blue dress that she was wearing was a perfect fit. The halter neck revealed a hint of cleavage but was still tasteful. Although the dress was form fitting, it stopped below her knees, and it was classy in its own right.

Kate grabbed her silver clutch purse and exited the hotel room, then she took the elevator down to the lobby. She felt her heart racing and was surprised that she was experiencing butterflies in her stomach.

Austin was standing in the lobby with a bouquet of red roses. He gave her a kiss on the cheek, and she thought that his cologne smelled delightful. He wore a starched white linen shirt and khaki trousers with brown loafers. He held her hand as they walked out to the car that was parked in front of the hotel. Austin gave the bellman a tip, then he opened the passenger door of the silver Audi Cabriolet.

Kate slid into the passenger seat. Her date asked her whether she was agreeable to putting the top down, to which she agreed. The night was cool and comfortable. The car left the boundaries of the hotel, and Austin directed the car toward Old Town Mykonos. Kate's perfectly curled locks were blowing in the wind, and she was worried about the state of her hair when they arrived. Midway through the drive, she considered asking Austin to put the top back up but then concluded that if her hair was going to be a mess, the damage had already been done.

Austin pulled into a small parking lot in front of a restaurant, tucked away from the crowds. There were four other cars there. He opened the passenger door and helped her out. Kate pulled down her dress and blindly tried to tame her curls. Her date held her hand and led her into the restaurant. The light was dim, and the candles, which were perfectly centered on the tables, illuminated the room.

Austin had made dinner reservations, and the waiter led them to a table next to a window. The waves could be heard splashing onto the rocks. Kate pulled out a compact mirror from her purse and looked at her reflection. Aside from a few strands that were out of place, her hair had mostly fallen back into place.

The waiter handed each of them a menu and recited the special of the evening. Austin requested the restaurant's best wine to be brought to the table. They ordered appetizers and requested more time to view the dishes listed for the main course. The waiter asked if the couple were celebrating a special occasion to which Austin replied, "I'm celebrating being in Mykonos with a special lady."

Kate was tickled pink, and she was almost certain that she was blushing. The waiter returned and poured them each a glass of red wine.

"I'll have the rib eye, medium, with the truffle macaroni and cheese and the asparagus," Kate ordered. She closed her menu and handed it to the waiter.

"Sir, have you decided?"

"Yes, I'll have the filet mignon, medium, with the loaded baked potato and the Greek house salad."

"Superb. I'll be back shortly with your appetizers." The waiter took Austin's menu and walked away.

"You look absolutely stunning. That blue dress looks perfect on you."

"Thank you," Kate replied with a smile. "You're not so bad yourself."

Austin smiled at her, and she felt her heart drop. It was a strange feeling that she'd never felt before, at least not to this magnitude. Ordinarily, she would be the enticer, or better yet the heartbreaker, but there was something different about Austin that casted a spell over her. She often enjoyed the company of the opposite sex, but never had she experienced these butterflies. What was it about Austin that was so different? Yes, he was handsome, but she had dated many good-looking men in the past. Was it his assertiveness and confidence? He came across fearless with the world at his feet, and he seemed to have his life figured out.

The waiter returned with the appetizers. He placed a plate of golden fried calamari, also known as kalamarakia tiganita, in the center of the table, along with the house-made hummus with pita chips. He placed the Greek house salad in front of Austin. "Enjoy."

"This looks great," Kate remarked. She scooped up some of the calamari and placed it on a small plate. She then squeezed a slice of lemon over the squid. "This is delicious. Calamari is one of my favorite things to order, if on the menu, and sometimes it is a disappointment. This, on the other hand, is perfect. It is crispy and flavorful."

"Did I tell you how beautiful you look?"

"Yes, you did," Kate replied. She could not contain her sheepish grin, and she felt a warmth to her cheeks.

Austin was staring at her as though she were the only other person in the room. He held the stem of his glass and swirled the red wine before smelling it and taking a sip. "This is a vintage red wine from Bordeaux, France. It is one of a kind." He focused his attention on her, and Kate felt as though he could read her thoughts.

"It's delicious. This is the best red wine I have ever tasted."

Kate swirled her glass and took another sip. She was intensely aware that Austin's eyes were fixed on her.

"Only the best for you," Austin replied. A few seconds of silence elapsed. "Kate, I want to know everything about you."

"Okay. Where do you want me to start?"

"Wherever you would like to start."

At that moment, the waiter returned with his assistant with a large tray holding the main course. The waiter opened a fold-out stand, and the assistant placed the tray with the food on top of it.

"Please, be careful," the waiter warned. "The plates are hot." He placed a plate, with the sizzling rib eye in front of Kate and a plate with the sizzling filet mignon in front of Austin. "May I get you anything else?"

"No, that will be all for now," Austin answered.

The waiter removed the empty plate, which contained the calamari and the salad bowl with only a couple halved grape tomatoes and three pitted black olives remaining. "Enjoy."

Kate cut a piece of her steak and took a bite. The meat was juicy and tender, and the flavor erupted in her mouth. They savored their food before continuing their conversation.

"So, you were about to tell me everything about yourself. I want to know you inside and out."

"I don't know where to start."

"What's your middle name? Tell me about your family. Where did you grow up?"

"My middle name is Miranda. Katherine Miranda Davenport. No one calls me Katherine. Only my mother, when she was angry at me. Everyone else calls me Kate."

"Do you realize that if we got married, your name would be Kate Bate?"

Kate laughed along with her date. "No, I didn't think about that," she lied. She definitely did not want Austin to know that she was already thinking about marriage.

"Tell me about your family."

"So, I was born in Brooklyn. I grew up in Park Slope, and I now live in Lower Manhattan. I've lived in New York City my entire life. A true New Yorker at heart."

"I love New York City. There's no place in the world like it."

"I have one brother who's three years older than me. His name is Kurt. My brother still lives in our home in Park Slope."

"He lives with your parents?"

"No. My parents divorced when I was twelve years old. I've seen my father twice after that. He lives somewhere in Connecticut with his new wife. He has a daughter with her whom I've never met."

"And your mother?"

Kate took a deep breath. "My mother died a little over a year ago."

"I'm so sorry, Kate." Austin held her hand.

"It's okay. My mother and I didn't have a great relationship growing up. I felt like she always blamed my brother and me for our father leaving. I don't know why she would, but she was never the same after my father left. We constantly butted heads, and I thought that she had been the worst mother in the world. I couldn't wait to go off to college and leave the house. I barely spoke to my mother after I left. My brother still maintained a relationship with her, though. My mother used to send me Christmas and birthday cards, but I never responded. I didn't want much to do with her. Then, a little over a year ago, my brother told me that my mother was diagnosed with metastatic pancreatic cancer. She couldn't eat, and she had lost about thirty pounds in one month. She had gone into kidney failure, and her body was shutting down. She didn't want anything else done. My brother took her home with hospice. I went to see her, and I almost didn't recognize her. She was frail and gaunt, and she looked like she was wasting away. It was sad and depressing, and I broke down in tears. I knelt by her bed, and she placed her feeble hand on my cheek. I remember her saying, 'Hello, my dear Kate. I've missed you, and I love you.' Her voice sounded like a whisper. I told her that I loved her and that I was sorry."

"Is there anything else that I can get for you?" the waiter asked, interrupting the conversation.

"No. Not at this time," Austin responded. The waiter poured them another glass of wine from the bottle, then he left the table.

Austin noticed that Kate's eyes were welling up. "I'm so sorry, Kate. Are you okay talking about this?"

"I'm okay," Kate replied. She lightly dabbed her eyes and hoped that her mascara had not run. "That moment gave me an understanding of true forgiveness. I felt as though a heavy weight was lifted off of my body. The doctors gave my mother days to weeks to live. She died three days later. I was at her bedside when she passed. She closed her eyes, and that was it. She looked so peaceful. She's at peace above."

Austin caressed her hand. "I'm glad that you and your mother were able to mend fences. It must have meant a lot to your mother for you to have been at her bedside."

Kate smiled at Austin. She loved his sensitive and affectionate side. She pulled out her compact mirror and looked at her reflection. Her makeup was still intact.

Kate took another bite of her truffle macaroni and cheese, and the creamy richness stimulated her salivary glands. The food was divine, but the form-fitting dress was immovable, which became an indication for her to slow down. Also, she did not want to come off as a glutton. "So, tell me a little more about yourself and your family."

Austin swirled his glass and took another sip of the wine. "Well, I was born and raised in Boston. I am a die-hard Patriots fan and a die-hard Red Sox fan. My father is a big-time attorney in Boston, and my mother is a pediatrician. They've been married for almost thirty-five years. I have two older brothers. My eldest brother, James, is a high school math teacher. My other brother, Conrad, and I are big into business and real estate. We both studied business at the Wharton School of the University of Pennsylvania. Conrad and I have always been competitive growing up, and we still are. He graduated cum laude, then I graduated summa cum laude, and I remember him being so upset. It's always about who could sell the biggest, most expensive house or who could generate the most exclusive clients."

"You both are competitive."

"Yes. I think we're both ambitious and motivated. We have both done well in real estate. This business can make you wealthy if you play your cards right and play the game with the right people. Right now, I'm planning to build the best hotel on one of these Greek islands. I'm looking for the optimal property, and I have three areas in mind. My vision is an eco-friendly hotel with spectacular 360-degree views, state-of-the art amenities, luxurious rooms, and premium foods. This hotel will attract the most exclusive clientele such as dignitaries and celebrities."

"Sounds great. I'm impressed with your vision."

"You could be a part of it too." Austin swirled his wine and took a mouthful, draining his glass. "I'm looking for investors. I'm looking for individuals who have their eyes set on the prize, and this is going to be a highly valued prize. This is going to be an award-winning hotel featured in magazines, and it's going to offer the best in guest satisfaction."

"May I interest you in dessert?" the waiter asked.

"No thank you," Kate replied.

"Certainly. I would love to see the dessert menu."

The waiter gathered up the plates, then he handed Austin a dessert menu before walking off.

"Kate, are you sure you don't want dessert?"

"No, thank you."

The waiter returned about five minutes later. "I'll have the galaktoboureko."

"Marvelous. I will be back shortly with your dessert."

"As I was saying, I'm looking for investors. I predict that the financial return will be rewarding. I'm talking double, triple, or even quadruple the investment."

"How much of an investment are we talking?" Kate asked.

"The minimum is fifty thousand, but the more the investment, the more the reward."

Kate pondered Austin's words. He seemed to be a savvy, successful businessman, and it would be great to be a financial stakeholder of something so grand and promising. She'd been awarded $125,000 from a life insurance policy after her mother's death. Her mother had a $250,000 policy that was equally shared between her and Kurt. The money was sitting in a money market account generating interest of less than twenty dollars a month. She thought to herself that her money might be better off invested.

"I'll have to think about it."

"Absolutely. It's a big commitment. Do you know of anyone who might be interested?"

"I could ask Giselle and Valerie."

"Sir, your galaktoboureko." The waiter placed the crispy custard-filled dessert on the table in front of him.

"Thank you."

"You are welcome. Is there anything else that I can get for both of you?"

"No, thank you," Kate answered.

"That will be all for now."

The waiter smiled and walked away.

"You have to try this dessert," Austin stated. He cut a piece with his fork and fed it to Kate.

"Delicious," Kate remarked. "So, you also have a house in LA?"

"Yes, I have a house in the Hollywood Hills with an amazing view of the skyline. Have you been to LA?"

"No, I've never been out west. I would love to go to LA and Las Vegas one day."

"I'll take you there. Just say the word."

Kate smiled at Austin, who was smiling back at her. She had never met anyone quite like him.

"So, what are you and your friends doing tomorrow?"

"I think we're going to relax. Maybe go to the beach."

"I would like to take you and your friends out on a yacht."

"Are you serious?"

"I'm serious. A buddy of mine rented a yacht, and we're planning on setting sail tomorrow with a handful of friends. What do you say?"

"That sounds amazing. Count us in," Kate said with excitement. "Wait, I'll first have to ask Giselle and Valerie."

"Of course. It'll be fun."

The waiter returned to the table, and Austin requested the check.

CHAPTER 9

Valerie took a sip of her orange juice. It was a beautiful morning, and an occasional light breeze brushed against their breakfast table on the hotel balcony. "Let me get this straight. Austin has a yacht?"

"Well, not exactly. His friend rented a yacht, and he's having a small get together. He's invited us."

"I don't know, Kate," Valerie continued. "I'm not in the mood to interact with strangers."

"Come on. It'll be fun. What about you, Giselle?"

"I'm okay with it, only if Val is willing to go. Otherwise, I say we spend the day together at the beach."

"Val, have you ever been on a yacht before? This is an opportunity to sail the waters in luxury." Kate brought out the puppy dog eyes again, and she hoped that Valerie would break.

Almost a minute of silence elapsed, and Valerie appeared to be in deep thought. "Fine, but you promise in Santorini that we'll spend time together, just the three of us."

Kate's eyes lit up. "You have my word. Austin said the yacht will set sail at noon and that we should be at the marina by 11:30. We should hurry. It's almost 10:00."

They finished their breakfast and got ready for the day excursion. Kate emerged from the bathroom in a tiny black bikini. "This little number is sure to get Austin's pulse racing," Kate commented with a wide grin. "Val, is that your grandmother's bathing suit you're wearing?"

"Kate, enough with the jokes. There's nothing wrong with my one-piece bathing suit."

Giselle covered her aqua bikini with a white beach wrap dress and secured her fanny pack around her waist. "Are you ladies ready to go?"

Kate and Valerie covered up with wrap dresses, and the friends were on their way. They took a taxi that dropped them off at the marina.

"I thought you said it was a small get-together," Valerie remarked as they walked toward the dock. There was a large group of people loitering on the dock, awaiting to board the luxury yacht named *Valiance*. There were already some partygoers on board. A young male in his twenties stood on the bow of the vessel with his arms outstretched to the side, shouting, "I'm the king of the world!" like Jack Dawson in the movie *Titanic*.

The ratio of women to men was drastically out of proportion. There was a gathering of bikini-clad women interspersed with men. The partygoers, who were still on dock, boarded the yacht along with the three friends. Austin Bate parted the crowd and walked toward them.

"Glad you all could make it," Austin said with excitement. He greeted Kate with a hug and a kiss on her cheek. He gave Giselle and Valerie a hug. "So, what do you think? Isn't this yacht absolutely amazing?"

"It certainly is," Kate remarked, as she looked around at her surroundings.

"I didn't expect so many people to be here," Giselle said. "Kate told us it was a small get-together."

"We have to do it big. This is Mykonos," Austin responded, as he extended his arms. "Can I get you ladies something to drink? Champagne?"

"No thanks," Valerie answered.

"I'm okay for now. But thank you," Giselle replied.

Kate took Austin up on his offer, and Austin left them to get her a glass of champagne. He returned a few minutes later with a male friend; he had a glass of champagne in one hand and a beer bottle in the other. "This is my buddy, Blake. He's the big shot who rented this yacht." Austin, in turn, introduced them to Blake.

"My, my, my. Aren't you ladies lovely," Blake commented. "I'm glad you made it. This is going to be one heck of a party."

Giselle looked at Valerie, who was clearly not impressed. Kate, on the other hand, was eager to get the party started.

"Ladies, it was nice to meet you. I'm going to check on a few things."

Blake dismissed himself. He weaved his way through the people gathered and disappeared among them.

The music came through the speakers, and the people who had gathered became fueled with more energy. The yacht moved away from the dock and sailed into the Aegean Sea. A male, who appeared to be in his late twenties or maybe even early thirties, popped open a bottle of champagne, and the contents erupted. He aimed the projectile alcoholic beverage toward a handful of bikini-clad women in close proximity, and the women screamed and laughed. The man then tilted his head back and poured the remaining champagne directly into his mouth.

Austin placed his arms around Kate's waist from behind and rested his chin on her right shoulder. "May I borrow Kate for a moment?" he asked. Before Giselle and Valerie could respond, he had whisked Kate away.

"Do you think I would make it to shore if I dived off now?" Valerie asked Giselle, who in turn laughed at her friend.

"We're stuck on this yacht for a few hours, so we might as well enjoy ourselves."

"Shrimp cocktail?" a server asked, as she balanced a tray with her right hand.

Giselle and Valerie both reached for a shrimp and dipped it in the cocktail sauce. There were other servers carrying trays with hors d' oeuvres.

The yacht sailed on the waters for about thirty minutes before it anchored. The alcohol flowed freely, and there were several party-goers who had had one too many. Some of the young men and women jumped off of the yacht and splashed into the water, and a handful did dives and flips. There were two obviously drunk women who took off their bikini tops and swirled the tiny articles of clothing in the air.

"It is a pleasant surprise to see you here," a voice said in a British accent. "Valerie, correct?"

Valerie turned, and her eyes fell on a shirtless man standing directly in front of her. It was Maxwell from the club.

He pointed at Giselle and had a reflective look. "Giselle, right?"

"That's right," Giselle answered.

"Man, I'm good." Maxwell smiled, evidently impressed with his memory. "You ladies seemed bored at the club. I'm quite surprised, actually, to see you both here."

"To be honest, we would much rather be somewhere else," Valerie responded.

"Since you're here, care to dance?" Maxwell asked, with his attention focused on Valerie. He had a broad smile, and his teeth were extraordinarily white. His dark skin glistened under the rays of the sun.

"No, thank you," Valerie replied.

"Oh come on Val. Don't be so stiff. Let your hair down."

"It's Valerie, and I'm not stiff. I don't feel like dancing."

"One little dance."

"No."

"Come on. Let me see your dance moves." Maxwell started to gyrate his hips, and he motioned with his hands for Valerie to join him.

"Look here, British boy. For the last time, I'm not interested, so get lost!"

"Whoa. You're a feisty one, aren't you?" Maxwell held his arms out as to indicate that he was backing off. "I'll leave you two ladies alone." Maxwell walked away and joined a small group of five that had gathered.

"Val, I've never seen that side of you before. You scared him away," Giselle commented with a look of surprise.

"That's the point. Now, where did Kate disappear to?"

"You are stunningly beautiful," Austin acknowledged as he gently moved the strands of hair that fell over Kate's face. They stood, facing each other, and the top of Kate's head leveled off around his shoulders. She looked into his eyes, and time appeared to stand still.

"Sorry to take you away from your friends and the party," he continued. "I wanted to spend some time alone with you away from everything."

Austin had taken Kate down some windy, carpeted stairs and down the hall into a room that was evidently a bedroom. A queen-sized bed was made up with cream-colored sheets and a comforter that appeared to be of high quality. Decorative pillows were meticulously placed at the head of the bed. A small circular table held up a tray of cheeses and fruits and a bottle of champagne. There were three small ceramic plates with hors d'oeuvres. A cylindrical glass vase contained a single red rose. Austin took the rose and removed the petals, and he scattered the petals on the bed.

Austin pulled out one of the armless chairs, and Kate sat down. He sat down on the chair opposite her. He opened up the bottle of champagne, and a mist of bubbles escaped.

What would Giselle and Valerie think if they knew I were in this provocative situation with Austin? Kate thought. After all, she had just met him, but she had never met anyone like him. The ambience was romantic, and it was just the both of them, even though there were at least one hundred people on board the vessel.

"I thought about you all night. I'm so happy that you made it."

Kate felt herself blushing. "I thought about you too last night."

"I could remain in your presence forever. You're an amazing woman, Kate."

Kate was almost speechless, which was unusual. "Thank you," she giggled sheepishly. *Get a grip of yourself, Kate,* she thought. Austin was staring directly at her. He smiled at her, and her heart instantly melted.

"So, did you give any more thought to the hotel investment? This hotel is going to be one of a kind. We're going to get a return on our investments and make a shitload of money."

"I did give it some thought. I mentioned it to Giselle and Valerie, but they weren't interested."

"So, what are your thoughts?" Austin asked, then he took a sip of champagne from his glass.

"Well, I think it sounds like a great investment, and you seem like the perfect person to invest with. You've had a lot of experience, and you're a successful businessman."

"Thank you," Austin responded with a smile.

Valerie had advised Kate to look at the business plan before nose-diving into a major investment. Kate had considered investing $50,000 of the money she'd received from her mother's life insurance policy.

"Do you have a business plan?" Kate asked.

"Of course I have a business plan," Austin replied with a smile. "I'm a businessman. That's like asking a painter if he has a brush or a medical doctor if he has a stethoscope." Austin took another sip of his champagne. He told Kate about marketing plans, industry trends, and tactics to create a competitive edge. He gave a financial analysis and the expected return of investment. Austin was rattling off numbers like a mathematical genius, and Kate was impressed. He promised to provide her with hard data to substantiate his claims.

"From what you're telling me, how could I not want to be a part of something so great? I'm in," Kate said confidently.

"Great!" Austin's eyes lit up. It was evident that he was passionate about the project.

Kate leaned in to feed him a strawberry. He reciprocated by taking a bite, then he went further by cupping his lips around her index and middle fingers. The warmth and moistness of his mouth and tongue were erotic and titillating. He stood up and held her left hand with his right. He led her to the bed adorned with red rose petals. Austin sensuously kissed her in a way that she'd never been kissed before. She fell captive to his power.

CHAPTER 10

The ferry left the port of Mykonos and was bound for the idyllic island of Santorini. A light rain started the morning, and now the sun was out and the clouds had scattered. The gray overshadowing of the skies had transformed to a soft shade of blue. The friends were seated below deck with Giselle seated in the middle. Almost every seat had been occupied. "I've been looking forward to going to Santorini since we bought the tickets," Giselle commented to her friends.

"Me too," Valerie agreed. "I think Santorini may be more my speed. Mykonos was a little bit too wild for me." Valerie leaned forward and angled her head toward Kate, who had her head buried in a romance novel. "Speaking of wild, where did you and Austin disappear to on the yacht? You were gone for a while."

Kate lowered her novel and smiled, which transitioned to a wide smile. There was definitely something hidden behind that mischievous grin. "We took some time to get to know each other better."

"Okay, what does that mean?" Valerie probed.

"It means we got to know each other better." Kate answered, evidently avoiding the question. "What did you two do?"

It was obvious that Kate was not willing to go into further details. "Well, Val gave a guy a piece of her mind," Giselle replied with a laugh, as she recalled the incident. "We met him before at the club, and he definitely had eyes for Val."

"Val, what did you say to him?"

"She said, 'Look here, British boy. For the last time, I'm not interested so get lost!'"

"Val, please tell me you didn't say that."

"Yes, I did," Valerie acknowledged with no regret. "He wouldn't get the hint, so I had to be blunt about it."

The ferry hit a rough patch of water, and the vessel swayed for several seconds. In front of them, a toddler seated on his mother's lap let out a high-pitched scream, then cried uncontrollably despite his mother's calming efforts. The mother opened a diaper bag and pulled out the magical pacifier, then she inserted it into the child's mouth. He immediately stopped crying. His long eyelashes were wet and clumped together, and the tears were still present on his cherubic cheeks.

God bless the person who invented the pacifier, Valerie thought. Her mind temporarily shifted to Donald and Bridget, and she wondered what they were doing. "I'm so glad it'll be just the three of us having fun for the next three days. No other people and definitely no men," Valerie commented. "Right?" She looked again at Kate.

"Right, Val. I gave you my word."

"Okay. I take you at your word."

Approximately two hours and forty minutes elapsed, then the ferry pulled into the port of Santorini. They exited the vessel with their luggage and hailed a cab to take them to the hotel. The island was as beautiful as Giselle had imagined. In fact, it was even more beautiful. The pictures of Santorini that she had looked at on the internet were absolutely beautiful but nothing compared to seeing the island in person. The caldera cliffs and the whitewashed buildings added character to the beautiful Greek island.

The taxi pulled up to the whitewashed hotel, which had an amazing view of the blue waters of the Aegean Sea. The warm sunshine, gentle breeze, and beautiful scenery created a peaceful paradise. Their bags were handled by the bellman, who wore starched white pants and a royal-blue linen shirt. There were a handful of tourists in the open-air lobby who were either checking in or lounging on the wicker chairs.

A middle-aged woman warmly greeted the friends; she was dressed in all white with the exception of the black, clumsy-looking shoes on her feet. Her black hair revealed strands of gray, and her hair was combed into a bun. Her thin lips appeared even thinner when she smiled. She offered them a choice of cucumber water or watermelon and mint water, which were already poured into glasses on a tray on a circular table covered with a white table cloth. The friends opted for the cucumber water, which was cool and refreshing.

They joined the short line for check-in to the hotel. The hotel clerk welcomed them with a broad smile that revealed prominent gums. The clerk entered them in a hotel raffle offered to all of the guests at check-in. The raffle was drawn once a week, and the lucky winner received a prize that ranged from a free night's hotel stay or a full course dinner at the hotel restaurant, Aphrodite, or a day cruise for two, just to name a few. Breakfast was a complimentary buffet open from 6:30 am to 10:30 am.

The bellman helped them with their luggage. He followed them into the elevator, which ascended to the second floor, and they made their way to room 212. The room was tiled, and the two double beds were made up with white sheets and white comforters. The air-conditioner was set to a comfortable temperature. The Greek Key navy blue curtains were pulled away, and the sunshine penetrated the thin transparent white curtains covering the windows. The room was clean and simple.

It was lunchtime, and their growling stomachs were fully aware of this. Valerie voted to have lunch at Aphrodite, but she was outvoted by her friends, who chose to have lunch in town. They caught a taxi and were dropped off in the heart of the vibrant town.

"Look at this restaurant." Giselle pointed to the structure that had a sign in the window claiming it had the best gyros in town. "Best gyros, huh. They all say that."

"Let's try it," Kate said. "It looks like a nice restaurant."

They entered the small eatery and were instantly greeted with a pleasant aroma. A television was stationed behind the bar broadcasting football, as the Europeans called it.

"Good afternoon, ladies. Welcome to Zeus Zest." The words came out of a man who may have been in his mid to late sixties. "My name is Demitrius. You may sit anywhere you like. You may also sit at the bar if you so choose. A great football game is on. Greece versus Belgium."

There were some diners seated at the tables, and two men, who appeared to be locals, sat at the bar. The friends opted to sit at the bar to take in the football culture that the Europeans were fascinated with.

The bartender took their drink orders and went on to serve Giselle a Coke, Valerie a Diet Coke, and Kate a Bloody Mary.

"No, no, no," Demitrius reacted almost in horror as one of the players on his team hit the ball off of the goal post. "Pardon me, ladies. As you can see, I'm passionate about football." The two other men at the bar also erupted in anger when the player missed the strike.

"We have fantastic gyros here," Demitrius commented to his guests. "And I'm not saying that because I own this restaurant. My wife is the mastermind behind every recipe on this menu, and everything is to die for, so you can't go wrong."

"We have to sample these fantastic gyros that you advertise," Giselle replied. The waiter took their orders, and the friends each ordered a lamb and beef gyro, which came with a small Greek salad.

"Where are you ladies from?" Demitrius asked. It was a question they'd been asked frequently while in Greece. "It's evident that you are Americans."

"We're from New York," Kate readily shared. Kate never hesitated to give an answer when she was asked this question.

"First time in Greece?"

"Yes. This is our first time," Kate continued.

"How do you like it?"

"We love it," Giselle replied. "Mainland Greece is a historical gem. Mykonos and Santorini are breathtaking. Words cannot truly capture the beauty of these islands."

"I'm glad you love it."

The food was served, and Giselle bit into the gyro. It melted in her mouth. The meat was tender, moist, and juicy, and it seemed to have extra flavor. She thought to herself that Demitrius may have been right. This easily could have been the best gyro she'd sunk her teeth into. Her friends seemed to be in agreement.

"Ah, what did I tell you," Demitrius commented, judging from the expressions on their faces. "Is this the best gyro you've ever tried, or what?"

"I will have to agree with you," Giselle replied. She took a napkin and dabbed the side of her mouth. Demitrius was pleased with his customers' reactions, then he made his way to one of the tables and chatted up some other diners. Next, he welcomed a party of four into the restaurant. About twenty minutes passed before he circled back to them.

Demitrius reminded Giselle of a Greek version of her grandfather, may his soul rest in peace. Her grandfather was full of energy, despite his years, and always the life of the party—a true social butterfly. Her grandfather had died of a massive heart attack while running a 5K. He'd been nearing the finish line when he suddenly collapsed.

Demitrius kept them well entertained. He had quite a sense of humor. His wife emerged from the back, and he gave her a kiss on the cheek. "This is my beautiful wife, Nikita, of fifty-one years and counting."

"Wow, fifty-one years." Kate replied. She seemed shocked and marveled at the same time. To Giselle's knowledge, Kate's longest relationship may have been six months, which could have even been a stretch. There was the on-and-off boyfriend, and maybe the combination of the time that they were together might have exceeded six months. Giselle thought to herself that she was not one to talk. She'd had terrible luck in the love department. In fact, some of her experiences could have easily turned her off of dating for life. She'd hoped that one day, that curse on her love life would be broken.

"So how did you two meet?" Kate inquired with full interest and attentiveness.

"Ah," Demitrius let out a long, deep audible sound. He stroked his bearded chin with his right hand, and his mind drifted deep into the past. "It was fifty-two years ago. It's almost as though it was yesterday. I was seventeen years old, a month or so shy of turning eighteen. I walked into a bakery when I beheld the most beautiful girl standing behind the counter." Demitrius paused and turned to Nikita, who was blushing. "Her father owned this bakery. I can still smell the bread baking, and I can still feel the warmth of the shop, which was a stark contrast to the chilly air outside. I felt like I was in a trance and that the beautiful lady in front of me was not real. Her smile was that of an angel. She had a shyness about her that was sweet and innocent. We looked into each other's eyes for what had to have been two minutes without saying a single word. There was a strong connection between us that was organic yet indescribable. Her father, who materialized out of thin air, interrupted the moment. Or maybe I was so captivated by her beauty that I did not realize he had walked in. I was instantly brought out of the trance as my eyes focused on a large man, six foot three, six foot four, somewhere in that ballpark. His arms were crossed over his chest, and his dark eyes were fixed on me like a target. There was not a hint of a smile. He was fully aware at that point that I was more interested in his daughter than buying bread."

Kate was fully amused by the story, and she encouraged Demitrius to go on. Giselle looked at Valerie, who was also thoroughly engaged. Demitrius sure had a way of making his customers feel relaxed and entertained at the same time.

"Her father told me that if I had no interest in buying, then I could see myself out of the door. I bought a loaf of bread and baklava. I then returned to the bakery every day at 5 pm and bought a loaf of bread whether I wanted it or not. Sometimes Nikita was there, and sometimes she was not. It was always a pleasant surprise when Nikita was there. Her father wore the same stern look when I walked in, almost as though it was tattooed on. Then, one day, I walked into the shop, and Nikita was not in sight. I was always hopeful, and my heart always sank like a ship when she was not there. Her father, on the other hand, was always there. I was expecting a cold interaction, as usual, when his face suddenly relaxed and his arms fell to his side, and he said, 'You've been coming to the bakery every day for almost three months. I know the bread is good, but evidently you're not here for the bread. You have taken an interest in my daughter. What are your intentions?' I knew that my answer to this question would hold a lot of weight, and that every word would be scrutinized."

"So what did you say?" Kate asked with anticipation.

"I told him that I had a connection with his daughter that I could not explain. I told him that I felt as if God had spoken to me and told me that this was the woman I needed to marry. I promised him that if he gave me the opportunity, I would love Nikita with all of my heart, and I would take care of her as I would my own body. I promised to give her the best I could offer."

"Aww. That's so sweet," Kate said. "I wish a man would say that about me."

"Her father smiled, which transformed his face. He was almost unrecognizable. He told me that the simple action of me coming to the bakery every day spoke volumes about my character. He said that my actions showed courage, heart, persistence, and determination. He then gave me his blessing. The next day, I asked Nikita out, and she said yes. The rest is history."

Demitrius turned again to Nikita and held her hand. He lifted her hand to his mouth and gently gave it a kiss. "She's as beautiful as the day I met her, and I fall in love with her more every day." Demitrius gave Nikita's hand another kiss. "I want what I want, and I get what I want."

Giselle was moved by Demetrius's story. She was in the same boat as Kate, and she wished that a man would feel the same way about her. She wished that a man would appreciate everything that she had to offer. Her mind went back to an intense therapy session that she'd had with her therapist. Her therapist had told her not to look for anyone else to complete her. She was encouraged to love herself completely and appreciate all of the great things she had to offer. She did not need anyone else to validate her.

Giselle's mind continued to drift as she pondered that therapy session. She had come a long way, but she still had work to do. She was a work in progress. Her mind refocused when Nikita placed a small plate of baklava in front of her. She had given each of them a slice and told them that it was on the house.

The friends stayed a few more minutes in the restaurant. Demitrius and Nikita encouraged them to return. "Our motto is this, 'You come as guests and you leave as family.' That is what we stand by," Demitrius stated with a smile.

The friends waved at Demitrius and his wife as they exited.

"They are so nice," Valerie remarked.

CHAPTER 11

"This ass smells."

Giselle laughed at her friend. "Kate, stop complaining and get on the donkey." The donkey handler helped Giselle onto the saddle, positioned on the bright coat that covered the animal's back. Valerie had already gotten on top of her donkey like the six other tourists. Kate finally allowed the handler to help her.

Two cruise ships sailed in the distance on calm waters from the caldera cliffs. One of the ships was heading in the direction of the island. The light blue sky had a few clouds scattered above.

The donkey handler again introduced himself to the group of tourists. He explained that the donkeys were bred in a humane manner, and they were well taken care of. He pointed out that all of the donkeys were healthy, and meaty, as he called it. "No skinny donkeys. No skin and bones."

The handler reiterated the safety instructions, then he struck his stick on the ground, which apparently was an indication for the donkeys to move. The donkeys fell into line and one by one, with their passengers, made their way up a pathway of innumerable steps. The pace was initially slow and steady, but that quickly changed. Kate's donkey fell out of line and appeared to have its own agenda. The donkey quickly accelerated, and Kate let out a shrieking sound as she held on to the handle for dear life. The donkey handler was able to get the animal under control, and the donkey slowed its pace. Kate's body still appeared tense, and she had a constipated look on her face.

Giselle thought to herself that the ride was not as pleasurable as she'd hoped it would be. The bottom of the caldera cliffs, to the town of Fira, seemed so far away. Kate let out another squealing sound as her donkey accelerated again. Valerie's donkey moved in a zigzag motion before straightening its path. Giselle had a visual of her donkey being trampled or, worse, falling over the cliff. She viewed the cable cars ascending to the top of the cliffs, and she wished that she'd chosen that route of transportation. After what seemed like an interminable journey, the donkeys made it to the top.

As Kate was being helped off of her donkey, balls of feces dropped in succession from the animal's rear end.

Kate looked repulsed. "Oh shit!"

They had an early dinner at the hotel's restaurant, Aphrodite, and surprisingly, Kate was agreeable to enjoying a relaxed and quiet evening. It was a beautiful time of day to sit outdoors and enjoy the beauty surrounding them. The donkey ride was enough action for the day. They sat on poolside chairs around a circular outdoor table. The infinite pool appeared to merge with the sea. Giselle thought to herself that she was looking at the most beautiful sunset imaginable. The sky manifested a shade of orange that almost seemed ethereal, and the beauty of God's meticulous hands was evident.

"I wish that I could stop time and remain in this moment," Giselle shared, as she watched the sun slowly disappearing behind the horizon.

"I know what you mean," Valerie agreed. "At this moment, I feel at peace with not a care in the world."

"Val, I know you're in love, but Giselle, do you think you've ever been in love?" Kate asked, switching the subject.

"I don't know. I thought that I may have been in love with Jerry, but it may have all been an infatuation. But you know my poor success rate with the opposite sex."

"I admire the relationship between Demitrius and Nikita. I would love a relationship like that one day," Kate thought out loud. "Did you see the way he looked at her? It was almost as though she were the only person in the room, and she was all his." A pause ensued. "Please don't think I'm crazy, but I think that I may be in love with Austin."

"Kate, you barely know him," Valerie commented. "You know I'm all about finding love, and I've been notorious in the past for being a matchmaker, but don't you think you're moving a little bit too fast?"

"Val, I thought that you would be happy for me. You seem to want to find everybody else love. You were so focused on finding Giselle love that you almost got her killed."

"Kate!" Giselle said in a raised voice.

"Kate, that's not fair!" Valerie retorted. She was obviously hurt at Kate's remark. "I still haven't forgiven myself for what happened to Giselle and what could've happened to her. That's a burden I'll always have to carry."

"Val, you're not responsible for what happened to me. You are not responsible for other people's actions."

"Val, I'm so sorry. Please forgive me for my insensitive words. I didn't mean it."

"You obviously think it because those words came out of your mouth." Valerie's eyes welled up, and she wiped her eyes before any tears could escape.

"I don't think that. Those words came out from a brief moment of… What should I say? Maybe a brief moment of hurt manifesting as anger."

"Kate, you know that I want only the best for you, and for you to think otherwise is hurtful."

"Val, I'm sorry. Please, I'm begging you to forgive me. I honestly didn't mean it." Kate gave Valerie a hug. After a few seconds, Valerie reciprocated.

Valerie had considered herself the big sister of the group. Giselle was the youngest. Kate was a year and a half older, and Valerie was three years older than Giselle. Valerie often came across as authoritative, but her intentions were pure. This sometimes created conflict between her and Kate because they were polar opposites. Kate was free spirited, uninhibited, and spontaneous. Although they were complete opposites, they somehow found a true friendship that seemed unbreakable, even if a few cracks appeared from time to time. Their friendship gave credence to the phrase "opposites attract." Giselle may have also played a role in keeping their friendship strong; she often played the role of mediator.

Valerie was born and raised in Baltimore, Maryland. She was the oldest of two sisters and a brother, and she'd played the role of a second mother to her siblings. Her mother, Beverly, held down two jobs and was often at work.

Her father, Benjamin Smith, passed away when she was fourteen years old. He was a hard worker and a provider to his family. Benjamin took care of others, but unfortunately, he did not take care of himself, and not taking care of himself later affected his ability to provide for his family. Benjamin was a poorly controlled diabetic. He'd suffered a stroke, which affected his left arm. He had regained some strength in that arm, and fortunately, he was able to continue his job as a warehouse manager. One day, he'd noticed a superficial ulcer underneath his right big toe. He ignored it, and it became wider, deeper, and ultimately infected. The infection spread up his leg.

Beverly drove him to the hospital, and he deteriorated quickly in the emergency room. He was septic and was admitted to the intensive care unit. A resistant bacterium was growing in his blood. His clinical status worsened and he had to be placed on a ventilator. After five days on the machine, he coded, and resuscitation efforts were futile.

Valerie was devastated, but she had to remain strong for her siblings. She also had to mature quickly. Her mother depended on her to help take charge of the household and watch over her siblings while she worked. Despite the extra load placed on her as a teenager, she'd managed to get good grades. By the time she'd gained entry into college, her sister Cecelia, who was two years younger, took on the role as second in charge of caring for their two younger siblings.

Valerie was the first in her family to go to college, and she'd graduated with highest honors. Her mother was so proud of her and could not contain the tears of joy at her daughter's graduation. Her mother was also pleased that she had found a good partner in Donald, whom she truly believed would take good care of her daughter.

When Bridget came a couple years later, Valerie thought that she would have had motherhood in the bag given her experience with her younger siblings. Little did she know what she would be in for.

CHAPTER 12

"Good morning. I hope that I've not disturbed you. This is the front desk calling. I have a message for Ms. Kate Davenport."

Giselle lowered the receiver from her ear. "Kate, it's for you. It's someone from the front desk."

"This is Kate." She listened to the caller for a few seconds. "Fantastic. I'll head down shortly." Kate hung up, and her eyes were filled with excitement.

"What was that all about?" Giselle asked.

"The front desk clerk told me there's a surprise waiting for me in the lobby. I must have won the raffle. I wonder what it could be." Kate combed her hair into a loose ponytail and tied the fashionable blue and white satin scarf that she'd bought in Athens around her neck. "Hurry up, Val," she called to her friend, who was still locked in the bathroom. "Please, Giselle, for the love of God, could you leave the fanny pack in the hotel? Just for today."

"The fanny pack goes. There's nothing wrong with me wearing it."

"I'm ready," Valerie stated. She emerged from the bathroom wearing a peach top and knee-length jeans.

"I won the raffle, Val. My surprise is waiting for me in the lobby."

"Congratulations. If you won a day cruise for two, we'll tell Giselle all about it."

"Very funny, Val," Giselle replied sarcastically.

"I don't feel like carrying my purse with me today," Valerie decided. "Could you please stick a couple items in your fanny pack?

I'm sure you have more pockets in there than you know what to do with."

"The same fanny pack that you and Kate heckle me about?"

"Come on, Giselle. My shoulders are aching."

"Only if you promise to never make fun of me again for wearing a fanny pack."

"Okay. I promise."

"Say it louder," Giselle said with a grin.

"I promise, I promise, I promise."

Kate laughed at her friends. "For the record, I did not make a promise. I'm still going to make fun of you for wearing a fanny pack."

Valerie handed Giselle her passport, fifty Euros, a ChapStick, a pack of Tic Tacs, and a map of Santorini.

"I thought you said a couple items."

"Giselle, I'm sure you could hide a small animal in that fanny pack, so I'm certain you can find room for my belongings."

Giselle looked at her friend and shook her head. "There you go again with the fanny pack jokes. You can't help yourself, can you?"

"Let's get out of here. It's almost noon," Kate stated as she looked at her watch.

They took the elevator to the first level and walked to the front desk. "Excuse me, sir. My name is Kate Davenport, and I'm in room 212."

"Ah, yes," the portly attendant replied. "Your surprise is behind you."

"I don't see what you're referring to." Kate looked around and was thoroughly confused. Seconds later, her surprise came into view. She could not believe it.

"Surprise!" an elated voice called out. Giselle and Valerie turned around almost simultaneously, and their jaws instantly dropped.

"Austin, what are you doing here?" Kate asked. She did not know if she should be excited or aggravated. She was certainly thrilled to see him, but she knew the feeling was not shared among her companions. Kate could feel Valerie's eyes piercing through her body like a sharp knife.

"You told me the hotel you were staying at, so I thought I would surprise you. I'm actually here to check out some property. What do you all have planned for the rest of the afternoon? I would love to show you all the property."

"Well, um…"

"We need a moment alone with our friend," Valerie interjected. She held Kate's arm and led her away from Austin; Giselle followed closely behind. "You need to get rid of him."

"Can you lower your voice? He can hear you."

"I don't care if he can hear me. Tell him to leave."

"Val, what do you want me to say? I don't have it in me to be rude like you."

"First of all, I'm not rude. I'm direct. All you have to do is tell him that this is a girls' trip and you want to spend time with your girlfriends. Simple. There's nothing rude about that."

"Giselle, you know I can't do that. This is a guy I actually like. What do you think?"

"I think that if he likes you as much as you like him, then he should understand."

"How about this? I would love to see the property that Austin has asked me to invest in. I'm actually seriously thinking about it. It seems like a smart investment. We can see the property, and I'll let him know that it's just us girls after that. Fair enough?"

There was silence among the group for almost a minute before Giselle interrupted the silence. "Fine. But please let him know that we would like to spend time together after that, just the three of us."

"Okay. I'll tell him after we see the property."

"Why not now?" Valerie inquired.

"I'll tell him. I promise."

Kate joined Austin, who was seated on one of the wicker chairs with a glass of cucumber water in his hand.

"Is everything okay?" Austin asked.

"Yes. Everything is great. We're excited to see the property."

Giselle and Valerie walked over.

"Well, let's get this show on the road. I can't wait to show you ladies what I have in store for you." Austin led the way outside the hotel lobby to a white Jeep Wrangler. The soft top was removed. Giselle and Valerie slid into the backseat, and Kate climbed into the front passenger seat. Austin reversed out of the parking space and he made his way out of the confines of the hotel.

"I hope I didn't put a damper on your plans."

"No, not at all," Kate readily responded. There was silence from the backseat.

"Sorry I didn't let you know I was coming. I wanted to give you all a surprise."

Kate let out an awkward laugh. "It was certainly a surprise." There was still silence from the backseat.

Austin directed the jeep along some narrow, windy roads. It was a beautiful day with barely any clouds in the sky. Kate's hair flew in front of her face, and she raked the loose strands behind her ear.

"I can't wait to show you ladies the property. This is prime real estate, and the view is spectacular." The Jeep Wrangler made its way up a few meandering roads until it made it to the top of an expanse of land with breathtaking views of the Aegean Sea. Austin parked, and they got out of the vehicle.

"Wow, this view is amazing,'" Kate commented after elevating her dropped jaw.

"What did I tell you? This place is secluded, and you couldn't ask for a better view. Santorini is a vacationer's paradise. We'll provide everything that a vacationer would want in a hotel. It will all be state of the art. It's a great investment. I have some bigwigs investing. We plan to start breaking ground in three months."

"You sold me on this property," Kate admitted. "This is absolutely beautiful."

Austin detailed the plans for the hotel and was passionate as he spoke. Giselle thought to herself that the property would be an ideal place to put a hotel, but she definitely did not have that kind of money sitting in the bank.

"I'm glad I got the chance to show you this amazing property."

"It truly is amazing," Kate concurred.

He looked at his watch. "It's about lunchtime. Let me take you all to lunch. My treat."

Kate felt her friends' eyes pointed directly at her. "Well, um. Well. We were hoping to have a girls' day today. It's our last full day in Santorini. I'm sorry, Austin."

"I can't say I'm not disappointed, but I understand. I'll drop you off whenever you want."

"Could you drop us off in the town?" Kate asked.

"No problem." Austin directed the vehicle toward Fira. He maneuvered along the serpentine roads. A few minutes into the drive, the jeep almost collided into an oncoming Fiat as it rounded the corner. The vehicles formed a "T" in the middle of the road.

Austin angrily jumped out of the jeep and approached the elderly couple in the other vehicle. The man, probably in his seventies, slowly got out of the car.

"You senile idiot! Don't you know how to drive?"

"I'm sorry," the man apologized, evidently shaken.

"You're the one who doesn't know how to drive!" shouted the woman in the passenger's seat.

"Please put your old lady on a leash," Austin retorted.

"Now, wait a minute, young man. I'm not going to allow you to speak to my wife like that."

"I can't believe Austin is talking to that couple like that," Giselle remarked to her friends. Valerie had a disgusted look. "Austin!" Giselle shouted from the backseat. "It's okay. Nobody was physically hurt."

After two more minutes of Austin giving the elderly couple a piece of his mind, he jumped into the driver's seat and slammed the door. "I'm so sorry that you all had to witness that. Someone could have gotten seriously hurt."

"Fortunately, no one did," Kate replied.

"I can't believe you spoke to that sweet elderly couple like that. It was an accident," Giselle added.

"Sweet elderly couple? That old lady had some fire in her. Did you hear her screaming at me?" Austin let out an irritated sigh. "I swear, when you get over a certain age, your license should be revoked."

They drove to their destination almost in complete silence. Austin dropped them off in the heart of Fira. "Thank you, Austin," Kate said. "We appreciate it."

"You're welcome." Austin had a smile that was not present half an hour ago. "Kate, I wish I could see you again."

Kate blushed, and she thanked Austin again for showing them the property.

"Kate, you know I love you, and I want only the best for you, but I don't trust Austin," Giselle commented. The friends leisurely walked side by side down a main street. Valerie was reluctant to offer her opinion given the incident that had happened the evening before, where Kate questioned her intent.

"Austin was upset. Someone could have gotten hurt or even killed."

"Stop making excuses for his actions," Giselle responded. "I get that he was upset, but the way he acted was not called for. It seems like he has some underlying anger issues."

"Everyone gets angry. That old man veered into our lane. Someone could have died. Do you get that?"

Giselle realized that she was not getting anywhere with Kate. She was still making excuses for Austin's actions. "Okay. Fine. Let's stop talking about it and enjoy the rest of the day."

"Sounds like a plan. I'm starving," Kate replied. "Where would you two like to eat?"

"Honestly, I wouldn't mind eating a gyro at Zeus Zest," Valerie said, as she broke her silence. "I have to admit that was the best gyro I have ever eaten."

"I agree," Kate commented. "Zeus Zest it is."

They walked in the direction of the restaurant, and the moment they entered, Demitrius welcomed them.

"My American friends! Great to see you all again."

"We could not leave Santorini without having one of your famous gyros again," Valerie said with a smile. "I don't know what Nikita adds to those gyros, but it's amazing."

"Thank you, thank you. I will relay your compliments to Nikita. So, did I hear you correctly? You're getting ready to leave Santorini?"

The friends sat at the bar, and the waiter gave them the menus. "Yes," Kate answered. "Tonight is our last night."

"I'm sad to hear that. You ladies just got here."

"I know," Valerie replied with a saddened look. "Three nights in Athens, three nights in Mykonos, and three nights in Santorini. It all went by so fast. Now it's time to get ready to head back home to reality."

The friends ordered the fried cheese as an appetizer, and they each ordered a beef and lamb gyro that came with a small Greek salad. Giselle and Kate ordered a Coke, and Valerie ordered a Diet Coke.

"So, what do you ladies have planned for your last day in paradise?" Demitrius asked.

"We're going to do some shopping," Kate answered. "Then we're going to head back to our hotel, have dinner, and watch the sunset. Our hotel has an amazing restaurant named Aphrodite. I heard the sea bass is delicious."

"Aphrodite at the Olive Branch Hotel? That restaurant has great food. May I also suggest the pan-fried trout if it's on the menu. Absolutely superb."

"I'll have to keep that in mind," Giselle responded.

The friends enjoyed their meals as they engaged in conversation with Demitrius, who was a skilled storyteller. Dessert was on the house, and the waiter brought out three small plates with generous servings of baklava.

The friends left the eatery and enjoyed the rest of the day in the town before heading back to the hotel. They had bags of souvenirs that they placed in the room.

"You know what I could drink right now?" Valerie asked rhetorically. "I could drink some of that refreshing cucumber water in the lobby. Do you guys want to head down for a few minutes?"

"Sure," Giselle chimed in. "I wouldn't mind a refreshing glass of that water."

"You both go ahead. I'm going to get a head start into the shower. But I wouldn't mind trying a glass of the watermelon and mint water."

"Okay." Giselle replied. "When we get back, one of us can jump in the shower next."

Giselle closed the door behind them. Kate took off her shorts. She was about to untie the blue and white scarf from around her neck when the phone rang on the nightstand. After four rings, Kate picked it up.

"Hello?"

"Hi, baby. I hoped that I would get you."

"Austin?"

"Yes, Kate. I miss you. I have to see you tonight."

"Austin, you know I would love to see you more than anything, but I can't. I promised Giselle and Valerie that we would spend our last night together. We have dinner reservations at eight."

"I need you tonight. I want you. I have a special surprise planned for you. Meet me for dinner at eight thirty at Eden's restaurant in town. I can send a taxi to get you. Kate, please say that you will spend tonight with me."

"Giselle and Valerie will kill me," Kate whispered, almost as if her friends were in the room and could have heard her conversation.

"Why are you whispering?"

"Giselle and Valerie will be upset. Valerie will literally be furious at me."

"Kate, I love you. I don't know what it is about you, but I can't resist you. Actually, I do know what it is. You're smart, you're beautiful, you're funny. I feel as if I can be my true self around you. I want a life with you, Kate."

Kate felt torn between Austin and her friends. She desperately wanted to spend more time with Austin, but she could not abandon her friends. Sure, she would see her friends back in New York. Who knew when she would see Austin again? He had an apartment in New York, but he also lived in Los Angeles, and he traveled a lot for his job.

"Hello? Kate, are you still there?"

"Yes, I'm still here."

"So, what do you say? Will you spend tonight with me?"

Kate was silent for almost half of a minute. "What about if I have dinner with my friends, then maybe they might be agreeable to me meeting you in town for an hour or so?"

"An hour is not enough Kate."

"We'll play it by ear. Let me first test the waters with Valerie."

"Fair enough. There's a lounge area at Eden's. I can send a taxi to pick you up. Let's say nine thirty? I'll wait for you."

"Nine thirty sounds good."

"Kate, I'm looking forward to seeing you tonight."

"I'm looking forward to seeing you too."

Kate sat on the edge of the bed, and she was torn. *How am I going to break this to Giselle and Valerie?* she thought. She was actually nervous. She had already committed to Austin. A few more minutes elapsed when the door opened.

"We have your watermelon and mint water," Valerie said as she walked through the door.

"Kate, you haven't showered yet," Giselle commented. "What have you been doing all of this time? Is everything okay?"

"Yes, everything is fine."

"Good," Giselle responded. "Well, since you're procrastinating getting into the shower, I'll go first. We need to hurry up if we're going to make our dinner reservations at eight." Giselle closed the door to the bathroom, and a few seconds later, the water was heard coming out of the shower head.

Valerie placed her suitcase on the bed and zipped it open. She pulled out a baby blue dress and lifted it up with both hands. "Does this dress need ironing?"

"Maybe a little bit toward the hem. It's a beautiful dress, Val."

Valerie looked at Kate with an incredulous expression. "Is that supposed to be a joke? This is the same dress that you laughed at in Mykonos when you said it looked like a church dress. Remember?"

"I was joking. It's beautiful. You're beautiful."

"What's going on, Kate? You've acted weird since we walked through the door. Is everything okay?"

"Yes, Val. Everything is fine."

"Have you decided what you're going to wear?" Valerie pulled out the iron and ironing board from the closet.

"No, not yet."

"Kate, what are you waiting for? We don't want to miss our reservation."

"Val, I really like Austin. I want you to like him too. I think we have something special, and I want you to be happy for us."

"Kate, I'm sorry about yesterday. I want only the best for you. I just want you to be careful. But if Austin makes you happy, then I'm happy."

"I'm looking forward to having dinner with two of my best friends. I'm also looking forward to spending even more time with you both in New York."

"Well, maybe we can have a girls' night out twice a month instead of once a month."

"That sounds wonderful," Kate replied with a smile. She paused for a few seconds. "Val, I was thinking, after we have dinner together, would you mind if I spent maybe an hour with Austin tonight? I'm not sure when I'll see him next. He's heading back to LA after he leaves Greece."

Valerie placed the steaming iron back on the ironing board. Her face was tense, and her lips quivered. "Kate, you promised we would spend our last night together, just the three of us. You can be so selfish! It's always all about you!"

"It's not always about me. I don't want to hurt your feelings, and I don't want to hurt Giselle's feelings. I also don't want to disappoint Austin."

"Austin! You don't want to disappoint Austin? You put us in the same category as this guy you met five days ago? This entire trip we have accommodated you. Kate wants to go to the club; we go to the club. Kate wants to hang out on a yacht; we hang out on a yacht. Kate wants to go here; we go here. Kate wants to go there; we go there. Kate wants to hang out with this Austin guy; we rearrange our plan. It's been all about you, and frankly I'm sick and tired of it!"

The bathroom door opened, and Giselle walked out with a towel around her and dripping-wet hair. "What are you two arguing about?"

"Kate wants to hang out with Austin tonight."

"For an hour, max. I want to enjoy dinner with you both then spend a little bit of time with Austin."

"Kate, since you've met Austin, you've spent more time with him than you have with us," Giselle said in a calm voice. "This is a girls' trip, and we came here to spend time with each other and enjoy the time together. You're being selfish right now."

"How am I being selfish? I'm trying to spend time with all of you."

"You don't get it; do you?" Valerie said rhetorically, shaking her head.

"I'm sorry. I can call Austin and tell him I can't meet with him tonight."

"You already told him you were going to meet up with him?" Valerie said in disbelief. "You know what? Meet him. Go. I'm no longer in the mood for having dinner tonight. I'm going to order in."

Kate's eyes teared up. "Val, please don't be like that."

Valerie sat on the bed and crossed her arms. She looked toward the window and away from Kate.

"Val, please don't be mad at me," Kate pleaded.

"Go!" Valerie said in a raised voice. "I don't even want to look at you right now."

The tears rolled down Kate's cheeks. She zipped open her suitcase and pulled out a pair of jeans that she squeezed herself into. She grabbed her purse and exited.

"Wait!" Giselle called out before the door closed. "Val, please don't let our last night end like this."

"She made the decision to let our last night end like this. She chose Austin over us."

"Maybe we should go after her. Suppose something happens to her, Val."

"Giselle, at this point, I don't care."

CHAPTER 13

Giselle opened the heavy curtains, and the rays of sunshine illuminated the room. Kate had not come back.

"We have to be at the airport in three hours to catch our flight," Giselle commented. "Where is Kate? She has not even packed yet."

Valerie lay on the bed in deep thought. "Do you think I was too hard on her?"

"I don't know. I completely understand how you felt. I felt the same way."

"I don't know if I should be angry at her or apologize to her. I'm hurt that she would choose to spend so much time with a guy that she just met over us. I feel as though she has been inconsiderate of our feelings and downright selfish. I'm also upset that she spent the entire night out with this guy."

"Well, Val, you did tell her to go. You told her that you didn't want to look at her."

"She had already made that decision. She had already committed her time to this Austin guy after we had dinner. I'm also upset that she is not back yet. I feel like she's still thinking of herself and not considering us. We have a flight to catch. I have a husband and a child to go home to."

Giselle pressed the restaurant button on the phone and ordered breakfast for both she and Valerie. After breakfast, they finished packing, and it was imperative that they leave for the airport in the next hour and a half.

"Where's Kate?" Giselle said in a frustrated tone. "This is absolutely ridiculous." She had paid for international usage of her phone and called Kate's cell phone number. The call went immediately to voicemail. "I have no way of getting in contact with her. Did she say where she was going last night?"

"No, she didn't." Valerie reflected. "We have no way of getting in contact with Austin. Did he mention the hotel he was staying at? Giselle, this is not good. Either she stayed out all night and overslept, or…" Valerie paused. "Or something happened to her. Do you think something happened to her?"

Deep down, Giselle felt that something might have happened to Kate. Yes, Kate had the tendency to be wild and free spirited, but she was also responsible when it came to important matters. There was no way that she would jeopardize them missing their flight.

"Val, I think we should go to the police."

"Checkout time is in thirty minutes. I'm going to throw Kate's belongings in her suitcase. Maybe the bellhops can hold our suitcases until we figure things out."

Giselle and Valerie checked out of the hotel but made a request for the bellhop to hold on to their luggage. They took a taxi to the police station. It had become evident that they were going to miss their flight.

They walked into the small, white building. "May I help you?" a young woman asked from behind the counter.

"Yes," Giselle answered. "We want to file a missing person's report."

The woman offered them a seat and informed them that someone would be with them shortly. Giselle and Valerie sat on the plastic blue chairs and waited impatiently. Valerie tapped her right foot repeatedly and fidgeted with her fingers.

Almost ten minutes elapsed before a police officer emerged through the door. He approached them and introduced himself as

Detective Pallis. The detective had a muscular frame, and he was very hairy. A layering of black hair covered his arms.

"My name is Giselle Bellamy, and this is my friend, Valerie Brooks."

The detective shook their hands, then led them through the door and offered them a seat.

"Something to drink? Water? Coffee?" the detective asked. Giselle and Valerie declined the offer. "So I hear that you want to file a missing person's report."

"Yes," Giselle responded. "Our friend is missing."

The detective pulled out a yellow pad and uncapped his pen. "Tell me when your friend went missing."

"We last saw her around 7:15 pm yesterday evening, and she didn't come back to the hotel this morning."

The detective put down his pen and sat back in his chair. He had a look of irritation, as though his time was being wasted. "Look, I understand that you are concerned about your friend, but it's only been about sixteen hours. Why don't you wait at least twenty-four to forty-eight hours before filing a missing person's report?"

"You don't understand," Valerie weighed in. "We're supposed to fly home to New York today. There's no way she would have missed the flight. That's why we believe that something is wrong."

Detective Pallis let out a deep sigh then sat forward. He picked up his pen with his left hand and positioned it on the writing pad. "Okay. I'll gather the information, but you would not believe the kinds of things that tourists do when they are here on vacation. Especially young ones like yourself."

It was evident to Giselle that the officer was not taking their concerns seriously.

"Okay. What is her full name?"

"Katherine Miranda Davenport," Giselle answered. "She goes by Kate."

"What is her age and date of birth?"

Giselle knew her friend's age. She knew the month and date of her birth, but she had to calculate her year of birth based on her age.

"Can you describe her? What is her height, approximate weight, hair color, eye color, that kind of thing?"

"I would say she's about five foot five. Maybe 125 pounds. Would you agree Val?"

"I would agree."

Giselle continued, "She has blonde straight hair about to the middle of her back. Her eyes are a light brown color. Actually, I have a photo of her in my camera." Giselle then realized that she'd placed her camera in the front zipped portion of her suitcase. All she had was her fanny pack secured around her waist.

Valerie pulled her camera out of her bag, and she looked through the photos until she found the best picture that captured Kate's features. She showed it to the officer, who jotted down some more information on his writing pad. He handed the camera back to Valerie.

"Okay. What was she last seen wearing?"

"She had on a white cotton short-sleeved V-neck top with light faded skinny jeans," Giselle answered. "She had a satin blue and white scarf with an image representing Athena tied around her neck. She bought the scarf in Athens."

Detective Pallis scribbled some more information on his writing pad. "Okay. Where did she go when she left the hotel?"

"We don't know," Valerie answered. "She had met this guy named Austin Bate, and she was meeting him somewhere. She didn't say."

"She did not tell you where she was going?" Detective Pallis asked, perplexed.

Giselle and Valerie looked briefly at each other, then Valerie continued. "We got into an argument last night. Kate met this guy Austin Bate when we were visiting Mykonos. She liked him. We thought that she was spending too much time with him when this was supposed to be a girls' trip. That was the root of our argument. We were supposed to have dinner and spend the rest of the night together. Just the three of us. It was our last night in Greece. She told us that she wanted to see Austin, and that's when the argument ensued."

"So, do you think that maybe she could be doing this out of anger? Maybe she does not want to see the both of you?" Detective Pallis reclined in his chair and swiveled the pen between his index and middle finger.

"Absolutely not," Giselle interjected. "We've gotten into many arguments, and that's all it is. We make up, and we move on. Kate would never disappear like that. She loves to have fun, but she is also a responsible person. We all have work to go back to in New York. Valerie has a husband and a two-year-old. I know my friend, and she wouldn't hide out in Greece."

"Maybe she caught a flight back to New York. We can check with the airport."

"Impossible! She would never do that," Giselle retorted. She was offended that Detective Pallis would suggest such a thing. "She left all of her belongings in the hotel."

"Okay. So what can you tell me about Austin Bate? What does he look like?"

"He's probably in his early or mid-thirties," Giselle responded. "He's about six foot. Average build. Caucasian. Tanned skin. Dark brown hair. His hair is cut short on the sides and fuller on top. He has hazel eyes. He's American. He's a real estate agent for the wealthy, and he's planning to build a hotel in Santorini."

"Does he have a beard or mustache?"

"He was clean shaven," Giselle responded.

"Any distinguishing marks. Scars, tattoos, anything that you can think of?"

Giselle and Valerie looked at each other. "Not that was apparent," Giselle answered.

"Any particular habits that you noticed?"

"What I can tell you is that he has a bad temper," Valerie interjected. "We witnessed it firsthand, and I'm scared that he may have hurt Kate." Valerie went into detail about the incident that took place the day before when Austin accosted the elderly couple.

"Okay, well you two did give me something to work with. I will inform you when we gather more information." Detective Pallis took down their contact information and the hotel they were staying at. They had already checked out, but they would have to check back in. Hopefully there would be a room available.

Detective Pallis walked them through the door into the waiting area. He requested that they inform the department as soon as possible if they found Kate.

Giselle and Valerie walked outside. Somehow, Giselle felt that Kate's case was going to be shoved to the bottom of the pile.

"Where could she possibly be?" Giselle asked, not expecting an answer from her friend. "Think, Valerie. Did Austin give a clue to where he is staying or where he likes to go in Santorini?"

"Not that I can think of."

"He does like to party and have fun. Maybe he might be hitting one of the top hang out spots tonight."

"Giselle, that's like looking for a needle in a haystack."

"You're probably right, but I wouldn't rule it out." Giselle tried calling Kate's phone again, and it immediately went to voicemail. "Val, let's go back to the hotel. There have to be cameras. Maybe the cameras can give us a clue."

"Good idea."

Giselle and Valerie took a taxi to the Olive Branch Hotel.

"Welcome back, ladies," the bellman greeted them as they exited the backseat of the taxi. "Do you need me to retrieve your bags?"

"Not yet," Giselle responded. She and Valerie walked to the front desk, and they were greeted by the same hotel clerk who had checked them in when they'd first arrived. His badge indicated that his name was Homer.

"We need to check into a room for the night," Giselle stated.

"I remember you two. Didn't I check you in three or four days ago?"

"It's a long story," Valerie chimed in. "Do you have a room?"

"Let's see." The clerk typed some information into the computer. "Is it for one night?"

"Yes. Just for one night," Valerie answered.

"Let's see. Do you want an ocean view?"

"We want the cheapest room you have," Valerie answered, slightly annoyed.

"Okay. We have a room with a king-size bed. It does not have a good view." He told them the price.

"We'll take it," Giselle responded. She provided her credit card information. "We would like to speak with your manager."

"Is everything okay? Did I do something wrong?" Homer asked nervously.

"No, you didn't. Our friend is missing, and we would like to speak with the manager," Giselle replied. "Maybe your manager can help us."

"I knew there was another person with you. Blonde hair."

"Have you seen her?" Giselle and Valerie asked almost in unison.

"Not since the day I checked you in. When did you last see her?"

"Yesterday evening. A little after 7 pm," Giselle answered.

"I'll get the manager for you." The clerk picked up the phone and pressed a number. He informed the listener that there were two guests needing to speak with the manager. "My manager will be with you shortly."

A young couple fell in line behind them, and Giselle and Valerie moved out of the way to allow them to check in.

Less than five minutes later, a middle-aged man of short stature appeared through a door behind the front desk, and he introduced himself as George, the manager.

"Good afternoon. How may I be of assistance to you both?" George asked with a smile. He offered them a handshake.

"We checked into this hotel with our friend three days ago," Giselle stated. "We last saw her in this hotel around quarter past seven yesterday evening. She was meeting a male friend. Our friend never came back. We were scheduled to fly back to the US today. We're worried that something might have happened to our friend. It's not like her to be irresponsible where she would miss her flight."

"I'm sorry to hear this," the manager responded. "Have you gone to the police?"

"We have," Valerie answered. "I don't think the police are going to take this seriously until at least twenty-four hours or maybe even forty-eight hours have gone by."

"Okay. So how do you think I can help?"

"We assume that you have cameras hidden throughout the hotel. We would like to see if there's any footage captured of our friend leaving the hotel," Giselle stated. "Maybe there might be a clue." She waited what seemed like a long time for the manager to respond.

"This is not a standard request, but I realize the predicament you are in. Follow me."

Giselle and Valerie followed closely behind. They were led through a door behind the front desk and down a hall to an end room on the right. George knocked, and a tall, burly man in a gray uniform opened the door.

"Hello boss," the security man acknowledged in a deep voice. He looked confused as he stared at Giselle and Valerie.

"Caesar, I'm going to need you to help these ladies. They are guests at the hotel, and they think that their friend has gone missing."

"What do you need for me to do boss?"

"They last saw their friend a little after seven yesterday evening. See what footage you have of her."

Caesar invited them into the dim room, which had six security monitors. He sat on a black leather chair and faced the monitors. "What does your friend look like?" Caesar asked. Giselle gave him a detailed description in addition to what Kate was last seen wearing.

The screens were equally divided into four smaller screens. There was a full view of all angles of the lobby, the stairwells, and the corridors of all four floors. A young couple appeared on the screen after emerging from their hotel room. They were laughing and overly affectionate. The man pressed his lover against the wall and passionately kissed her. Another screen displayed the corridor of another floor. A woman appeared to have difficulty controlling her child. The little boy, four or five, got loose from his mother's grip and ran wildly down the hall. The mother ran after him, and the boy did not get too far. She spanked him, and the boy wailed.

Screenshots of the lobby displayed tourists arriving and leaving. Some were mingling in the lobby. There were two attendants at the counter, both assisting guests. One of the attendants was Homer. The bellmen were in view. Some helped the tourists with their luggage, while others awaited the arrivals of guests.

"Okay, let's see," the security guard remarked as he clicked the mouse. "Your friend was last seen in your hotel room shortly after 7 pm. What's your room number?"

"Two twelve," Giselle answered. "Our room number was 212."

"Okay, let's see," the security guard continued. "Let's set the date back to yesterday at 7 pm." The guard went to a menu screen, and he entered a password that showed up on the screen as asterisks. He then entered the date and start time in the designated slot. "Okay, let's go to each channel and view the playback."

Giselle felt motionless as she waited for what would appear on the screen. She glanced over at Valerie, whose eyes were fixed on the screen. George, the manager, remained close by, as he was evidently curious as to what was taking place.

The security guard forwarded the recording. "That's her!" Giselle exclaimed, pointing at the screen. The security guard immediately paused the image then played the recording. Kate walked down the carpeted corridor. She stopped and turned back, retracing her steps. She stopped in front of the door, and it looked as though she pulled out her card key. She stood facing the door, almost as if she were deciding whether to enter. She put the card key back in her purse and walked to the elevator.

Kate exited the elevator into the lobby. She sat on one of the wicker chairs for several minutes. She then walked outside the lobby and took a left turn.

"Where did she go?" Giselle asked the security guard. She noticed a slight panic in her voice. "Did she get into a taxi?"

"The surveillance camera capturing the front entrance to the hotel malfunctioned three days ago," the security guard commented.

"Are you serious?" Valerie interjected, annoyed.

"Do you have any other cameras along the perimeter of the hotel?" Giselle asked.

"We have a camera capturing the rear of the hotel." The security guard switched to the rear camera. There was no evidence of Kate. He fast forwarded the recording, and after thirty minutes of footage went by, it was evident that Kate was not there.

"Are you telling me that there's absolutely no footage from the moment Kate stepped out of the lobby?" Giselle asked. "There's no way to see if she entered one of the taxi cabs?"

"Let's see again." The security guard switched back to the surveillance footage of the lobby. He rewound the recording until Kate appeared on the screen. "Your friend took a left when she exited the lobby. It's hard to tell from this footage if she got into one of the taxis."

"I'm sorry for this misfortune," George commented. "We are in the process of updating our surveillance system to a hi-tech system that is weather resistant with panoramic views."

Who cares, Giselle thought. *How's that going to help us now?*

"I will speak to the bellmen and staff who were on last night. Maybe someone can provide us more information on your friend."

"We would greatly appreciate it," Giselle replied. She looked over at Valerie, who had a despondent look. George led them back to the lobby.

"If there is anything else that I can do for you both, please let me know," the manager stated. He shook their hands, then he walked away.

"What now?" Valerie asked her friend. "I don't know what else to do."

"Let's head into town. Maybe we might run into Austin."

"There's no way we're going to run into Austin."

"Do you have a better idea?"

Valerie sighed. "Okay, let's go."

They requested a taxi, which arrived about fifteen minutes later. The friends slid into the backseat. Giselle asked Valerie for her camera. She clicked through the images until she found a close-up picture of Kate, and she showed the image to the taxi driver. "Have you seen this person?"

The driver reached behind for the camera, and he studied the image for a few seconds. He told them that he had never seen the person before. It was discouraging to hear, but Giselle hoped that someone in town may recognize Kate from the picture.

The taxi driver drove them to the heart of Fira.

Giselle and Valerie walked through the town of Fira, randomly showing strangers a picture of Kate. No one recognized her. They stopped by Zeus Zest, and Demetrius cheerfully welcomed them as they entered.

"I thought you ladies had left paradise by now," he said with a smile. "What's wrong? Why the dismal mood?"

Valerie informed him that Kate had gone missing, and she told him what had transpired. Demetrius was dismayed to hear that Kate had gone missing. He promised to keep his eyes vigilant and ask around. They thanked Demetrius for his kindness and left the eatery.

They walked for another half an hour, showing strangers a picture of Kate, but still made no headway. No one claimed to have seen her.

It was after 5 pm, and they agreed that they needed to sit for a moment and get something to eat. The last meal they'd had was around 8 am. They settled on a café and sat outside where they had a good view of the people walking by.

"Giselle, this is all my fault."

"You can't keep blaming yourself. This isn't your fault."

"This would've never happened if I had not lost my temper. I told her to leave," Valerie said in dismay. Her eyes welled up, and she dabbed her eyes with a napkin.

"This isn't the time to play the blame game."

The waitress approached the table and took their orders. They both ordered a sandwich and a side salad. She took their menus and walked away.

"As I was saying, this isn't the time to play the blame game. Our next step will be to go to the US embassy in Athens."

"Is that Maxwell?" Valerie asked, looking across the cobblestone path.

Giselle looked in the direction that her friend was pointing. Maxwell was walking out of a souvenir shop.

"Maxwell!" Valerie called out. "Maxwell!"

Maxwell walked across the street. He was wearing a beige shirt with palm tree designs, knee-length cargo pants, brown leather sandals, and a fedora hat, looking like a true tourist. His dark skin was glistening.

"Valerie. Giselle. Fancy seeing you two here," he said in a British accent. "Are you both following me, or is this all a strange coincidence?"

"We need your help," Valerie said, getting straight to the point.

"I'm doing well, by the way," Maxwell stated sarcastically. "May I at least sit down?"

"Please have a seat," Giselle replied. "How are you doing?"

"I'm doing great. Enjoying another beautiful day in Santorini. How long are you two here?"

The waitress returned with the sandwiches and side salads. She acknowledged that there was an additional person at the table. Maxwell asked for a glass of water. The waitress took a glass from an adjacent table and filled it. She filled the other two glasses as well, then she excused herself.

"We were supposed to head back to New York today," Giselle replied. "Our friend did not come back to the hotel, and we're trying to find her."

"So, how do you think I can help?"

"Kate was on the yacht with your friends Austin and Blake," she continued. "We think she's hanging out with Austin. We need help getting in touch with Austin."

"Austin. Who's Austin?"

"He was on the yacht. He's good friends with Blake. Caucasian, tall, average build, tanned, dark brown hair, hazel eyes, American," Giselle responded.

"That describes a lot of the guys on that yacht." He paused then continued. "Blake is my buddy, but I don't know the other bloke."

"Can you get in contact with Blake and find out some information about Austin?" Valerie chimed in. "What hotel is he staying at? Is he even still on the island?"

Maxwell chuckled. "What ever happened to 'get lost British boy'?"

"Look Maxwell, I'm sorry. It was rude of me to talk to you like that. You didn't deserve it. Please accept my apology."

He thought for a few seconds. "I know how you can make it up to me." He wore a mischievous smile, and the whiteness of his teeth was dazzling.

Valerie looked apprehensive. She had no idea what Maxwell was going to ask of her.

He seemed to relish the look on her face. "I want you to dance with me, Val."

"What?" Valerie said in disbelief. Her look of apprehension transformed to confusion.

"You did not dance with me in the club. You did not dance with me on the yacht. Now I want you to dance with me."

"Where?"

"Here. Right now."

"You want me to dance with you right here with all of these people walking by? They're going to think we're crazy."

"Who cares what they think? You don't know them, and you're never going to see them again in your life."

"There's no music."

"We don't need music." Maxwell extended his left hand to Valerie. She reluctantly gave him her right hand, and she stood. She looked around, expecting the impending embarrassment.

"Okay, Val. So the movement is all in the hips. Follow my lead." Maxwell secured his left hand around her waist and held her left hand with his right. He swayed his hips from side to side.

Giselle observed her friend attempting to dance. Valerie looked stiff as a board. Maxwell, on the other hand, had some impressive moves. He tried unsuccessfully to spin his dance partner, but Valerie's two left feet got in the way. They drew the attention of some of the people walking by. Some stopped and observed the spectacle. There was a middle-aged man who started taking pictures.

"Can we stop now?" Valerie pleaded. Maxwell ignored her and continued the performance. His energy level was not slowing down. He tried again to twirl Valerie around. She almost made a full circle before losing her balance. She fell backward, and Maxwell fortunately caught her before she embarrassed herself even more.

The show generated a few claps from the spectators. "Now we can stop," Maxwell said with a smile.

They both sat at the table, and Valerie appeared traumatized.

"Relax Val. Don't be so tense. Now how can I help you?"

Valerie tried to dismiss her humiliation and suppress her aggravation. She knew that Kate's life was at stake. "We need you to get in contact with Blake. We need to find Austin."

"So you want me to call up my friend and randomly ask him the whereabouts of someone I don't even know?"

Giselle thought out loud. "Austin was making a big investment in a hotel on Santorini. Say you're interested in investing in the property, and you would like to discuss being an investor."

Maxwell leaned back in his chair and eyed both of them. "You want me to lie about being interested in an investment? What's going on?"

"We think our friend is with Austin," Giselle replied.

"Okay. So why don't I ask Blake to call this Austin guy to find out if your friend is with him?"

There was silence for several seconds. "Can we trust you?" Giselle asked.

"Yes, you both can trust me."

"We think that something may have happened to our friend," Giselle continued. "We think Austin may know something."

"So, you think this Austin guy harmed your friend?"

"We definitely think that she is in danger," Valerie stated, as she cut back into the conversation.

"Why don't you go to the police if you think your friend is in danger?"

"We went to the police this morning," Giselle replied. "I don't think Kate is even on their radar right now."

"So, you want to confront someone you think is potentially dangerous?"

"We want to ask him a few questions," Valerie answered.

"I don't like the sound of this. Maybe I need to be around to protect you."

"Could you please call your friend? We would be extremely grateful," Valerie responded.

Maxwell stared at them for a few more seconds. "Okay." He pulled his cell phone out of his pocket and scrolled. He pressed a button and placed the phone to his ear. After a few seconds, he spoke through the receiver. "Blake. Hey, bud. This is Maxwell. Give me a ring when you get this message."

Giselle and Valerie had barely touched their sandwiches. The waitress inquired whether the meal was not to their liking to which they assured her that that was not the case. They forced themselves to eat their meals despite not having much of an appetite.

Maxwell's phone rang, and he picked it up after the second ring. "Blake, what's going on, my man?" A pause took place. "Nothing much. Enjoying the beautiful weather in paradise." Another pause ensued, then Maxwell laughed and tilted his head back. "Man, you are living the life. In my next life, I want to come back as you." He laughed again. "I'm serious. You live the life that many men only dream of living." Another laugh followed. "Anyway, I have a favor to ask of you. Your friend Austin, who was on the yacht in Mykonos, I hear he's planning to build a hotel in Santorini. Let him know that I'm interested in investing. I'm actually here in Santorini, so the sooner he can call me, the better." He listened for a few seconds. "Absolutely, give him my number." There was another pause. "Thanks again, man. I owe you one." They spoke for a few more minutes, then the call was terminated. "Now, we await the call."

"Thanks," Giselle responded. "We appreciate you calling. Now, hopefully, Austin calls."

"Don't take this the wrong way, but I think I should get your numbers or at least have a way of reaching you both in case I'm able to obtain information."

Giselle gave him her cell phone number. Valerie also gave him her cell phone number as a backup.

"What hotel are you staying at?"

Giselle and Valerie glanced at each other, and there was no immediate response to his question. He picked up on their hesitation.

"I'm only asking in case I can't reach you by phone. I'm staying at the Villa Breeze."

"We're at the Olive Branch Hotel," Giselle replied.

"Should I stay close to you guys for now in case this Austin guy calls, or do you want me to contact you if I hear from him? Maybe I can even offer more help."

They pondered for a moment. "It wouldn't hurt to have another set of eyes and ears," Giselle said. "We can put all of our minds together."

"I'm fully in," Maxwell commented. "I want to help you find your friend." A pause followed. "What do we do in the meantime?"

The waitress returned to the table. "Can I get you anything else?"

No one wanted anything else to eat or drink, so they requested the check. Giselle and Valerie paid for their meals. They remained at the table trying to lay out their next steps and formulate a plan. Almost twenty minutes went by when Maxwell's phone rang. It was an unidentified number.

"Hello." There was a pause. "This is he." Another pause. "Thanks for calling." Maxwell gave a thumbs-up indicating that the expected caller was on the other end of the line.

Giselle realized that she was holding her breath. She could feel her heart beating. She hoped that Austin would lead them to Kate and prayed that Kate was unharmed.

"I heard that you're planning to build a hotel in Santorini, and I heard you're looking for investors. I'm interested in hearing more."

There was a long silence, and Giselle could envision Austin rattling off information about the hotel. His favorite phrase was "state of the art."

"That all sounds great," Maxwell said. "I would like to meet up with you, and we can discuss more in person." Another pause ensued. "Fantastic, 7 pm at Eden's sounds great." He hung up. "I guess I've committed myself to dinner with this bloke. Do I pretend I'm interested in this hotel?"

Valerie momentarily excused herself from the table. She had to call Donald to let him know that she had not made it onto the flight. She gave him enough information to let him know the circumstances but refrained from telling him too much, as she did not want him to worry. She promised that she would be back in New York soon. At least, she hoped. Donald voiced his concern, but she assured him that everything would be okay and that she would keep him abreast.

Giselle looked at her watch. It was 6:15 pm. They had to come up with a plan soon.

CHAPTER 14

Maxwell walked into the restaurant and removed his fedora. He looked at his watch. It was 7:01 pm. "Good evening, sir. I'm meeting up with Austin Bate. We have 7 pm reservations."

"Yes. Please follow me."

Maxwell followed the waiter to a table in a corner of the room. Most of the tables were occupied by diners.

"Austin Bate. I'm Maxwell."

Austin stood and shook Maxwell's hand. "Nice to meet you. Have a seat." They both sat.

"British accent. Where in England are you from?"

"London borough of Hackney."

"Nice. I didn't catch your last name."

"It's Adeyemi."

"Adeyemi. What's the origin of your name?"

"It's Nigerian. My parents moved to London to attend university. I was born two years later in London."

"Is your family still in London?"

The waiter interrupted the conversation momentarily as he took their orders.

"My sister and I live in London. My parents moved back to Nigeria almost eight years ago. But enough about me. Tell me more about yourself and your business."

"So, how exactly did you hear about this business deal?" Austin asked. He intently eyed Maxwell, then he took a sip from his glass of water.

"I overheard a couple of people on the yacht in Mykonos talking about it. I must say, you were portrayed as such an astute and ingenious person that I said to myself, Maxwell, you have to meet this guy."

Austin evidently relished the compliment, and his smile broadened. He placed his hands behind his head and leaned back in his chair. "I didn't realize that you were on the yacht. I was a little," he paused. "Let's just say that I was a little bit preoccupied on the yacht."

"There's something more behind that smile," Maxwell said with a laugh. He playfully pointed his index finger at his dining companion. "I can tell. Spill it."

Austin smiled then took another sip from his glass. He intentionally changed the subject. "So how do you know Blake?"

"I met him during my first semester at the University of Cambridge. He was in my accounting class. We hit it off almost immediately. A Yankee studying in England. What's not to like? When he moved back to the US, we kept in touch."

"So Maxwell, what is it that you do?"

"I'm an investment banker. I work for a bank back home in London."

"So you're in the business of dealing with money. That's exactly what I need. People who work with money or people who have a lot of money."

"Well then, you've met the right person. So tell me about yourself and your business."

The waiter brought them bread with an olive oil and pesto dip. He placed a glass of rum and Coke on the table in front of Austin and a Coors Light in front of Maxwell. He assured them that their meals would be ready soon.

Austin described himself as a successful real estate broker for wealthy clientele and multimillion-dollar companies. He proudly listed all of his accomplishments, not to mention his achievement when he graduated with highest honors at the Wharton School of Business. He shared his vision for the hotel that he planned on naming Utopia Hotel and Resort. The name said it all. Austin had big plans and high standards, and he was determined to transform his vision into a reality.

"So how much money are you looking for your investors to invest?"

"A minimum of fifty grand. I actually have investors in my pocket who are willing to dish out some major cash." Austin went on and on about his potential investors, and he dominated the conversation as they ate dinner.

Maxwell switched the conversation to a lighter subject. "Aside from work, how have you been occupying yourself in Santorini?"

"My focus has mainly been on work, but I found some time to enjoy the beauty of the island and mingle with tourists."

"Excuse my candor, but the women here are hot. Smoking hot."

Austin laughed. "I have to agree with you my friend. There have been a few that have caught my eye."

"No one woman in particular?"

"Not really. I'm not looking to settle down right now. I have a lot on my plate, and I'm always traveling. I don't think it would be fair to put my lifestyle on anyone right now. I was actually engaged a few months back, and my fiancée couldn't keep up. It took a toll on our relationship, and we grew distant. We decided that the best thing to do was to break off the engagement and go our separate ways." Austin paused. "I still love her though. We met in college."

The waiter returned with another glass of rum and Coke for Austin and a Coors Light for Maxwell.

"So, what about you? Are you in a relationship, or are you living the single life?"

Maxwell took a gulp from the beer bottle. "I'm single, but I wouldn't mind settling down, if it's with the right person."

"I hear that."

"So how much longer are you here in Santorini?"

"I'm leaving the day after tomorrow. Maybe I can show you the property tomorrow?"

"Sounds good. Give me your number, and I'll give you a call tomorrow morning," Maxwell replied. Austin gave Maxwell his number. "Name a meeting spot or maybe I can come to your hotel. Where are you staying, by the way?"

Without hesitation, Austin told Maxwell that he was staying at the Blue Grecian Hotel.

Austin and Maxwell walked out of Eden's Restaurant and Bar. They stood outside and continued their conversation. The sun had gone down, but the street was lit and lively. A group of people were gathered together, immersed in loud talk and heavy laughter.

"Austin. What a surprise to see you here," Giselle said, interrupting their conversation. Valerie was standing close by. "Where's Kate?"

Austin was evidently caught off guard. "I have no idea. I thought you all left for New York."

"Well, we're still here." Valerie said. She crossed her arms across her chest. "Kate met up with you, and she did not come back to the hotel. So where is she?"

"Look, the last time I saw her was yesterday afternoon when I dropped you all back in town. When did you last see her?"

"Don't play this game with us," Valerie accused him with clear indignation. "She left the hotel last night to meet up with you."

"Austin, is everything okay?" Maxwell chimed in.

He ignored the question. "Okay. Hold it right there. Kate never met up with me. I waited for her, but she never showed up."

"Liar!" Valerie said in a raised voice. "Tell us where Kate is right now, or we're going to the police."

"Is everything okay?" Maxwell asked again, inserting himself into the heated discussion.

"Everything is okay," Austin said. He appeared slightly irritated. "I'm so sorry you're witnessing this. All of this is a big misunderstanding. I don't know what's going on. Why the accusation?"

"We're not accusing you," Giselle replied, trying to get a hold of the situation. She had repeatedly told Valerie to keep her cool and not to convey to Austin that he was being incriminated. "We want to know if you've heard from Kate."

"Are you telling me that Kate is missing?"

"Don't act so surprised," Valerie retorted.

Giselle tried to calm her friend down. "Austin. Last night, Kate left the hotel, and she was meeting up with you. We have not heard from her since then. She wouldn't disappear like that. We had a flight to catch."

"I'm telling you the truth. I hoped that she would meet up with me, but she never did. I waited at the bar for almost three hours, but she never showed up. I figured she stood me up. The bartender can vouch for me." Austin pointed at the restaurant. "I was at Eden's last night. I sat at the bar the entire time and downed a few drinks. The only time I got up was to take a piss."

"Austin, do you have any clue as to where our friend could have gone," Giselle replied. "Anything she might have said. Anything?"

"She didn't tell me or hint at anything indicative of her whereabouts. I wish I could help, but I have no answers. I don't know where Kate is. I hope she's alright and you find her soon." Austin turned his attention to Maxwell and extended his hand. Maxwell reciprocated and shook Austin's hand. "It was a pleasure meeting you, and don't be a stranger."

Austin disappeared into the night. Giselle was momentarily frozen. It was strange that someone who Kate claimed to have feelings for was so untroubled by her disappearance. Frankly, his hope of them finding her seemed disingenuous.

"Can you believe that son of a female dog?" Valerie said, exasperated. "He knows something. He knows where Kate is. He's behind all of this. I hope he has not laid a finger on her."

"I don't think we handled this the correct way," Giselle said as she reflected on the last ten minutes. "He knows we're on to him. Who knows where he went off to or when he's leaving the island?"

"You both are not giving me any credit," Maxwell interrupted. "Of course I led the dinner conversation in that direction. He's leaving the day after tomorrow. He's staying at the Blue Grecian Hotel in Fira."

"Strong work," Giselle replied. "Let's contact emergency services." Giselle took her phone out of her fanny pack. "What's the equivalent to 911 here?"

Maxwell and Valerie shrugged their shoulders. She accessed the internet on her phone and discovered that the emergency number was 112 and the number for police was 100. She dialed 100, but the call went to voicemail. The voice spoke Greek, which was followed by a message in English. The police department was closed, and for emergencies, the caller was instructed to dial 112. Giselle dialed the number, and after a few seconds, a male voice spoke Greek in her ear.

"I speak English." Giselle replied.

The voice immediately changed to English. "One-twelve. What is your emergency?"

"Yes. My name is Giselle Bellamy, and I want to report a missing person and a suspected kidnapping."

"Who's the person, and what is your relationship to this person?"

"Her name is Katherine Davenport. She goes by Kate. She is my friend."

"Who has kidnapped her?"

"I highly suspect that it is a guy she just met named Austin Bate."

"When did Kate go missing?

"She was last seen at the Olive Branch Hotel yesterday evening. A little after 7 pm."

"Do you know where she went after that?"

"I don't. She was meeting up with Austin Bate."

"What information do you have on Austin Bate?"

Giselle told the operator everything she knew about Austin from his place of birth to his physical description to his business dealings in Santorini. She told the operator the hotel where he was staying. She mentioned that she had gone to the police. She even mentioned the encounter outside of Eden's.

"Please send the police to investigate Austin."

The operator assured her that he would communicate with the police and have them go out to the Blue Grecian Hotel.

———

Two police officers entered the Blue Grecian Hotel. One of the officers inquired about the hotel room of Austin Bate. The officers took the elevator to the fourth floor and knocked on room 403. The door opened but was halted by the chain lock on the door.

"Are you Austin Bate?" one of the officers asked.

"Yes, I am. What's this all about?"

"Could you please open the door?" the same officer asked.

Austin removed the chain lock and opened the door. He was shirtless and wearing only boxers.

"Do you mind putting on a shirt and some pants." the other police officer said, more of a statement than a question.

"Not at all officer." Austin unzipped his suitcase and took out a white T-shirt. He inserted his arms through the sleeves and pulled the shirt over his head. He pulled out a pair of faded jeans and stepped in one leg at a time. "Now is someone going to tell me what this is all about?"

"This is about Kate Davenport," the officer that first spoke answered. "The woman you met up with last night."

"I didn't meet up with her. We had plans last night at Eden's Restaurant and Bar, but she never showed. I waited at the bar for her for almost three hours. She stood me up. Or at least I thought she stood me up."

"Can anyone corroborate this story?" the same police officer asked.

"Yes. I was at the bar the entire time. Joe, the bartender served me. I even told him my name. Also, I met a cute waitress. I think her name was Hestia. She said she was named after the Greek goddess of home, family, or something like that. She wanted to know what a handsome guy like me was doing at the bar all alone. I told her that I was waiting for someone, but I thought I had been stood up."

"When was the last time you saw Kate Davenport?" the officer who had dominated the interrogation asked.

"The last time I saw her was yesterday afternoon. I dropped her and her friends off in town around 2 pm."

Austin was interrogated for about twenty more minutes. The officers had nothing on him, and their next course of action was to check out his alibi. He was instructed to call 112 if he remembered anything.

The officers walked into Eden's. The restaurant hostess appeared nervous at the sight of the police officers, and she asked permission to get the manager.

The manager was a heavyset middle aged woman of short stature, and her brunette hair was cut short. The police officers told her that a customer reportedly dined at the restaurant last night and they needed to verify this information with the staff. One of the officers inquired about Joe, the bartender, and a waitress by the name of Hestia. The manager informed them that Joe was on duty but Hestia had the night off. She led the officers to the bar.

There were six customers at the bar. The manager pulled Joe to the side and told him that the officers had a few questions for him concerning a customer he may have seen last night.

Joe evidently was not intimidated by the officers, and he asked if they could hurry it up; he had customers to attend to. The officer leading the investigation asked if he remembered a Caucasian male in his early thirties spending almost three hours at the bar last night. American. Roughly six foot. Dark brown hair. Hazel eyes.

Joe immediately blurted out the name Austin. He told the officers that the customer arrived at the bar around 8 pm. He had struck up a conversation with the customer after Austin asked him about the Europeans' profound fascination with soccer, known as football. Joe countered that it was analogous to the Americans' fascination with their version of football. Then they debated which sport deserved to be called football. Austin felt that there was only one sport that deserved the name, which was American football. Joe shot back, declaring that American football should be renamed handball because the ball spends most of the time in the player's hand compared to European football, where the players use their feet primarily. They shared a laugh. The customer introduced himself as Austin. He had served him a shot of whiskey and two glasses of rum and Coke. He hung out at the bar until the restaurant was about to close, which was 11 pm.

The officers left the restaurant. Austin Bate had a strong alibi. The officers deduced that it was unlikely that the missing person met up with Austin immediately after leaving the hotel.

CHAPTER 15

"The officers ruled out Austin Bate as a person of interest based on his strong alibi," Detective Pallis remarked. He sat behind his desk, and Giselle and Valerie were seated across from him.

"You have to do something," Giselle pleaded. "Something has happened to her. This is not like Kate."

"We're doing everything we can. We're searching the area where she was last seen. We're checking the hospital. We're checking security footage. We've entered her name into the database. As soon as we get more information, we will contact you."

"So we're supposed to sit back and wait?" Valerie asked rhetorically.

"As I said, we're doing everything we can." A pause ensued. "Would you consider your friend a threat to herself or others?"

"She's not a threat to herself or others, but there is a threat to her," Giselle replied.

"And what proof do you have? Who is a threat to her?"

"Austin Bate is the threat," Valerie answered. "Either he's done something to her or he knows something."

"As I said, Austin Bate is not a person of interest at this time. His alibi was rock solid. It so happens that Eden's has a security camera, so we will verify this."

"So you're okay with the fact that our friend is missing?" Valerie asked sarcastically.

"Look. It's not a crime to go missing. We will follow procedure. Again, if we obtain any information, we will get in contact with you." Detective Pallis stood, indicating that the conversation was over. Giselle thanked him for his assistance, and she and Valerie left the building.

"There's something not right about Austin," Giselle commented. It was disheartening to find out that Austin was not on the investigative radar. "He's definitely up to something, and we need to find out what it is."

"What do you suggest we do?"

"Let's head over to the Blue Grecian Hotel. Austin is not leaving until tomorrow. We need to find out what he's up to." Giselle looked at her watch. It was 8:46 am. At that moment, her phone rang. She unzipped her fanny pack and took out her cell phone. She did not recognize the number.

"Hello." There was a pause. "Oh, hello, Maxwell." Another pause. "Val and I are leaving the police station right now." Another pause. "Well, the police do not suspect Austin. They said he has a strong alibi. Apparently he was at Eden's from about 8 pm to closing." Another pause. "I don't trust Austin, and I know there is something that he is hiding. We're going to catch a cab to take us to the Blue Grecian Hotel." Giselle switched the phone to her other ear. "Honestly, I don't know what our plan is. He's denied that he had anything to do with Kate's disappearance, and I don't think he's going to change his story. We're going to have to follow his footsteps." There was another pause. "That's perfect. Call Austin and let him know that you want to meet up with him and that you're interested in seeing the property." Another pause. "Great. Let's say we meet at the same café as yesterday." Another pause. "We're heading there now. See you there." She terminated the call.

Giselle and Valerie caught a taxi. They were dropped off down the street from the Mediterranean Earth café. They walked in the direction of the café, and as they got closer, they recognized

Maxwell coming from the opposite direction. He was wearing the same fedora but with a different outfit.

"I definitely need to eat something," Valerie said. "I barely ate the sandwich we had here yesterday."

"I agree. Did you eat breakfast?" Giselle asked Maxwell.

"I did, but I wouldn't mind seeing what's on the menu."

"Okay, let's grab something quickly," Giselle responded. "We need to devise a plan."

The waiter seated them at a table in one of the corners of the small café. He gave each a menu.

"I tried calling Austin twice. It rang a few times and went to his voicemail. I left a message. Maybe he's sleeping. Hopefully he'll call back soon."

"I hope so," Valerie replied. She opened the menu and eyed the options. For such a small café, the list was impressive. The waiter took their orders. Valerie ordered scrambled eggs with tomatoes and feta with a side of whole wheat bread. She ordered a cup of coffee too.

"And for you?" the waitress asked, turning to Giselle.

"I'll have the scrambled eggs with spinach and feta and the yogurt with honey and walnuts. And to drink, I'll have a glass of orange juice."

"Very well. And for you sir?"

"I'll have a bowl of assorted fruits. Water will be fine."

The waiter took the menus and walked away.

"So, what's the plan? Are you ladies going to stalk him?"

"If that's what it takes," Valerie responded.

"Suppose you both are looking in the wrong direction. Suppose Austin had nothing to do with it."

"Oh, he had something to do with it alright," Valerie retorted. "He has a nasty temper, and I can definitely see him acting out if put in a predicament."

"Okay. What would be his reason for harming your friend?"

"Who knows," Giselle replied. "Kate was falling for him. She was even talking about marriage, and if you know Kate, that is unlike her. Maybe she was pressuring him for a commitment."

Maxwell let out a loud sigh. "Austin did mention to me that he wasn't looking to settle down. He said that he had a lot on his plate. His lifestyle would not accommodate a serious relationship. That's why he and his fiancée broke off their engagement a few months ago."

"He was engaged?" Giselle and Valerie said in unison. It was jarring to hear that Austin was once engaged and not too long ago at that.

"Yes. He said she was his college sweetheart. He said he still loves her."

"Did he mention Kate?" Giselle asked.

"Not quite. At least he didn't mention her by name. I asked him if anyone in particular in Greece had caught his eye and he said 'not really'."

Giselle was speechless. It saddened her that her friend had thought so highly of this guy and even thought that she may have been in love with him, just to find out that the feelings were not reciprocated.

The waiter brought a tray and placed the breakfast items in front of them accordingly. Maxwell took his phone out of his pocket. He keyed in a password then he pressed a button. He put the phone to his ear and waited. "Hey Austin. This is Maxwell again. I hope I'm not bothering you. I'm hoping to see the property before you leave the island. Please give me a call when you get this message. Thanks." Maxwell disconnected. "I guess we'll have to wait."

"Suppose he doesn't call back," Valerie noted.

"I say we go to the hotel and see what Austin boy is up to," Giselle replied. "Let's eat quickly. We need to follow him."

"Then what?" Maxwell asked with skepticism. "You follow him and then what?"

"Right now, I don't have much more of a plan. There's not much that I have to work with. The police are only willing to do so much. My hands are tied. The only thing I can hope for is that some clue will manifest itself."

Maxwell insisted on taking care of the bill and would not take no for an answer. They left the café and walked in the direction of the hotel. The walk took them a little over ten minutes.

"I was thinking that you may be the best person to go in," Giselle said, addressing Maxwell. "You can tell the hotel attendant that you are meeting with Austin Bate and if Mr. Bate could be notified that you're in the lobby. We'll wait outside."

"What have I gotten myself into," Maxwell said with a smile. "If this is what it takes to get you closer to finding your friend, then I'm willing to do whatever I can."

"We appreciate it," Giselle responded with a smile. "We really do."

"Yes, we certainly do appreciate it."

Maxwell walked to the hotel lobby then entered through the sliding glass door. He was no longer in sight.

"Kate, where could you be?" Valerie thought out loud. "I pray that you're okay. I'm so sorry for letting you leave us. Especially in a foreign country. I should have stopped you. I should have never allowed you to walk out of that hotel room."

"Valerie, you're going to have to stop blaming yourself. We need to focus."

"Suppose she's dead," Valerie stated as she thought about the frightful possibility. Her eyes welled up, and a tear fell down her cheek.

Giselle hugged her friend. "She's not dead. You have to believe that. We're going to find her and bring her back home."

Maxwell walked out of the hotel lobby and approached them. "Bad news. Austin checked out of the hotel this morning."

CHAPTER 16

"I bet he's leaving the island," Giselle said with exasperation. She was frustrated and scolded herself for not being quick enough. How could she let him outsmart her? She knew that Austin was aware that they were on to him. Now he had slipped right through her fingers like a stream of water, unhindered with no revelation of its final destination.

She waved down a taxicab, and the three of them slid into the backseat. The taxi driver headed in the direction of the police station. The taxi chugged down the road at snail's pace as though it were reluctant to reach its destination. After a few minutes elapsed, Valerie ordered the driver to speed up. There was clear annoyance in her voice, and the driver immediately acquiesced. He accelerated and the car lunged forward, causing them to fall backward into the seat. It ran across a deep pothole, and the cab jolted a foot into the air before landing harshly on the asphalt.

"Hey, mate, can you take it easy?" Maxwell said, rubbing his lower back with his right hand. "When we asked you to go a little faster, we didn't mean go crazy."

The taxi driver apologized. He drove more cautiously at a reasonable speed. The cab pulled up in front of the police station, and they exited. Giselle was about to pay the driver, but Maxwell again was insistent.

"If you keep insisting on paying for everything, we're going to have to do this by ourselves."

"I'm sorry. I'm a gentleman, and the man always pays."

"Valerie and I don't expect you to pay for anything. You're helping us out, and we appreciate it."

"Okay. Understood."

They walked into the police station. The cool air from the air-conditioned room greeted them as they entered.

"May I help you?" the attendant asked. It was the same young woman who was behind the desk earlier in the morning.

"Yes. Is Detective Pallis available?" Giselle asked.

"I'll check to see if he's available. Please have a seat."

They sat on the blue plastic chairs. A humming noise came from the water fountain in the corner of the room. Giselle was aware of every noise around her. She observed the nervous tapping of Valerie's left foot on the tile. A brown and white bird pecked its beak on the exterior part of the glass window. She could even hear the beating of her heart inside her chest.

A door in the partitioning opened, and Detective Pallis was in full view. "Hello again, ladies. It's been how many hours since I last saw you?" He looked at his watch. "I take it that you have not found your friend."

"No we have not, and we know who's responsible," Valerie replied.

"Okay, follow me."

At that moment, a middle-aged man limped into the station assisted by a younger man holding onto his arm. They both spoke in Greek.

Giselle and her companions followed behind Detective Pallis through the door.

"Is he with you?" the officer asked with a perplexed look.

"Yes he is. This is Maxwell. He's been trying to help us find our friend," Giselle replied. At that moment, she realized that she did not know Maxwell's last name. She did not know much about him except for the fact that he was from England and he loved to dance. Her main focus was on finding Kate, so she did not even think to ask him any details about himself.

They were led into his office, and Detective Pallis excused himself. He brought in a blue plastic chair for Maxwell to sit on. Detective Pallis situated himself behind his desk and placed his hands behind his head. "So, you say that you know who's responsible for your friend being missing. Enlighten me."

"Austin Bate is responsible," Valerie spoke with confidence. "The same guy we told you about before."

"I understand that this is frustrating for you. Believe me, I do. You want to reach for anyone who had any association with your friend. That is completely understandable. But like I stated earlier, Austin Bate is not a person of interest at this time. We were able to access the video surveillance at Eden's, and Austin's alibi checked out. He was seated at the bar most of the time from a little after 8 pm to closing at 11 pm. He left the bar three times for a short period of time, presumably going to the bathroom; he headed in that direction all three times. Again, I know this is difficult for you, but we are actively looking for your friend."

Valerie was persistent. "With all due respect to you and your colleagues, there's something up with this guy. He was supposed to leave Santorini tomorrow, but he all of a sudden got up and left. He checked out of his hotel this morning. It's because he knew we were on to him."

"And how do you know that?"

Valerie did not answer the question.

Detective Pallis ignored it. "Look. We have no reason to hold him. Maybe something came up. He is free to leave as he chooses."

Detective Pallis stood again, indicating that the conversation was over. "As soon as we get more information, I'll be the first to let you know. I have your numbers."

Valerie wearily stood up. Her body felt heavy like a large bag filled to the brim with sand, and it took every bit of strength for her to stand firmly on her feet. Her eyelids were heavy from lack of sleep, and she was almost certain that the stress was evident on her face. Her hope of finding Kate abated as the minutes passed by. She felt a sickening feeling in the pit of her stomach, a feeling that something terrible had happened. Her mind went back to the moment that Kate left the hotel room. She was enraged that her friend had gone back on her word once again. It was disappointing that Kate chose a guy over her friends. She was more hurt than anything, and her hurt manifested as anger. What she would have done to be able to rewind time to the moment Kate walked out the door. She would have urged her to stay and try to convince her that Austin was bad news. Instead, she allowed her friend to walk out into the stealth of night in a foreign country. She tried to ease her guilt by acknowledging that Kate was determined to meet with Austin whether she approved or not. Kate felt that she was in love. For such a smart girl, she always wore blinders when it came to men. Kate's blinders were closely secured over her eyes with Austin. There was no shift to allow visibility into his deceit and lies. Kate had believed that Austin was genuine. Valerie thought to herself that little did Kate know that Austin's feelings were not mutual and he'd had a fiancée not too long ago. Giselle snapped Valerie out of her daydream with a firm shake.

"Valerie, are you listening to us?" Giselle said, concerned. "You looked like you were paralyzed."

"I'm fine."

"As I said, I will update you as soon as I get more information," Detective Pallis reiterated. He led them out to the waiting area. "I'll be in touch." He waved at them before disappearing behind the door that led to his office.

They walked out of the police station into the warm sunshine. Giselle looked around at her surroundings. It was such a beautiful day outside, which contrasted the dark cloud that figuratively hung over her head emitting a heavy downpour of rain.

"What now?" Maxwell asked. His dark skin glistened under the rays. Giselle was convinced that he rubbed some type of oil on his skin. Maxwell stared directly at her, and she had no idea how to answer his question.

"I don't know. I don't know what's the next step. I don't know if he took a flight out or a ferry off the island."

"Maybe we can split up. Maybe Maxwell can go to the airport, and Giselle and I can go to the ferry terminal."

Maxwell looked at Valerie as though she had three heads. "Let's say by chance one of us spots him. Then what? Do you want me to jump on top of him or, better yet, kidnap him? You heard the detective. Austin Bate is not a person of interest, and he is free to leave as he wishes."

"Whose side are you on anyway?"

"Val. I mean Valerie. Please don't get defensive. I'm trying to help. I don't see how us going to the airport or ferry terminal is going to help."

"Val, he's right. We have to come up with another plan."

CHAPTER 17

"**S**ir, we're going to need you to come with us."
Austin became defensive as the customs officer tried to detain him. "What did I do? This is ridiculous." He looked around and noted that a few travelers were staring at him.

"Sir, you don't need to cause a scene. We need you to come with us. Officer Trakas will escort you."

"I have a plane to catch. This is absurd."

"If you do not cooperate, we will be forced to arrest you."

Austin looked around again, and he let out a loud sigh. "Fine."

A middle-aged man dressed in a dark blue uniform led Austin into a sterile-looking room. A dark brown oak desk took up most of the space, and a computer was situated on top of it. "Have a seat, Mr. Bate."

Austin looked around again as though he were trapped with no opportunity to escape. He reluctantly sat on the chair. "What's this all about?"

"I will ask the questions," Officer Trakas stated authoritatively. "May I see your passport?"

Austin reached into his Burberry carry-on bag and pulled out a United States passport. He handed it to the officer. Austin looked at his watch. "How long is this going to take?"

Officer Trakas ignored the question as he looked through the passport. "Where are you going?"

"I'm heading to New York City with a layover in Frankfurt."

"I see." Officer Trakas continued to page through the passport. "You have visited Shanghai five times in the past year. Can you explain that?"

"I wasn't aware that that was a crime. I love my dim sum." There was an awkward pause. "Hey, I'm kidding. I met a beautiful Chinese lady over there, and I go to visit her from time to time. It's also an extraordinary city. Have you ever been?"

"Again, I will ask the questions," Officer Trakas replied. He gave Austin a stern look. "Mr. Bate, I'm going to get straight to it. Your name was flagged in our system. It looks like you have been involved in an international money laundering scheme, and you're trying to use that dirty money to buy property and build real estate on our beautiful Greek islands."

"I don't know what you're talking about. You must have the wrong person."

"Oh, do I? I don't think so. You're not boarding that flight today."

"What? I need to catch that flight. I'm telling you that you have the wrong person. You can't do this. I have rights."

"It appears that you have been working for Hu Peng."

"Who?"

"Do you want me to play this game with you?"

"Look. I don't know a Hu Peng or Hu Pong or Hu Pang. I don't know anyone by that name."

"Well, let me refresh your memory. Hu Peng is a big shark in Shanghai. He owns several businesses, such as gentlemen night-clubs, massage parlors, and nail salons, to name a few, which appear to be legitimate to the outside world, but in reality, he is hiding illegally obtained funds. He has extended his influence to real estate, and he has obtained prime real estate in Shanghai, Hong Kong, Dubai, London, Paris, New York, and Los Angeles, that we are aware of. He's using crooked people like you in the real estate business to do his dirty work. But in actuality, Peng is the ultimate owner. So, how much money did he give you in cash to buy property in Greece under your name? Let's face it. He pays you a nice sum of dirty money that you can't refuse. You purchase property and build your hotel. But Hu Peng is the owner. I must say, that is a smart plan. Why would anyone raise an eyebrow? You seem on paper to be a hardworking, successful real estate broker who graduated from a prestigious university. So, why would you be a red flag?"

"I don't know what you're talking about."

"There was a sting operation that brought Hu Peng down. He had a bulldog of a lawyer who was able to get him out on bail, but he is on the no fly list. Unfortunately, for some of his crooked employees, they weren't as lucky. One of his boys spoke under pressure, and your name came up. That may explain why you're so anxious to leave paradise."

Austin looked Officer Trakas directly in his eyes. "I still don't know what you're talking about."

"Okay Mr. Bate. I'm tired of playing this game. You're going down to the police station. Maybe they will be able to extract a confession out of you."

"Look, for the last time, I don't know what you're talking about. You have me mixed up with some other person." Austin leaned back in the chair and placed his hands over his head. He was exhausted from the repeated questioning. He had been in the police station for almost an hour.

Detective Pallis eyed Austin with an incredulous stare. He observed every eye movement and body gesture. "Mr. Bate, I'm going to ask you this question again, and this time, I want you to tell me the truth. What is your involvement with Hu Peng?"

"I don't know Hu Peng, and I sure don't work for him. I work for Pepperidge and Lane Premier real estate in New York City."

"I get that that's your legal job. What I'm talking about is the illegal job, the job that Peng is paying you a hefty amount to build a hotel on this island."

"I'm a well-educated, successful businessman with a lot of contacts and influence. I have a résumé that would make most people green with envy. I have a reputation that speaks for itself. My bank account has a lot of zeros in it, if you know what I mean. I don't need to muddy the waters with any underhanded dealings."

"Speaking about your finances, three years ago, you were accused of tax evasion, but somehow, you were able to pay the government its due taxes and avoid jail time. And now, it looks like you're in debt again." Detective Pallis paged through a stack of papers. "Living above your means Mr. Bate? A $2 million condo in SoHo, Manhattan. A $2.5 million home in the Hollywood Hills. A boat. A Porsche 718 Boxster. A Range Rover."

"Where did you get that information?" Austin snapped. He was defensive, and he reached for the stack of papers.

Detective Pallis slammed his hand onto the pile. "This information belongs to me." For the first time during the interview, Austin seemed flustered. "Now, are you going to tell me everything you know about Hu Peng and the work that you're doing for him?"

Austin sat back and remained silent. After almost a two-minute pause, Detective Pallis broke the silence. "Mr. Bate, the information is coming in as we speak, and when we connect all of the dots, and believe me we will, we'll see that you were one of the links in Hu Peng's chain. But this can be further pursued in front of a judge in Athens. You have the right to an attorney."

"Am I being arrested?"

"Before I get to that, let's switch gears a little; shall we?"

"Okay," Austin replied cautiously. He had no idea where Detective Pallis was about to go with his questioning.

"Where's Kate Davenport?"

"What?" Austin said in disbelief.

"You heard me. Where is Kate Davenport?"

"I don't know where she is. The police have already interrogated me, and I told them the truth. I planned on meeting with her at Eden's Restaurant and Bar, but she never showed up. I waited for her until the bar closed. I thought she stood me up, so I went back to my hotel. The police also verified my alibi."

"It has been brought to my attention that you tried to persuade Kate Davenport to invest money in your hotel. Does Hu Peng know about this side dealing to put extra money in your greedy pockets? You were trying to scheme her out of money; weren't you?"

Austin was silent again.

"So, I'm going to ask you again. Where's Kate Davenport? What have you done with her?"

"I swear to you. I don't know where she is."

"Is she alive?"

"For goodness sakes, I am not a murderer." Austin was becoming increasingly emotional. He was unnerved and fidgeted in his chair.

"Are you okay? You seem a little nervous."

"Look, I'm a lot of things, but I am not a murderer. I would never hurt Kate."

Detective Pallis pressed on with his questioning, and his words became more accusatory. He had thrown Austin off- kilter.

CHAPTER 18

"Kate! Kate!" Giselle shouted to the top of her lungs. She recognized her friend from the back. Her blonde hair was swept up into a ponytail, and it swung from side to side as she walked ahead. She had on the same white shirt and faded, fitted jeans when she left the hotel on that ill-fated night. The satin blue and white scarf was knotted around her neck. The movement of her steps was familiar, and it was definitely Kate walking ahead of her down the narrow alleyway. "Kate, slow down! It's me, Giselle. Slow down! Wait! It's me!"

Giselle quickened her steps, and Kate accelerated. She wished that Valerie and Maxwell were with her. She had left them at a café two blocks away. "Kate! Slow down! It's me!" She realized that she was running, and Kate in turn took off running. She evidently knew that she was being followed. Why was Kate running away from her? It was strange. It made no sense.

Kate took a sharp left turn and ran down the narrow path. She bumped into an elderly man and almost knocked him to the ground. Giselle ran after her and appeared to be gaining ground, narrowing the gap between them. The sun was setting, and the remaining light in the sky was rapidly disappearing. Her lungs burned, and she felt out of breath as she tried to catch up with Kate.

Kate suddenly slowed down and came to a halt, her back still turned. Giselle slowed then stopped a couple feet behind Kate. She bent over momentarily, trying to catch her breath. "Kate, why were you running from me?" She noted that her voice was choppy as she tried to fill her lungs with much-needed air. "Val and I have been looking all over for you. We even went to the police. We should have never allowed you to walk out of that hotel room. Thank goodness you're alive and safe." Giselle placed her right hand on Kate's right shoulder. "Kate, look at me."

Kate slowly turned. Giselle instantly screamed. Her voice ricocheted off of the walls. Nefarious shadows emerged around her. Kate's face was hollow, almost as if it were dug out with a sharp object. Maggots crawled out in large numbers, one on top of the other.

"Giselle! Giselle! Are you okay!" Valerie screamed as she tried to shake her friend out of a nightmare. She snapped out of it, but Valerie was on her bed, still shaking her.

"I'm okay. I had a terrible nightmare." Her cotton T-shirt was drenched with sweat, and it clung to her body.

"It must have been. You're soaked. Do you want to tell me about it?"

Giselle wiped her face with her hand. She was dripping with sweat. Valerie turned on the light to the bathroom. She handed Giselle a hand towel. She then turned the knob at the base of the lamp on the night table. A dim light spilled across the room.

"You look like you were running a race."

Giselle wiped her face with the towel. "You could say that. In my dream, I felt like I was."

"What was so terrifying?"

"It was Kate."

"What about Kate?"

"She was walking down an alleyway. Her back was to me, but I knew it was her. She had on the same clothes as the night she left the hotel room. She even had the satin scarf around her neck. The shape of her and the way she moved, it was definitely Kate. I called out but she would not respond. I walked toward her, but she walked away. The faster I walked, the faster she walked away from me. I started to run, then she started running. I called her name, but she would not stop. I knew that she knew it was me. It was all so strange. She finally stopped, and I placed my hand on her shoulder. She turned around."

"And? What happened?"

"She had no face. It was a large hole filled with maggots. There were these shadows emerging from the ground, closing in on me. I felt as though I was being suffocated. I could not breathe."

Valerie had a horrified look on her face. She did not know what to make of it all. Truthfully, she did not want to have to interpret it because construing the dream would only bring to life what she feared the most. They sat in silence. The air-conditioner came to life and blasted cool air throughout the room. The digital clock on the night table displayed 3:07 am. Valerie was the first to break the silence.

"What do you think all of this means?"

Giselle zipped open her suitcase and pulled out a T-shirt. She took off her sweat-drenched top and placed it in a plastic bag. She pulled on the clean T-shirt and situated herself back in the bed.

"Val, it was the scariest thing imaginable. I felt as though I were falling into a dark abyss, and the hands of Satan were trying to grab me. It was as if they had already gotten a hold of Kate, and I couldn't save her. The maggots represent decay, and I'm afraid that she might be dead or at least in grave danger."

Valerie could not contain her tears, and the drops streamed down her face. Giselle hugged her friend. Valerie's body shook as she cried; she was inconsolable.

CHAPTER 19

The light of dawn seeped through the opening of the curtains. Giselle squinted her eyes as she tried to focus on the digital clock. Her eyelids were heavy. The time was blurry, but the numbers eventually came into focus. It was 6:04 am. Her head was throbbing, and it felt as if someone had taken a jackhammer mercilessly to her head. She rubbed her temples, hoping that it would alleviate the pain and intense pressure behind her eyes. She knew she had not slept after being frightfully awoken from that nightmare. It was the worst thing imaginable, and it felt real. It seemed like pure evil. There was no other way to explain it. She had tossed and turned all night. Her body could not relax, and she could not remove those horrific thoughts from her consciousness.

"Val. Are you sleeping?"

"No, I'm up," a muffled voice came from under the covers. "I couldn't sleep."

"I couldn't sleep either."

They lay in bed for almost another hour, barely saying a word. Giselle dragged herself out of bed. Her body felt like a ton of bricks, and it took every bit of energy left in her to stand on her feet. She shuffled toward the window and opened the curtains. The light entered her eyes, and it almost struck her down, as if she were a vampire, except that she had a soul.

"Where are you, Kate?" Giselle said under her breath. "Where could you possibly be?" She looked out at the expanse of the sea.

It seemed so calm and peaceful, and the light hitting it at certain angles made it sparkle like precious jewels.

"Do you want to order in breakfast?"

Giselle's thoughts were interrupted. "Sure."

"I need at least two strong cups of coffee to even start the day. I'm so exhausted." Valerie looked through the hotel room service menu. "What do you want?"

"I don't know."

"Do you want to look through the menu?"

Giselle kept her gaze out the window. She rubbed her temples again in a slow, deliberate motion.

"Giselle, are you listening to me? What do you want for breakfast?"

"I'll have whatever you're having."

"Do you want Tylenol?"

"Yes. I think I may need two."

Valerie reached for her handbag on the floor next to the bed. She took out a small bottle of Tylenol. She removed the cotton and gently shook two pills into the inner cap. "Here you go, and here's a bottle of water. It's unopened."

Giselle swallowed the pills with a sip of water. She probably would have needed something stronger to knock out the headache, but hopefully the Tylenol would do the trick.

"I'm ordering a mushroom, spinach, and gruyere omelet with a side of whole wheat toast and a pot of coffee. What do you want?"

"That sounds good. I'll have the same thing."

Where could you possibly be? Giselle thought. She heard Valerie's voice in the background ordering room service. She shuffled back to the bed and crawled under the sheets. Hopefully the Tylenol would take effect soon.

"Room service will bring the food in about forty-five minutes."

"Okay."

"So, what next? Where do we go from here?"

"I wish I knew the answer to that question. I'm out of suggestions. I pray that Kate is okay."

"If she's okay, then why hasn't she contacted us? That is what scares me. I told Donald last night that Kate is missing. I didn't want to create fear and worry in him, but as expected, I did exactly that. He's not only worried about Kate, but he's worried about me. He's worried about us. He's scared that we could be putting ourselves in danger."

Valerie's cell phone rang, and she immediately reached for her handbag. She fumbled through the contents of her bag, and after about the sixth ring, she answered the phone. "Hi, honey." This was followed by a brief pause. "Yes, I'm okay. I'm fine. Everything will be fine. I promise you."

Giselle observed her friend talking on the phone. Valerie's face looked worried as she simultaneously tried to convince her husband that everything was fine and that the police force was working tirelessly to find Kate.

"How's Bridget?" There was a pause. "Tell her that Mommy loves her, and I'll be home soon." There was another pause. "But honey, I have to go. I love you too. I have to go now. I'll talk to you again soon." She disconnected.

"You didn't appear convincing at all."

"I know. I was trying to convince myself at the same time."

"We have to hold out hope that Kate will return safely."

"Giselle, can we pray?"

"Please do. I have been offering up my prayers to God, but there is power in united prayer."

Valerie sat up in the bed and assumed a cross-legged position. "Dear God, we want to offer a prayer for our dear friend, our sister, Kate. Wherever she is, I pray that she is safe. Please protect her from harm, and please bring her back safely to us. All this we ask in your name. Amen."

"Amen."

They tried to come up with a plan, but there were no foreseeable roads to follow. Whatever suggestions they threw out led to a dead end. They heard a knock at the door followed by the sound of a male's voice. "Room service."

Valerie opened the door, and the waiter rolled a cart in and situated it next to the desk. He uncovered the stainless steel platters and revealed two perfectly folded omelets. "May I pour you both some coffee?"

"Yes, please," Valerie answered.

The waiter poured the hot coffee into two teacups. The aroma of the coffee was strong, and the steam arising from it danced from side to side. The waiter arranged miniature glass bottles of condiments in the center of the cart, including four different flavors of jams. Giselle gave him a tip. He thanked her then exited.

"How's your headache?"

"It's actually much better. I no longer feel like my head is about to explode."

"I'm glad your headache is better. Your eyes are a little red."

"I know. I fell asleep in my contacts."

"Did we decide on our next course of action?"

"No, we didn't." She thought for a moment. "I know the hotel manager said that none of the workers could recall seeing Kate leave the hotel, but I think we should ask around ourselves. We should do our own investigation."

"I think you're right."

They ate breakfast. The hot coffee was exactly what they needed to infuse some energy into their bodies. They quickly got ready.

"Giselle, must you bring this silly fanny pack everywhere we go? Did you even bring a handbag?"

"Valerie, this is not the time for fashion advice. It's convenient, and it's secured firmly around my waist. Both of my arms are free."

"Okay. Fine. I won't mention it again." She picked up her handbag by the strap and placed it over her right shoulder. "Let's go."

Their efforts were fruitless. A couple of the bellmen recognized Kate from the picture, but they had no knowledge of where she could have disappeared to. None of the hotel guests could offer any information on Kate's whereabouts.

They walked out of the hotel. The heat from the sun was already intense. It was going to be a sweltering day. They walked through the streets without a mental road map, hoping that some clue would manifest itself and lead them in the right direction. There was nothing. The hope that they were holding onto was diminishing by the day or even by the hour. They walked up and down the streets of Fira, showing strangers a picture of Kate, hoping that someone would recognize her and offer some valuable information. Their efforts were to no avail. They decided to walk back to the hotel. The heat drained the energy from their bodies. They took a different route back to the hotel.

"Giselle, maybe we should go another way. This alley looks a little run-down."

"It'll be fine. The hotel is only two blocks away."

The alley was lined with old buildings defaced with graffiti. A strong stench of urine greeted them as they walked further through the narrow passageway. They were startled. A large, black trash bag, which appeared to be filled to capacity, moved from side to side, and a homeless man came into view. He grinned broadly at them. He had a few missing teeth. His brown hair was thin and straggly with a few strands of gray. He had a full, unkempt beard. The man's shirt, which was likely white at one point in time, was dirty with several holes, and his worn jeans had several stains. Despite the heat, he had on a tattered plaid jacket. The vagrant extended a clear plastic cup in their direction, evidently begging for some change.

"Let's get out of here," Valerie said in a low tone. It was apparent that she was uncomfortable. There were no other people in sight.

The homeless man walked to the middle of the alleyway as the friends attempted to walk by. He kept his right hand extended with the plastic cup. A grin was still etched onto his face.

"Get out of our way!" Valerie snapped. She tugged at Giselle's shirt, trying to pull her away from the stranger.

"Wait." Giselle pulled back from her friend and remained stationary. She eyed the homeless man's right arm. "Where did you get that scarf?"

A blue and white scarf with images of the goddess Athena was tied around his arm over the sleeve of the plaid jacket. A gold pin of the letter K was attached to the scarf.

"Answer me! Where did you get that scarf?" She awaited an answer, but the man did not respond. His remaining teeth were brown and decayed as he grinned at her. "Do you understand English?"

"I watch things. I know things."

"So you do speak English. What is it that you know?"

Valerie was surprisingly speechless as she stared at the homeless man.

He let out a raucous laugh. An offensive odor emanated from his body. He stroked the scarf gently with his left hand, almost as though it were a prized possession.

"The god has come back for his wife."

Giselle looked at him with a perplexed look. "Who has come back for his wife?"

"The god, Hades. He came to save her."

"Save who? What are you talking about? Where did you get that scarf?"

"His wife gave it to me as a gift." The vagrant stroked the scarf again.

"Who gave it to you as a gift? I don't understand what you're saying." Giselle unzipped her fanny pack and pulled out a picture of Kate. "Have you seen this person?"

The man reached for the picture, and she pulled the picture back from his attempted grasp.

"Take a look at this person." She moved the picture closer to his line of vision, hoping that he would not reach for it again.

He laughed again for at least a full minute. "She's beautiful."

"So, have you seen her?"

"Hades has come back for his wife. Zeus has the sky, Poseidon has the sea, and Hades has the underworld. Hades has taken Persephone to be his wife and queen."

"Giselle, let's go. He's obviously crazy."

"That scarf around your arm belongs to the person in this picture. Have you seen her? Answer me! Where is she?"

Valerie tugged at her friend's shirt again. "Let's go."

Giselle did not budge. Instead, she tried to get information from the homeless man. Valerie took out her phone to take a picture of the vagrant, and at that moment, the man reached for Valerie's bag and aggressively pulled it off of her shoulder. He took off running down the alleyway.

"Give me my bag!"

They ran after the homeless man, screaming for him to stop. As they inched closer, he swung the bag around by the strap, grazing Valerie's face and propelling her backward onto the ground. He stumbled before regaining his balance as he ran away from them. He took a right turn and disappeared from view.

Valerie stood then dusted herself off. Her phone had fallen out of her hand, but thankfully, the screen hadn't cracked. She placed her hands over her face and cried. "Can anything else go wrong? Kate is missing or worse. I don't even want to acknowledge the fact that she could be dead. My husband is worried sick about me. I'm away from my two-year-old. Now this homeless man has stolen my bag with all of my important belongings—my wallet and ID, all of my money. Oh my goodness, my passport was in my bag."

Giselle jogged to the end of the alleyway. She looked around. The homeless man was nowhere in sight. She jogged back to Valerie. Her friend was crying.

"I thought you placed your passport in the hotel safe."

"I was going to, but I didn't."

Giselle hugged her friend. "Val. Everything is going to work out. We're going to find Kate. Please don't give up hope." She felt Valerie's body shaking as she cried. "Let me hear you say that we're going to find Kate."

Valerie wiped the tears from her face and looked at her friend. "We're going to find Kate."

"Let me hear you say it again."

"We're going to find Kate."

"Good. Don't worry about the money. I have Euros and American dollars, and I have my credit card. We'll go to the police to file a report and contact the US embassy in Athens. Everything will be okay. I believe that."

Valerie hugged her friend. Her tears were soaking her friend's shirt.

"Val, I know this isn't the right time, but he had no chance of getting my fanny pack."

CHAPTER 20

Giselle and Valerie walked into the police station. The same receptionist was seated behind the desk. There were about eight or nine people scattered throughout the room seated on the plastic blue chairs.

"I need to report a theft. My bag was pulled right off of my shoulder, and the thief ran away with it. All of my money and identification was in that bag."

"What's your name?"

"Valerie Brooks."

"Please have a seat, and your name will be called."

The friends took a seat near the water fountain. The hum from the fountain was again audible. Valerie's nervous twitch returned. Her right foot tapped repetitively on the floor.

"Val, please try to relax. You're making me uneasy."

"I'm making you uneasy? This entire situation is about to make me have a meltdown. Kate is missing or, worse, dead. My whole identity has been stolen. My husband is worried sick about me. My child needs her mother. And you tell me that I'm making you uneasy?"

"I didn't mean it like that. I'm sorry. This is taking a toll on me too, but I'm trying my best to keep it together. We have to keep it together for Kate's sake. I have to hold out hope that we'll find her. We'll get you back your documents, and you'll get home safely to Donald and Bridget. You have to believe."

"That's easier said than done. We're no closer to finding Kate since she walked out of that hotel room."

"It's not easy, but we have to remain optimistic."

Valerie's nervous twitch subsided. Minutes later, she started to tap her right foot repeatedly again. Her name was called, and Giselle followed behind her through the door. It was a new person who greeted them, and he introduced himself as Detective Christou.

"Is Detective Pallis here?" Giselle inquired.

"No, today is his day off. I'll be assisting you. Please have a seat."

They sat across from the detective.

"How may I be of assistance to you?"

"My bag was pulled right off of my shoulder by some homeless man. All of my money and credit cards were in that purse. My driver's license and passport were in that bag. I have no form of identification on me."

"Okay. Let's start from the beginning. Where were you, and what did this person look like?"

Valerie did her best to describe the alley that they were walking through with landmarks and its close proximity to the hotel. Her memory was a little inaccurate as she described the homeless man and the scene, and Giselle had to periodically intervene.

"We'll try to track this man down, but it may not be that easy unless he happens to return to the same alley. We'll get in touch with you if we find him. In the meantime, I suggest you get in touch with the US embassy in Athens." He scribbled some information on a sheet of paper. "Will that be all?"

"No," Giselle remarked. "There's something important that we didn't mention to you. Our friend, Kate Davenport, has been missing for the past three days. We've been working with Detective Pallis trying to find her."

Valerie interrupted, "We believe that a man by the name of Austin Bate may have had something to do with it. He suddenly left the island."

"Ah, I'm well aware of this case. Austin Bate was prohibited from leaving the island. He was interrogated extensively, and there's no concrete proof that he had anything to do with your friend's disappearance."

"Are you telling us that Austin is still in Santorini?" Giselle asked. She felt a sense of relief that he had not left the island. If the police were wiping their hands of him, then she would have to take matters into her own hands.

"Yes, he's still on the island, but he has other problems to worry about."

"What do you mean?" Giselle probed.

"I've shared enough. This is an ongoing investigation."

"But you said that there was no proof that Austin had anything to do with Kate's disappearance," Valerie said. "Then why is he still being investigated?"

"As I said before, I've shared enough. But someone will get in touch with you if we find the man who stole your bag." The detective stood, indicating that the time was up.

"There's one more important thing," Giselle stated. The detective slowly sat and leaned back in his chair. "The homeless man had Kate's scarf tied around his right arm over his jacket. It's a blue and white scarf with images of the goddess Athena."

"How do you know it's her scarf?"

"There's a gold pin of the letter K attached to it. It's her scarf," Giselle responded. "The alley is right next to our hotel. I don't know how he would've gotten her scarf, but he knows something."

"Go on. I'm listening."

"He told us that he watched things, and the god has come back for his wife. I kept asking him to explain himself. Who came back for his wife? He mentioned the god Hades and that Hades's wife gave him the scarf. I showed him a picture of Kate, and he looked as though he recognized her. He mentioned Zeus and Poseidon. Nothing made sense, but at the same time, I got a strong inclination that he knew something. It's my intuition, and I've learned to trust my intuition."

"This man seems like a crazy homeless person, but if we can validate what you're telling me, then this is more than a case involving theft. We'll reach out to you when we get more information."

A police officer shouted at a man whose head was buried in a large, black garbage bag. The man appeared startled as he looked at the two police officers. He had on a worn plaid jacket despite the heat, and a scarf was tied around the sleeve of his right arm. He had returned to the alleyway, like a bird drawn back to its nest. A piece of bread fell from his hand, and he took off running. One of the officers pounced into action and tackled him to the ground. The man let out a profanity-laden verbal attack. The officers held his hands behind his back and secured them in handcuffs.

The homeless man was brought into the police station. His stench followed him like a shadow. He was placed into the interrogation room. His hands remained in handcuffs, but now they were cuffed in front of him. The man sat in a wooden chair with Detective Christou seated across from him at a table. The interrogation room one-way mirror allowed Giselle and Valerie to watch. Detective Christou was reluctant at first, but after the unrelenting pleas, he allowed them to observe the interrogation.

The detective eyed the man up and down. He observed the straggly hair that covered the man's head like a dirty mop that had been overused and worn out. The man's teeth looked like a child had colored them with a yellow crayon. He yawned loudly, revealing a thick, white-coated tongue. His unkempt beard had a few bread crumbs lodged between the bushy hairs. A filthy shirt with several holes peeked from under his plaid jacket. There was dirt under his ridged fingernails.

"What is your name?" Detective Christou asked, breaking the silence. "I'm aware that you speak English."

"Ajax."

"Ajax what? What is your last name?"

"It's just Ajax."

"Where did you get that scarf?"

The man looked at the scarf and stroked it gently with his left hand. "It was a gift."

"A gift from who?"

"A gift from Persephone."

"Who's Persephone?" the detective inquired.

"My queen. She gave it to me as a gift when she left with her lover."

"Who is her lover?"

"Don't you know who's her lover? His name is Hades, god of the underworld, leader of the dead," he stated in a depraved voice.

Detective Christou felt himself getting irritated. The man was evidently a nutcase and he was not in the mood to play along. "Ajax, I'm well aware of Greek mythology. But that's all it is. These are myths. Now, where did you get that scarf?"

The man looked up at the ceiling. He looked like he was focused on an object, then his gaze moved horizontally, back and forth, without him moving his head.

Detective Christou looked up at the ceiling. "What are you looking at?"

The man lowered his head and focused his gaze on the detective. "Do you hear that? Listen."

There was no sound. "What is it that you're hearing?"

"Wedding bells. Persephone has married Hades." Ajax let out a loud repulsive laugh. His laugh went on for at least a minute and grew exponentially louder. "My queen has married her king. My queen has married her king. My queen has married her king!" He erupted in laughter again.

Detective Christou was thrown off of his game. He did not know what direction to go. The man's laughter sent chills down his spine. He decided to switch the line of interrogation. "Where is the bag that you stole today in the alleyway?"

The man's wide grin disappeared. "I don't need it anymore."

"What did you do with it? What did you take out of the bag?"

"I don't have it."

Detective Christou's frustration began to intensify. He eyed Ajax intently. It was near impossible to extract any useful information from him. He took out a picture from a manila folder. It was a photograph of Kate Davenport. "Have you seen her?"

He looked at the picture with an eerie kind of admiration. "My beautiful Persephone."

"So, you have seen her."

"My Persephone, I know you made a beautiful bride."

"Who was she with?"

"She was with Hades."

The detective became exasperated. Ajax evidently recognized Kate from the picture, but who was she with? "Can you describe Hades?"

"He is strong and powerful. Zeus and Poseidon can't stop him. They will try, but they can't stop him. He is too powerful. His power is unstoppable. He will destroy anyone who tries to stop him."

"Okay, but what does he look like?"

Ajax looked up again and stared at the ceiling. Or maybe he was seeing things. He appeared to be having visual and auditory hallucinations. Frankly, Ajax needed to be committed to a mental institution right away.

Detective Christou tried another approach. "Ajax, I want you to answer specific questions."

Ajax looked at him. It was a blank stare, almost as though he were lost in his own world, a state of mind filled with delusions that only he had access to.

"What color was the man's hair?"

"Black."

"Are you sure?"

"Hades's hair is black."

Detective Christou skeptically jotted it down. He did not know if the information was reliable. "Okay. Was his hair curly or straight?"

"Hades's hair is straight."

"Does he have short hair or long hair? Or is it medium length?"

"Hades has long hair."

"Okay. Is it this long?" Detective Christou placed his hand at the level of his chin.

"Longer."

"This long?" He placed his hands at the level of his shoulders.

"Yes."

"Okay. Can you estimate how tall he is?"

Ajax again produced that blank, unnerving stare. There was no telling what was going through his mind. Detective Christou stood. "Is he taller than me, shorter than me, or around my height?"

"Hades is taller than you."

The detective sat and jotted down the kidnapper's height as taller than five foot ten. "Okay. Is he bigger than me or smaller than me?"

"Hades is bigger than you. He is stronger than you and more powerful. He can crush you with the might of his hand. He can consume you with his breath. He can annihilate you from this world. My god rules the dead." Ajax erupted in laughter. The sound could easily be used in a horror film.

Detective Christou paused momentarily, the pen still in his hand. He decided to play along. "What was Hades wearing?"

"He was wearing all black. Everything was black."

"Can you tell me what was going on between Hades and Persephone? Was he hurting her?"

"Hades would never do that," Ajax stated angrily. "He would never hurt his queen. He loves her. He made her his wife."

Detective Christou backed off. He needed to approach this subject cautiously and delicately. "You're right, he would never hurt his queen. Do you know where he took her?"

"He took her to his kingdom in the underworld."

"Where is the underworld?"

"You can't go there unless he takes you there."

"Okay Ajax, is there anything else you can remember about Hades? Anything?"

"Hades has the mark of a creature that was looking at me."

"A mark? Do you mean a tattoo?

Ajax nodded his head yes.

"Where is his tattoo?"

Ajax pointed to his right arm where the scarf was tied.

"What does it look like?"

"Give me the pen."

"What?"

"Give me the pen."

The detective reluctantly turned the sheet of paper over that he was jotting on and moved it toward Ajax. He placed the pen on top of the paper. Ajax reached for the pen, with his hands in cuffs and drew an image.

Detective Christou observed the stroke of the pen and the ink that it produced on the paper. His eyes widened. It couldn't be. The image was a pentagram, and in the center was an eye. It was the symbol of a dangerous and notorious gang, the Bulgarian mafia.

CHAPTER 21

Giselle and Valerie made their way to Zeus Zest. Food was the last thing on their minds, but it was essential for them to eat. They had forgotten to eat dinner the night before, which later became an afterthought.

The weather again seemed perfect. The sun was shining, and there was barely a cloud in the sky. Giselle felt a stark contrast inside her body. She felt as though a current of heavy rain was pouring down in torrents over her head. The gentle breeze that caressed her skin should have been a treacherous wind causing destruction in its path. She was trapped in an interminable nightmare.

The atmosphere in the restaurant was similar to before. The television broadcasted a football game, and the spectators at the bar were fully engrossed. Among them was Demitrius, who immediately noticed them as they entered. He personally escorted them to a table and sat next to Valerie, who was seated across from Giselle.

"Where's Kate? Please tell me that you have found her."

"No such luck," Giselle answered. "The detectives are still trying to collect information."

"Any leads so far?"

Valerie told Demitrius about her run-in with the vagrant and the interrogation at the police station. As always, Valerie gave more information than she should. After all, it was an ongoing investigation. "The detective thinks that the Bulgarian mafia is involved."

"The Bulgarian mafia?" Demitrius reiterated in disbelief. "That can't be." He lowered his voice, although there was no one at the adjacent tables. A family of four was seated at a table at the opposite end of the restaurant, and two young female companions sat in close proximity to the family. There were five men at the bar, apparently oblivious to their surroundings. "I find it hard to believe that the Bulgarian mafia is in Santorini. For what purpose?"

"I don't know," Valerie responded. "The man who kidnapped Kate had a tattoo identifying him as part of the mafia."

"That's crazy. My beautiful Santorini?" Demitrius looked away and shook his head. A glassy film formed over his eyes. "I'm so sorry about your friend. I want to help in any way that I can. I know this island like the back of my hand. What does this guy look like, so I can keep an eye out?"

Valerie answered, "He is taller than five foot ten, well built with dark, straight, shoulder-length hair. He was wearing all black when he kidnapped Kate. He has a tattoo of a pentagram, with an eye in the center, on his right arm."

"That's pretty detailed. Are you sure this guy isn't crazy?"

"Oh, he's definitely crazy," Valerie continued. "But there seemed to be some truth in what he was saying."

"Like I said, I know this place like the back of my hand, and this person or group of thugs will not stay hidden for long. They will not be left alone to corrupt and defile Santorini. I consider Santorini my island, and I'll protect it at all costs. I have connections, and this person you described will be found, and he will pay for what he has done to your friend. In the meantime, I want you two to remain safe."

"Thank you, Demitrius," Valerie stated. She was happy that there was someone else who had an interest in finding Kate.

"Don't mention it. Nikita and I are here to help. Please keep us up to date."

"Thank you," the friends replied in unison.

"What can I get you both to eat? Lunch is on the house."

"That's so kind of you," Giselle replied, "but please, we want to pay. You've been so kind."

"Well, at least let me provide dessert."

They agreed.

Moments later, the waiter brought out a tray with their meals. As usual, the food was delicious—lamb and beef gyros and two generous servings of baklava. Their conversation focused on the next course of action. Kate was last seen with a man presumed to be associated with the Bulgarian mafia. This was three days ago. A lot could've happened in three days. And what would the mafia want with Kate? Where did they take her? Was she alive? If she was, she must be scared and helpless.

Giselle suggested going back to the hotel. There was a computer with internet access in one of the corners of the lobby, away from the front desk. She had to know more about the Bulgarian mafia and the illegal activity they were wrapped up in, although the list was likely long. The biggest question surrounding Kate was what illegal activity could she be involved in? Sure, the best thing to do would have been to allow the trained authorities to handle the situation, but Giselle knew that she could not sit back and do nothing. It was the curious nature that she was inherently born with. It was the seed that grew and eventually led her to pursue a career in forensics.

They thanked Demitrius and left the restaurant. The warm sunshine landed on their faces. It was truly a beautiful day.

"Val, we have to be careful sharing such sensitive information with others. The Bulgarian mafia being involved escalates this to a higher level. This is a matter of international security. We're talking about organized crime. This should go to the Cyber Crime Unit and Interpol."

"I know, but we need all the help we can get. Each day that goes by is another day that Kate is missing. The clock is ticking, and every minute counts."

"Believe me, I get it, but let's be more careful. We probably should not even share this information with Maxwell."

"You're probably right."

Giselle fumbled through her fanny pack, looking for her ChapStick. She unzipped the inner pocket and slid her hand from side to side. "Oh my goodness, Val!"

"What?"

"You're not going to believe this."

"What am I not going to believe?"

Giselle pulled out a passport, and Valerie immediately screamed with excitement. "I forgot you had given me your passport to hold. You remember that day that you and Kate were making fun of my fanny pack and then you had the audacity to ask me to hold some of your belongings?" She pulled out a ChapStick, a pack of Tic Tacs and fifty Euros belonging to Valerie.

"I can't believe this." Tears of joy formed in Valerie's eyes, and she wiped them before the drops could escape. "That's some good news for the day."

Although they could have walked to the hotel, which may have taken them thirty minutes, they opted to take a taxi. Giselle paid the driver, who grunted an unintelligible response. She could not tell whether he was rude or indifferent. Maybe he was having a bad day.

Fortunately, the sole computer in the lobby was not occupied. Giselle sat at the computer, and Valerie pulled up a chair next to her. She entered her username, which was her last name, and the password, which was her room number. In the Google search box, she typed "Bulgarian mafia." Wikipedia information on the Bulgarian mafia came up. There were other links generating information too. Which mafia kidnapped Kate, and again, the burning question remained, what did they want with her? Was she pulled into a drug cartel or human trafficking? All of the possibilities were heinous and bloodcurdling.

CHAPTER 22

Demitrius headed home shortly after 11 pm. The restaurant was closed, and business for that day had been modest, to say the least. It didn't matter. He had other aspirations, and the restaurant was something he did to occupy some of his time. The restaurant was for Nikita. It was her dream to have a menu display her delectable creations that she had perfected throughout the years. It was dark outside, and the air was balmy. Nikita had already gone home. He had stuck around the restaurant for another hour to tie up some loose ends—work that he was doing, not related to the restaurant.

He entered through the back door into the kitchen, and a dim light from the living room barely seeped through, creating faint illumination. A mug was in the sink with a tea bag, and the kettle was still warm. He called out Nikita's name, but there was no answer. She must have already fallen asleep. It did not take much. A hot cup of chamomile tea and a warm shower was all she needed. Once her head touched the pillow, she was out like a light.

He cracked open the bedroom door, and as expected, a silhouette of Nikita's body was tucked under the sheet. She was asleep. He gently kissed her forehead. She mumbled "good night" before drifting off again. She looked like an angel and smelt of jasmine, a fragrance she sprayed over her body after her nighttime shower. She had worn that fragrance for years.

Demitrius quietly left her and walked into the bathroom. He looked at his reflection in the mirror. He was sixty-nine years old, less than a month away from turning seventy. He admired his reflection and thought that he could easily shave off five years from his age. Age, after all, was nothing but a number. He was still in good health, minus some high cholesterol and what his doctor referred to as borderline diabetes. Fortunately, he was able to manage his medical issues with diet and exercise, although his doctor warned him that he was close to starting medications. And there were the occasional aches and pains that come with age. But overall, he was doing well. His looks certainly did not fade with age. He considered himself a handsome man aging like fine wine, only getting better over time. In fact, the grayness of his hair and manicured beard made him look astute and distinguished. His eyes, on the other hand, conveyed warmth and kindness, a feature that he was always able to use to his advantage. It allowed him to gain the confidence and trust of others. But most importantly, he considered himself a high achiever, driven by money, status, and success. He was a go-getter, and the word "no" was never an option. It was a word that only he was entitled to use. His determination and persistence was how he got Nikita, although he had to sprinkle these attributes with sweetness to make her his wife.

His lower back was a little bit achy but nothing that two tablets of Tylenol couldn't take care of. A shower was all that he needed at the moment, and he was looking forward to curling up next to Nikita, enchanted by her fragrance. Maybe he might get lucky tonight. He reached into the medicine cabinet and shook out two tablets of Tylenol into his palm. He chucked them into his mouth and washed them down with some water from a bottle that he kept on the bathroom counter.

He ran the water from the shower head, waiting for it to achieve the perfect temperature. He took off his shirt and admired his frame. *Not bad*, he thought for a man swiftly approaching seventy. His eyes focused on his right shoulder. The reflection from the mirror was clear—a tattoo of a pentagram with an eye in the center.

CHAPTER 23

D emitrius Botsaris was born in Sofia, Bulgaria. He was born Demitrius Borislavov. His father, Sabin Borislavov, was born into the Bulgarian mafia. The Borislavov family was one of the most notorious and influential mafias, a criminal empire that had infiltrated businesses and had its tentacles in drugs and prostitution. Despite growing up in a life surrounded by crime, Sabin decidedly maintained a moral compass. His uncle was the boss, and his father was a captain in the empire. His two older brothers were heavily involved as well. Sabin was no stranger to witnessing crime and bloodshed. Rules were made to be broken, except when it came to the mafia's rules and the structure of the family. Loyalty was everything. It meant life or death. It was the glue that bonded the family together.

Sabin fell in love with his neighbor's daughter, Petya Andonov. He dreamed of a life with her, away from the condemned stain of his family. His eagerness to leave was accelerated after witnessing the gruesome murder of his cousin, who was a soldier in the organization. His cousin Dimo had spared the life of a friend whom he was ordered to kill. As a punishment and a learning lesson to the other members, his father shot Dimo cold-bloodedly in the head. There was no evidence of contrition on his father's face. Sabin felt like he was watching a demon manifested in human form.

Sabin was conflicted because he loved his father. It was as though his father took on two different forms. He was the underhanded, vicious, diabolical man when dealing with the mafia, but at other times, he was the loving father, that is, following his father's own definition of love. Sabin lived a life of plenty. All of his wants were met thanks to his father's earning power through illegal businesses and criminal activity. To continue surviving in his family, one had to be without a conscience. Unfortunately, or maybe fortunately, Sabin had a conscience.

His relationship with Petya evolved at a rapid pace. It was a whirlwind romance with no signs of slowing. She was everything he wanted in a woman; she was intelligent, smart and sophisticated, charismatic, and a world-class beauty. She was perfect. He asked her to marry him, and she said yes. With Petya at his side, he felt like he could do almost anything. Petya found out she was two months pregnant, and they moved up the wedding. Demitrius Ivan Borislavov was born seven months later. He was a bundle of joy, and Sabin did not want him exposed to the immorality and odious nature of his family, which would have been inevitable.

Sabin had been developing an exit strategy. He had fully gained the courage to escape the tight grip and looming cloud of his family. In the dead of the night, he packed up his car with essential belongings and fled with his family to Athens. He had enough cash on him to survive at least six months. He kept a low profile initially, but then slowly, he started to integrate into the Greek culture. He even changed his last name to Botsaris to sound more Greek and less Bulgarian. Sabin got a job working at a convenience store. A few months later, he picked up another job as a taxi driver to supplement his income.

Demetrius grew up an only child with a vivid imagination. That's what happens sometimes as an only child. One develops a colorful and dramatic imagination to fill the loneliness. His father was working twelve-hour days to ensure there was food on the table and a roof over their heads. His mother complained often. It was one thing after the next. She complained that his father was always working, but she also complained that there was not enough money coming into the house. She chastised him with guilt-laden rants for dragging her away from Sofia to a cramped, two-bedroom apartment in a rundown neighborhood in Athens. His father tried to appease her and reassure her that things would get better. She had to be patient. Patience is a virtue that his mother did not possess. It was as foreign as pigs flying.

Demitrius once overheard his mother denigrating his father through the thin walls of his bedroom. Despite covering his ears, the verbal abuse spewing out from his mother's mouth filtered through his hands. She had called his father a pathetic excuse of a man who would never make anything of himself. Sabin would unsuccessfully try to defend himself, falling drastically short of convincing her that he was working hard to make a better life for them. His words fell on deaf ears. Demitrius often wondered what his father ever saw in his mother to marry her. Then again, he did see the softer, kinder side of her. She appeared sweet and attentive. She would bake his father's favorite Bulgarian dessert with fresh apples for no reason at all. She would plant him with kisses when he walked through the door from a long day at work, telling him how much she appreciated him and the dedication he had to his family. Everything would be well again until the next round of devaluation. It went on for years.

The degradation trickled down to Demetrius. Nothing was ever good enough for his mother. She would always find fault or something to be critical of. He had come home one day from school, blissfully exhilarated after achieving an A on a mathematics final exam—ninety-six percent to be exact. Mathematics was not his strong suit. It did not come naturally, and a great deal of focus and long hours of practice were put into achieving that grade. He excitedly shared the news with his mother when he got home. Her first words to him were, "Did anyone score higher than a ninety-six percent?"

"Only one person who scored a ninety-eight percent."

"Then you're not the best. Try harder next time."

It was as if his mother took a pin and poked a hole in him, deflating his body like a balloon. Or maybe it felt like a boxer who had the air knocked out of him after a defeating blow. His father on the other hand was thrilled with the news. He had proudly attached his son's report card with a magnet to the buzzing refrigerator. Demitrius had gotten four As and two Bs.

The next morning, his report card was no longer on the refrigerator. It was in the trash, not buried underneath the rubbish but laying on top in plain sight. He knew it was his mother. He wanted to confront her so badly, but he knew she would either deny it—although who else could have been the perpetrator—or it would have resulted in an argument. She would argue her point until she won. It was always about winning for her. If you weren't a winner, you were a loser. He decided to let it go.

His father was always proud of his achievements, big or small. He was loving and encouraging. The only problem was that his father was rarely home. He was working two jobs while trying to get his business off of the ground. When Demetrius was not in school, he was antagonized by the presence of his mother. It was tantamount to a looming dark cloud that could burst open at any moment with a torrential downpour. He would much rather hang out with friends, but he was instructed by his mother to come home immediately after school. She disguised her intentions as love. It was her way of supposedly protecting him from the temptations of the streets. In actuality, she wanted him to share in her miserable existence. How could she not be miserable? She created misery in her own family and others, and misery sure loves company. She didn't care about him having friends. The fewer people he had in his life, the more attention he could give to her. That was a part of her devious plan.

Demitrius had heard his mother tell the story of how she could have become a model at least a hundred times—not just any model but a high-fashion model walking the runways of Milan, Paris, and New York. She bragged about her striking good looks and her shapely figure before she sacrificed it all by getting pregnant and having a child. Now her hips would never be the same, and the stretchmarks would never go away. She felt that Demitrius was not appreciative of the existence that she gave him and made him aware that she had other choices.

On one rare family outing, his father took them out to dinner at a nice restaurant downtown. His mother wore a sequin black dress that was way too tight for her wide hips, which she blamed him for. Strangely, it felt nice going out as a family. It felt like a piece of normalcy. His mother was in the front passenger seat, and her hand rested on his father's thigh. She complimented his freshly cut hair, the intoxicating fragrance of his cologne, and the new shirt he was wearing that she'd bought him. She told him how much he was appreciated, and the compliments dripped off of her tongue like honey.

Demitrius rolled his eyes as he observed the spectacle. It was almost as though the verbal abuse that his father had to endure the night before never happened. She sure had a way of controlling him, like a skilled puppet master. The nauseating show went on until his father parked the car.

His parents walked hand in hand into the restaurant as Demitrius trailed behind. His father was lapping up the attention. Who knew how long the attention and admiration would last before the monster would be released? It was inevitable. It may take days or weeks, but the monster was only asleep, soon to be awoken, taking on a destructive path. Then the monster would eventually be harnessed and contained, cradled to sleep, while being housed in a shell of a person.

The wait for a table was not long and they were led to the far end of the restaurant. Of course it was not good enough, and his mother insisted on another table. Once a table was found to her liking, they were seated, and the waiter handed them their menus. The nauseating spectacle resumed, and his mother showered his father with compliments. Demitrius wondered if his father actually believed all of the lies. His father probably did not care. He wanted to experience the Petya he fell in love with years ago in Sofia.

His mother ordered the filet mignon, medium rare, with clear instructions on the amount of pinkness and the amount of redness. The sizzling steak came, and when his mother cut into it, her face instantly showed disgust. She tasted the au gratin potatoes and quickly spat them into her cloth napkin. *Here we go*, Demitrius thought. She snapped her fingers, ushering the waiter. The steak was too pink and not enough red. It wasn't enough to simply request another steak prepared to her liking and another side item. Her words had to be intertwined with insults. The waiter repeatedly apologized and promised a steak prepared exactly how she wanted it. She ordered the steamed broccoli and carrots instead. Demitrius had also ordered the au gratin potatoes with his meal, and he thought they were delicious. It was warm, creamy, and flavorful. His mother had to complain. No matter how good the potatoes were, she would have found fault.

The steak came to the table sizzling on the plate. The manager had accompanied the waiter and offered his sincerest apologies. His mother cut into the steak. Demitrius caught the look on his mother's face. The entire evening of trying to be a normal family was about to be ruined. The monster had awoken. The steak was now too red and not enough pink, and she accused them of insinuating that she was an animal, eating meat with so much blood. Again, the manager apologized and instructed his waiter to take the steak immediately and put it back on the grill. The manager assured her that the steak would be free of charge. His father tried his best to calm her down. The look of embarrassment was written all over his face. Petya turned her vitriolic speech toward her husband, accusing him of never sticking up for her. As much as his father tried to convince her otherwise, his words fell on deaf ears. He had turned into the enemy. Thankfully, the third attempt at the steak was pleasing.

The rest of the evening was dreadfully painful. A word here and there was said to fill the awkwardness of the silence. His father paid for the meal, and they got up and left. The ride home was in silence.

CHAPTER 24

Demitrius was aware that he was becoming hardened. He had a charismatic way about him that drew others to him like a moth to a flame. The sad thing about it was that he did not care. People were objects to be used and to be discarded when they no longer served a purpose. He did not know the true meaning of love. Maybe he loved his father. He certainly did not have respect for him. His father was weak, vulnerable, and easily manipulated. Those were characteristics that he never wanted to possess. He was strong, and if anyone was going to be manipulated, it was the other person.

His heart was temporarily softened when he walked into a bakery at the age of seventeen and beheld the beauty of a young lady, Nikita, who later became his wife. Others may have said it was infatuation, but in his mind, it was love. He thought about Nikita day and night. It became an obsession. Her father was not going to get in the way of him having her as his wife. He needed to show respect to her father because it was evident that her father meant a lot to her. He had to give the illusion of respect; otherwise, he would have threatened him to the point that he had no other option than to give away his daughter. Her father conceded on his own and labeled Demitrius as a fine, upstanding young man with dedication and perseverance.

Demitrius became more intrigued by his heritage. His father rarely spoke about his past, and when he did, he was vague. In a burst of rage, his mother had revealed to him that he came from a line of mafia men from Bulgaria. She stated that evil and corruption were flowing from his veins, back to his heart, and pumping throughout his body. She once called him Satan's spawn.

Demitrius believed that there was something inherently different about him. He wasn't like his friends. All of his friends seemed normal and appeared to come from good homes. His father was working longer hours and was seldom home, not that he blamed his father. Home seemed tantamount to what hell would be minus the flames of fire, and his mother was the devil incarnate. That may have been an exaggeration, but it was pretty close. His mother also started to see a man on the side. Demitrius had known for a long time that his mother was having an affair or possibly multiple affairs. He was torn as to whether to tell his father, but he had a strong feeling that his father would be in denial. His mother in turn would have retaliated and made him regret the day that he was born.

Demitrius desperately wanted to feel accepted and to have a sense of belonging. He wanted to be a part of a brotherhood. He had developed an intense fascination and preoccupation with the Bulgarian mafia. He wanted to know more. Mafia blood pumped through his body, and it gave him life. He wanted to know the family tree and where he branched off. Demitrius researched every-thing he could get his hands on related to the Bulgarian mafia. He read news clippings and conducted exhaustive internet searches. The violent crimes did not deter him, but instead, they drew him closer and sparked his intrigue even more. He wondered what it felt like to take the life out of a body. The thought made him feel godlike and powerful.

He convinced Nikita to move away with him to Bulgaria. It was not an easy task, and she gave him a great deal of resistance. All of her family was in Greece, and Greece was the only country she had known. Demitrius conveyed to her that there were skills that he needed to develop that were only available to him in Bulgaria. He was vague but tried to communicate enough information to satisfy her decision to move. He promised her that they would return to Greece, and their lives would be wealthy and prosperous. He even promised Nikita her own restaurant in Santorini, which had been a dream of hers, even as a little girl. Some people want to be doctors, some lawyers, some teachers; Nikita wanted to own her own restaurant. She had picked out a name when she was twelve years old. The restaurant was going to be named Zeus Zest.

That summer, after tying the knot in April, they moved to Sofia. Demitrius did not have much money to his name, and the change was striking. Nikita went from living in a comfortable home with her father to a cramped, roach-infested apartment. Demitrius did his best to console her and reassure her that life was going to get better. He had big plans for them, and this less than ideal change was only temporary. She had to believe in him.

Demitrius lay on the bed looking up at the ceiling. It was dark outside, and Nikita was sound asleep next to him. He knew the names of some of the big dogs in the mafia. There was an internet article he found that detailed a sting operation leading to the arrest of some of the members. The article went into great detail about the Borislavov family. One of the high-ranking members was Ivan Borislavov, who had three sons, Yosif, Marko, and Sabin. Demitrius's heart stopped when he read the name Sabin. He knew that his father had changed his surname to Botsaris when he moved to Greece. The article did not make much mention of Sabin, but now he was convinced that he belonged to a powerful organization. Ivan Borislavov was his grandfather, and Andrey Borislavov, who was the head of the organization, was his great uncle.

There was one big question that occupied his mind. How was he going to integrate himself into the order? It was his birthright. Was that enough to be accepted? How would he go about finding members of the mafia? Were these people even accessible?

CHAPTER 25

L ocating members of the Borislavov family was not as difficult as he'd thought. A little research and talking to the right people led him in the right direction. It turned out that the Borislavov family had not intended to be hidden. If they wanted to be obscure, they would have achieved that goal. They were respected in the community or, better yet, feared. It was an unspoken awareness that members of the family were not to be crossed or there could be a steep price to pay. They had often intimidated the police force, and several members of the department would turn their heads the other way when a Borislavov was involved in any illegal activity.

Demitrius wanted to bypass the lower-ranking members of the family and go straight to the head of the serpent, Andrey Borislavov, his great uncle. After much investigation, he discovered that the Borislavov family owned one of the most frequented casinos in Sofia and that Andrey was usually there, especially on the weekends. Demitrius decided to try his luck at blackjack on a Friday night, and hopefully he would be able to try his luck with Andrey. Hopefully, he would not get himself killed in the process.

The strong smell of tobacco smoke greeted him as he walked into the casino minutes after 8 pm. The smoke held onto the molecules in the air; it made his eyes start to water and his throat itch. He instinctively had a coughing fit and was somewhat embarrassed. He definitely did not want to seem out of place. All of the patrons appeared to be relaxed and at ease, many with cigarettes or cigars hanging out of their mouths, emitting smoke and adding to the thick fog that encompassed the room.

He sat at one of the blackjack tables. His Bulgarian was not good but he was able to engage in rudimentary conversation. There were four other players around the table who all stared at him as though he had three heads. It must have been obvious that he was not from Bulgaria. Little did they know that his roots dug deep into the soil of Bulgaria, and the blood of the Borislavov family was pumping through his arteries and flowing through his veins.

The dealer looked up at him without lifting his head. A cigar was pressed between his thin lips. It was almost as though the dealer were trying to read his mind. He looked down at the stack of cards and dealt Demitrius a hand. Demitrius's first two cards were a jack and an ace, and he called blackjack. The dealer was not impressed. He removed the cigar out of his mouth and blew a smoke ring into the air. He placed the cigar back in his mouth and glided the chips on the table. The dealer dealt the cards to the gamblers, and on the second round of play, Demitrius came the closest to twenty-one.

Demitrius won again on the third and fourth play. The dealer maintained a straight face, but his eyes revealed the truth. There was disdain there. One of the gamblers slammed his hand on the table and belted out an expletive before regaining his composure.

Demetrius felt that he had played enough, and it was time to get down to business. It was time to come face-to-face with the serpent whom he felt was lurking somewhere out of plain sight. He took a deep breath and blurted out that he needed to speak with Andrey Borislavov. The entire table instantly became quiet and again focused their attention on him. Ten penetrating eyes, including that of the dealer, were pointed directly at him. The dealer did not appear to blink as his eyes remained affixed. He puffed on the cigar and held the smoke in his mouth for a few seconds before puffing it out. In a strong Bulgarian accent, he asked Demitrius what his interest was in Andrey Borislavov.

Demitrius looked around at the occupants at the table, and he felt trapped. He realized that he had to be careful with his words. He decided to be vague but brief and told the dealer that it was a personal matter. The dealer was not satisfied with the response. After a few seconds of silence, the dealer's gaze moved upward, and he directed his line of vision toward a camera. He then placed his right hand horizontally, palm down, to his neck. Demetrius wondered what that gesture meant but he knew it was not a good sign.

Moments later, two men in suits stood by him, one on each side, and one demanded that he follow them. They each tightly gripped an arm, one on each side, and forcefully led him away.

Demitrius felt a tight knot in his stomach. His palms became sweaty, and he felt as though he was going to pass out at any moment. He focused on his breath and tried to calm himself down. He was led behind a thick red velvet curtain and directed along a narrow passageway. Where were they taking him?

They led him down the dim passageway. He asked the men where they were going, but they ignored his question. One of the men led him down a dingy stairwell, while the other kept closely behind. They walked a few more feet before stopping in front of a door. The man who was grabbing him tightly around his right arm knocked on the door. In a loud voice, a man authoritatively instructed in Bulgarian for them to enter. Behind a round table were six men engaged in a round of poker. They had all directed their attention to the door. A thick layer of tobacco smoke had formed in the room, and two of the men continued to smoke, adding to the layer in the air, while their gaze remained firm.

Demitrius was aware of the intensity of his heartbeat. His heart felt as though it would beat out of his chest. Beads of sweat formed on his forehead, and his armpits were moist. The moment felt like an eternity as he watched the men, who were evidently dangerous, stare him down. They were analyzing him. They were studying him. They were reading his body language.

Demitrius desperately tried to appear assured, but he knew that these men could smell fear in him. They were like lions in a den ready to pounce on their prey. The king was seated in his direct line of vision. He instantly recognized the man as Andrey Borislavov from a couple newspaper clippings. His larger-than-life presence was palpable in the room.

Andrey's dark, mysterious eyes were narrow and penetrating. Andrey placed his cigar back in his mouth and sucked on the rolled tobacco, filling his mouth with the smoke. He allowed the smoke to linger in his mouth for a few seconds before blowing it out gently.

The silence was finally broken once the head of the criminal organization demanded that he state his name and the reason for his presence. Although his Bulgarian was not perfect, Demetrius was able to comprehend and speak the language basics, thanks to months of studying and integrating with the locals.

Demitrius cleared his throat. He told the gang of criminals his name. After a deep breath, he stated that he wanted to join the organization.

Andrey's intimidating eyes were unwavering. He sucked again on the cigar. As he slowly blew out the smoke, his mouth formed a wide grin. The look on Andrey's face was menacing. His smile appeared devious and calculating.

Andrey asked where he was from. Demitrius replied that he was from Athens, but he had Bulgarian blood flowing through him. He had left his world behind and had fully embraced his Bulgarian heritage.

Andrey then asked him what he knew about the organization. Demitrius felt all eyes on him. He was the center of attention, and he wondered whether he had made a grave mistake entering the building. After another deep breath, he told his audience that the

Borislavov name was one of power, influence, respect, and most importantly loyalty. He was loyal, and he was willing to die for the brotherhood.

Andrey's eyes had not deviated. He studied Demitrius intensely. Nothing had gone unnoticed. Demitrius felt as though he were on a stage with the lights shining down on him. He was an actor auditioning for a role, and he had to appear believable and put on the performance of his life. He had to get the role. He explained to his audience that he was willing to do anything to prove himself and show his loyalty.

Andrey's expressionless face again transitioned to that sinister stare, and that menacing grin had returned. Demitrius had no idea what was behind that grin. Was Andrey warming up to the idea of letting him in? If he was, Demetrius knew that the path would not be easy. Or was he merely amused, allowing Demitrius to entertain him before striking? There were numerous possibilities.

Andrey invited Demitrius to come closer. The request was unexpected, and a trickle of urine escaped his bladder. Reluctantly, Demitrius walked around two of the members and stood next to Andrey an arm's length away. Andrey invited him to come closer and again a little closer. Demitrius inched closer and again tried his best to seem unbothered. As he inched closer, he felt a hand force-fully grab him by the neck and thrust his head sideways onto the table. It was one of Andrey's sidekicks who had stood up unnoticed and attacked him from behind. Demitrius had come face-to-face with the venomous serpent, who was staring him directly in his eyes. It was not noticeable before from a distance, but the irises of Andrey's eyes were two different colors. One eye was menacingly dark, and the other eye strikingly gray.

In Bulgarian, Andrey disgustingly reprimanded Demitrius for entering his territory and boldly making the request to join the organization. He instructed his men to take Demitrius away and get rid of him. Before his men could follow through with the orders,

Demitrius belted out that his last name was originally Borislavov and that his father is Sabin Borislavov. He told Andrey that his grandfather is Ivan, Andrey's brother.

For the first time since Demitrius had entered the room, Andrey seemed momentarily unnerved. Then Andrey seamlessly regained his authoritative demeanor and instructed Demitrius to take a seat. The man who had forcefully attacked him obligingly gave up his seat.

Andrey demanded that he explain himself. Demitrius informed him that his father had escaped to Athens with his bride Petya when he was a baby. Demitrius relayed the information that his mother had begrudgingly shared with him, although the reason that his mother had divulged such information was to further attack his father for uprooting the family from the comforts of their life in Sofia. He told Andrey that once he had learned about his family history, his focus had been to integrate himself into the fabric of the order and fulfill his birthright. He was willing to prove himself and to do whatever it took to show his loyalty.

Andrey did not reply. Deep in thought, he looked at Demitrius. The wheels in his head turned. After a few moments of dead silence, he voiced that Sabin had been disloyal and had abandoned the family. It was Demitrius's job to bring Sabin back to Sofia and make him pay gravely for his disloyalty.

Demitrius crawled into bed beside Nikita. She was already asleep, and the fragrance of jasmine still lingered on her body. He reached over and gently kissed her on the head before lying on his back, staring at the ceiling through the darkness. A faint light seeped into the room from one of the street lights outside. Their apartment building was located in a rough neighborhood in Sofia. Rent was cheap, and it was only going to be temporary lodging until

Demitrius could get his feet firmly fixed to the ground. It was not uncommon to hear the chatter of tenants at all hours of the night.

It was almost 2 am. Demitrius reflected on the past six hours, from the minute that he walked into the casino to the moment he walked out of the building unscathed, minus some discomfort to the back of his neck and the right side of his face. It was a terrifying moment, and the ordeal still seemed surreal.

His mind raced as he tried to devise a plan to lead his father to Sofia. He was fully aware of the devious undertaking that he was plotting, but he did not care. He believed that his father loved him, but at this point in his life, it meant nothing. The irreparable damage to his soul had already been done. His father was a puppet. He was a defenseless, vulnerable puppet pulled by strings. He allowed his own wife to use and abuse him. His father could not even protect his son from his mother. Because of this failure on his father's part, he was left with emotional wounds that ultimately hardened him. His body was covered with emotional scars. His father was weak and powerless. These were traits that Demitrius would never want to possess. Survival was for the fittest. After all, isn't that what Darwinian evolutionary theory was built on?

The plan suddenly came to him, and he experienced an intense, adrenaline rush. He was going to use his father's love to his advantage. For once, his father's love would serve a purpose. It was going to get him into the order.

He was going to lure his father to Sofia under the guise that he was in trouble. His father was gullible, and he did not anticipate that much convincing or much craftiness would be needed. It was rather surprising that his father was even a product of the greatness of the Borislavov family. In everything, there is always a weak link. His father was evidently the weak link.

The rays of the sun illuminated the bedroom. The streets had already come to life. Demitrius lay in bed, still looking at the ceiling. He realized that he had not slept. The smell of bacon permeated through the gap underneath the door, and the crackling sound was audible as the fat from the bacon merged with the heat. Demitrius could not wait to find out what all Nikita was preparing for breakfast. He hadn't eaten the night before because his nerves were on edge. Now he was ravenous. The smell of piping-hot coffee was now intermingled with the delectable smells in the apartment. Demitrius got up and put on his blue robe. Soon it would be time to get ready for his demeaning nine-to-five job. He opened the bedroom door, and there was Nikita, with her back toward him, frying the bacon. He admired the beauty of her hourglass shape. She was wearing only a form-fitting transparent white T-shirt. He approached her from behind and wrapped his arms around her waist. He softly kissed her neck, and she adoringly lay her head on his head. He started to caress her as she playfully knocked his hands away while trying to finish breakfast. She set two placemats on the table, with a knife and fork, and she prepared two plates with bacon, scrambled eggs, and homemade bread. She placed a bowl of fresh fruit on the table and poured coffee into two mugs.

Nikita always insisted on praying before a meal, and Demitrius always obliged. She was Christian Orthodox, and he was an atheist, a secret that he never divulged to her. He often appeased Nikita by going to church with her. He often wondered what she would do if he ever admitted to her that he did not believe in God. Nikita was the only important person in his life, and he often wondered why she held such importance. Maybe because she represented the other side of him if he wasn't so defiled, and he strangely wanted to hold onto that notion. He loved the way that she looked at him. It was a look of love and admiration, and she made him feel that he could do anything. She was also smart and witty, elements that he admired. She could easily engage in a conversation on any subject. She was also undeniably beautiful.

Nikita inquired about his night. She had fallen back asleep at almost 1 am, and he still had not returned. She had not expected him to be home so late, but she'd figured that he and his coworkers were having a great time at one of the bars downtown. After all, that is what he had told her. He would be hanging out with some of his coworkers after work. Little did she know that he was associating with the most notorious family in Bulgaria. She accepted the fact that he had a late night with his colleagues and did not inquire any further. Demitrius sometimes wondered if she actually believed him, but he loved the fact that she rarely questioned him or put up a fight.

Nikita took the empty plate in front of him and made her way into the kitchen to wash the dishes. Demitrius stopped to give her a kiss before walking into the bedroom to get ready for work. He got dressed, kissed Nikita goodbye, and walked out the door, making his way down the dingy steps of the apartment building. He climbed over a drunk who was sprawled on the concrete floor of the lower level of the building. He walked to the nearest pay phone, which was defaced with graffiti, and he made an international phone call to Athens. Luckily, his father picked up on the second ring. Demitrius had rehearsed this conversation in his mind throughout the night. He told his father that he was in danger and that he needed to come to Sofia right away. Despite his father's desperate attempts to garner more information, the response was the same. He could not divulge any more information over the phone, and time was of the essence. Sabin reassured his son that he would be on the next train to Sofia. It would take about fourteen hours. Demitrius gave his father the address to meet him. He would be waiting. Demitrius hung up the phone and smiled.

At midnight, Demitrius walked into the casino with a box in his hand. He told the guard that he had a gift for Andrey and that Andrey was expecting him. The guard gave him an incredulous look as he eyed the box. He instructed the guard to tell Andrey that Demitrius Borislavov was waiting for him with an important gift. The guard made a phone call then ordered Demitrius to follow him. They walked behind a red velvet curtain along a narrow passageway, down a stairwell, then a few more feet before stopping at a door. The guard knocked on the door, and a loud voice ordered the knocker to enter. The door opened to a similar scene from the night before.

Demitrius asked permission to approach the table, and permission was granted. Demitrius placed the five-kilogram box on the table and invited Andrey to open it. Andrey stood and looked Demitrius straight in the eyes. The stark contrast of the coloring of his eyes was grossly apparent. Andrey slowly removed the lid. There lying in the box was the head of Sabin Borislavov. Andrey turned to Demitrius and smiled. It was a smile that said welcome to the brotherhood.

CHAPTER 26

Demitrius proved himself to be a vital player in the game constructed by Andrey Borislavov. He was a skilled chess player strategically moving his pieces on the board. His innate ability to manipulate and exploit others with no remorse compounded with his shrewd intellect made him indispensable. He was cunning and fearless. He was a quick learner and had gained mastery of human emotions and body language. He was often able to predict what others were thinking or anticipate their next move, which ultimately put him one step ahead of the game. Demitrius quickly accelerated the ranks of the notorious organization and was informally regarded as Andrey's right-hand man.

Demitrius was in charge of many of the illegal operations, and his subordinates had to report to him. A lower-ranking member, known as Dragan, was less than impressed. He despised the fact that Demitrius was able to implant himself into the organization and worm his way to the top. He abhorred taking instructions from someone who was almost twenty years his junior.

One Saturday, Dragan was instructed to carry out a task that he felt to be demeaning. Although he tried to conceal it, Dragan knew that Demitrius was aware of the disdain he had for him. He knew that Demitrius was intentionally ordering him to do degrading jobs, and he'd reached his breaking point. He barged into Demitrius's office and verbally attacked him while waving his index finger violently toward his boss. Demitrius sat calmly behind his desk with a devious smirk etched onto his face. He conveyed to Dragan that he'd been expecting him. Without saying another word, Demitrius abruptly got up and took hold of Dragan's right hand. He forcefully planted Dragan's hand onto the oak desk, took his army knife out of his pocket, and cut off his subordinate's index finger. Dragan screamed out in horror as he watched his blood stain the oak. The act was a stern warning, and from that moment forward, Dragan knew his place.

Nikita saw another side of her husband. She saw the loving, caring, adoring side of him. He worked a lot, but when he was home, he showered her with attention and expensive gifts.

Demitrius allowed Nikita to see the side of him that he wanted her to see. He'd fabricated a Monday to Friday job that sometimes called him in on the weekends. As far as Nikita knew, he was involved in important business activity at a prestigious establishment in downtown Sofia, and the details went over her head. She knew that he held an important position and that he was successful, but most importantly, he loved his job, and she was proud of him. His success was evident by his financial earnings. They'd moved into a nice, spacious, two-story home with four bedrooms and four bathrooms, south of the city, in an exclusive neighborhood. The money was flowing in unhindered.

Nikita was living a life that she'd only dreamed of. Demitrius took her on spontaneous trips to London, Paris, Venice, and Rome. For her birthday weekend, he called her from work and asked her to pack a weekend bag with clothes for warm weather and to include a couple of swimsuits. He would not tell her where they were going, and the anticipation was thrilling.

Demitrius's surprise did not disappoint. He had a weekend planned for her in Monaco aboard a luxury yacht. It was surreal where their life had taken them. They went shopping in fashionable boutiques and designer stores. They were drinking expensive champagne and indulging in caviar and escargot. They were surrounded by beautiful people and extravagant wealth. Money was no object.

Nikita was reserved. Demitrius, on the other hand, was sociable and tended to be the life of the party. His great sense of humor and undeniable charm drew people toward him, and they delighted in his company. His charm gained them an invitation to an elite party held aboard a diplomat's yacht.

Rorey Wood, a famous Hollywood actor, was at the party. Rorey was tall, dark, and handsome, and he was the definition of masculinity from his chiseled jawline to his sculpted physique. He'd started on a soap opera, *The Young and the Beautiful*, before taking a leap into the movie industry. He was considered one of the leading heartthrobs on the big screen. His date was a slender female who exuded old Hollywood glamour. Her wavy blonde hair cascaded down to the mid portion of her back. Her long, white, silk dress hugged her curves, and she completed her look with silver-studded shoes and dangling diamond earrings that dazzled in the night.

Demitrius had struck up a conversation with Rorey, and they had hit it off. Nikita listened in on the conversation but did not speak much. In actuality, she was quite nervous being in the company of Hollywood royalty. She grew up watching Rorey on television. *The Young and the Beautiful* was her favorite soap opera, and she'd had a crush on Rorey, who played the character Danny Love, a young Casanova. She'd been upset when Danny Love had broken Madison's heart. Rorey's character was killed off after being involved in a fatal motorcycle accident. Rorey then transitioned onto the big screen and played a leading role in several blockbuster hits. Her favorite movie he'd been in was *Omen*, where he'd played Robert Doss, a high school teacher who'd developed premonitions after a head injury, and he was able to prevent bad things from happening before they occurred.

Rorey's date was immaculate. Her makeup was flawless, and her red lipstick was perfectly painted on her pouty lips. She was introduced as Linda. Nikita hadn't recognized her, but she easily could be mistaken for a Hollywood movie star. Linda carried herself with an air of importance, and she completely disregarded Nikita's presence. She had a flirtatious way about her, and her laugh seemed inauthentic. Linda caught the attention of a waiter who dutifully brought over a tray of champagne glasses. She placed her empty glass, stained with her lipstick, onto the tray and took another glass. She turned and instantly inserted herself back into the conversation.

Nikita felt like a fish out of water. Everyone around her seemed important and influential. She couldn't help but to draw comparisons between herself and the other women on the yacht. She felt completely disconnected and invisible. At that moment, she even felt invisible to her husband. Demitrius was thoroughly engrossed in a conversation with Rorey and Linda, and another couple had joined in. Demitrius had briefly introduced Nikita before striking up a conversation with the other couple.

Nikita tried to adjust her posture by standing straight and putting her shoulders back. She viewed the moment as an opportunity to start breaking away from her shyness. Deep down, she did not believe that she belonged among the company of people with such importance. It was a notion that she had to get rid of quickly or suppress to the point of oblivion. Nikita went into observation mode and tried to imitate Linda. At first, she felt stupid. She was pretending to be a character. She arched her back and held in her stomach. Most of her energy went into looking the part, and she lost focus of the conversation. She tilted her head back and laughed at a joke that she'd missed the punchline to. She struggled to maintain a smile, and her mouth tensed and quivered. She felt like an imposter, but this was now her life, and she had to embrace it fully.

Upon their return to Sofia, Demitrius engulfed himself into his business. He worked longer hours and was home less and less. Nikita had voiced her concerns about his prolonged absence. He reminded her that his job had paid for their lavish home, the expensive jewelry around her neck, and the luxurious hotels during their extravagant weekend getaways. Nikita was still uncertain about the details of his job. Demitrius often stated that his dealings were classified and confidential, and Nikita accepted his words with no further questioning.

The money rolled in, but Nikita still felt a deep void. All of her costly possessions could not fill it. She felt lonely. Her relationships outside of her husband were superficial. She had no one in Sofia with whom she could be transparent and be herself. Her relationship with her husband became less recognizable as they spent less and less time together. When they were together, he often told her that he loved her, and he showered her with kisses and expensive gifts, but the connection was no longer there. She yearned for the time that they'd spent together in Athens during the early part of their marriage. She missed the long talks and the laughs. It was a simple life, but they had each other. Now, she felt as though she were sleeping with a stranger.

Nikita had had her third miscarriage. It was a devastating loss, and she felt alone. She had been two months along. Her dream of becoming a mother seemed as though it would never come to fruition. Deep down, she also hoped that a child would bring her and Demitrius closer together. Maybe he would spend more time at home.

The years went by, and nothing changed. Demitrius continued to work long hours, and the money continued to roll in. Despite the vast material possessions, Nikita felt hollow inside. The emptiness of her existence was present upon awakening and lingered throughout the day until she went to sleep at night.

Demitrius came home one night to find Nikita crying uncontrollably on the bed. Her tears had soaked the gray pillowcase, leaving behind a large, wet stain. The more that Demitrius tried to console her, the more she cried. He could not understand why she would be unhappy given all of the wealth they had accumulated. Her lifestyle would have made most women envious. She confessed to her husband that she was lonely. She missed him. She missed the talks and the laughs. She missed the closeness.

Demitrius offered to take her to Hawaii for a week, just the two of them with no interruptions. His cell phone would be off, and she would have his undivided attention. He waited for a response as she dried her eyes with tissue paper. Nikita told him that she needed fulfillment. She needed a purpose. Her dream had been to own a restaurant in Santorini, and she would call it Zeus Zest. He'd promised her when they'd gotten married that they would return to Greece after he'd accumulated the knowledge and experience that he needed in Bulgaria. Years had gone by, and she wanted to return home.

Demitrius sat on the edge of the bed, pondering Nikita's words. He did make her that promise, and he considered himself a man of his word. He loved Nikita, and he wanted her to be happy. At that moment, he made the decision for them to return to Greece. He would talk to Andrey the following day. His plan would be to expand the business there.

CHAPTER 27

Giselle and Valerie were having lunch outside a café. Maxwell had taken a flight back to London earlier that morning. He'd offered to stay and help them with the investigation, but Giselle encouraged him to return home.

The friends discussed their next steps. They kept hitting dead ends. There weren't too many leads that they could tackle on their own. The National Intelligence Service would be handling the leads related to the Bulgarian mafia. Their hands were tied.

Ajax, the homeless man who'd stolen Valerie's purse, was sent from jail to a mental facility for further evaluation and treatment. Giselle suggested going to the facility and convincing the medical staff to allow them to speak with him. She then acknowledged that that plan would not work. There was no way that the doctor would allow them to interview a patient, more so one who needed intense psychiatric treatment.

Giselle took a bite of her salad and sat back in her chair. She was not hungry. She forced herself to think. Were there any clues that they'd missed? This was a puzzle, and she had to find the pieces and put it together. She and Valerie sat in silence for over half an hour. The waitress had come by three times to see whether they'd needed anything.

"Val, I don't want you to look. First, promise me that you're not going to look."

"Look at what?"

"I'll tell you, but first, you have to promise me that you won't look."

"Okay, fine. I won't look."

"And you have to promise me that you'll remain calm," Giselle cautioned.

"Okay. Now you're scaring me."

"Val, promise me."

"Okay, I promise."

"I think a guy in a white car is looking at us."

"What!" Valerie exclaimed.

"Val, keep your voice down. You promise you'd remain calm."

"Are you sure it's not some random guy sitting in his car?"

"It could be, but I have a gut feeling that something is wrong. He's looking ahead now, but he's been looking in our direction way too many times."

"What does he look like?" Valerie pressed her friend.

"He's well built, and he has shoulder-length black hair."

"Oh my goodness. Do you think that could be the person Ajax was describing?"

"It very well could be."

Valerie turned and locked eyes with the driver. The man turned on the ignition and quickly drove off.

Giselle watched intently as the car drove away. "Quick, I need a pen," Giselle stated hurriedly. She rummaged through her fanny pack and found a black ink pen. She scribbled the license plate number on a napkin. "Val, I told you not to look!"

"I'm sorry. Please don't be upset. I was looking back casually."

"We need to take this information to the police station right away."

———

They took a taxi to the police station. Fortunately, Detective Christou was on duty, who was familiar with the case and had interviewed Ajax.

"I know you are deeply worried about your friend and understandably so," Detective Christou stated behind his desk. His eyes diverted between Giselle and Valerie. "But you can't randomly see a guy and think that he's involved. Why don't–"

"But you don't understand, Detective," Giselle interrupted. "This man was acting suspicious. He fits the description that Ajax gave you."

"You're taking this from a homeless nutcase who thought that Hades had come to rescue his queen?" Detective Christou gave them an incredulous look. "This is a man who needed serious psychiatric attention and needed to be in a mental ward. In fact, that's exactly where we took him."

"Then why did this man quickly drive off when I locked eyes with him?" Valerie asked rhetorically. "I'll tell you why. He knew we were on to him."

"With all due respect, I think your minds are playing tricks on you. You've probably not been eating well or sleeping much. You're desperate to find your friend, and you're probably overly suspicious of everyone."

"And with all due respect to you, Detective," Giselle responded, "we're not delusional. I know what I saw. This was a man who was observing us for almost half an hour. Something was off about the situation. I have a gut feeling, and over the years, I've learned to trust my gut. It has steered me in the right direction."

"So what do you want me to do with your gut feeling?" Detective Christou asked sarcastically.

Giselle took the napkin out of her fanny pack where she'd written the license plate number. "I want you to look into this license plate number. He was driving a white hatchback Peugeot. This may give you a clue into the man driving that vehicle."

The detective stared intently at Giselle while twirling his pen between his thumb and index finger. Giselle continued, "You saw that pentagram symbol Ajax drew. You acknowledged that it was the symbol of the Bulgarian mafia. Ajax may have had psychiatric issues, but you can't deny that he saw something dangerous. How else would he have gotten our friend's scarf? Believe me, that was her scarf. That man in that car could be involved. We're pleading with you. Please look into this plate number."

Detective Christou scribbled the number onto a sheet of paper. He assured them that he would look into the plate number. "I want you both to remember that if the Bulgarian mafia is involved, this would be a matter of national security and indeed a dangerous and potentially deadly situation." He instructed them to leave it to the experts.

They shook hands with the detective and left the police station.

CHAPTER 28

They walked side by side along one of the narrow streets of Fira, contemplating their next move. "Giselle, maybe Demitrius can help us."

"Val, I've told you. We should be careful with this sensitive information."

"We can't depend on Detective Christou. He probably placed that piece of paper with the license plate number at the bottom of his pile."

"Val, I don't know if we should get Demitrius involved. You heard the detective. This is a matter of national security."

"Do you have a better idea?" There was a long pause. "I didn't think so." Valerie stopped in her tracks, and Giselle did the same. "Look Giselle, I understand that this is a matter of national security, but we can't remain idle and leave it in Detective Christou's hands."

"I agree with you, Val. I just don't know what is the next right move."

"And that's where Demitrius might be able to help us. You heard him. He knows this island like the back of his hand. He said he has connections. Maybe he could help us find out who this guy is." Valerie held her friend by her shoulders. "I know you don't want to get Demitrius involved, but we have no choice. We need all the help we can get."

Giselle reluctantly agreed, and they made their way to Zeus Zest. Upon entering the restaurant, Demitrius was not visibly present. There were two people dining at a table in a corner, but otherwise, the restaurant was relatively empty.

One of the workers greeted them at the bar. Giselle remembered him from their last visit to the restaurant. His name was Alec, and he'd turned eighteen the day before. Demitrius had congratulated him on becoming a man.

"Where's Demitrius?" Valerie asked.

"He took the day off," Alec responded. "How can I help you both?"

"We need to speak to Demitrius," Valerie continued. "Any idea where we could find him?"

"I don't know where he is. Is it something that I can help you with?"

"No, you won't be able to help us," Valerie replied. "Can you call him? Tell him that Valerie and Giselle need to speak with him. It's urgent."

Alec picked up the phone and dialed a number. After a few seconds, he hung up. "Sorry, he didn't answer."

"Try again," Valerie urged.

Alec picked up the receiver and dialed. Several seconds passed before he hung up the phone. "Sorry, no answer. It's not allowing me to leave a voicemail. Can I take your number? I'll have him call you when he gets in tomorrow morning."

"Tomorrow is too late," Valerie responded.

"May I ask what this is about?"

Valerie ignored his question. "Can you tell us where he lives?"

"I'm sorry, but I'm not at liberty to share that information."

"He won't mind," Valerie continued. "He wants us to contact him with this information."

"And how do you know him?"

"Don't you remember us?" Giselle chimed in. It was the first words she'd spoken since walking into the restaurant. "Demitrius introduced us to you last Monday. You turned eighteen."

"Yes, I remember."

"We've become friends with Demitrius," Valerie said, as she took hold of the conversation. "I wish I could share this information with you, but it's personal, and Demitrius would want to know right away. Trust me."

Alec was hesitant. "Uh, I don't know. He's a private person. Extremely private." He had a deep look of uncertainty. "I don't want to get involved."

"You won't get involved," Valerie reassured him. "He'll never know that you gave us the information."

Alec paused. "His house is huge and well guarded. If I were you, I probably wouldn't go unless he's expecting you."

"Can you tell us how to get there?" Giselle asked.

Alec took a blue ink pen out of a plastic cup and wrote the directions on a napkin. He'd been to Demitrius's house once, a few months back, when he'd been ordered to deliver a package. "Here are the directions. This is the best that I can do. The cell phone service isn't too good in certain spots, so be careful."

They thanked Alec and walked in the direction of the street that the taxicabs frequented.

"Val, maybe we should rethink this. We don't know Demitrius too well. Alec stressed that he's a private person, and he may not like us showing up at his property."

"Every day that goes by is a day that Kate could be in more danger. She might be suffering wherever she is. It could be worse, but I don't want to think of the worst-case scenario."

"Take a left here," Valerie instructed the taxi driver. "No, the other left."

"Are you sure you know where you're going?" the taxi driver asked, almost annoyed.

"Yes, we know where we're going. Now take that left."

The taxi driver increased his speed after slowing down to almost a snail's pace. He turned onto a narrow street on a slight incline. There was a marble statue of a sculpted man and his dog raised in the center of a fountain. It was exactly as Alec had described. The grass desperately needed to be mowed.

"Keep going straight." Valerie instructed. They had come to a dead end, and the taxi came to a stop.

The driver turned. "Look, I'm not trying to be rude, but do you know where you're going? This is a dead end. I'm not going to go around in circles. It's going to cost you."

Giselle turned to her friend. "I think this is it." It was exactly as Alec had described. The directions led them to a dead end. On the left was a gravel road with a large sign that said *No Trespassing*.

"I think you're right," Valerie acknowledged. "This is it."

"What is it?" the driver asked confused. "I'm not going down that road. You see the sign."

"Val, maybe we should rethink this."

"Giselle, we have to do this."

"Look, I don't know what you two Americans are up to. I suggest that you let me take you back, and you can pay me the price we agreed on."

"No, we're getting out." Valerie opened the door.

"Okay. Suit yourself. But I'm not waiting for you. And just some advice, the phone reception is not always good."

"Val, let's go back."

"I've made my decision," Valerie stated. She paid the driver, got out of the cab, and closed the door. Reluctantly, Giselle got out too.

The taxi driver made a three-point turn and went on his way.

Giselle and Valerie started down the gravel road. As they walked farther, a two-story, whitewashed house came into view, peeking above a white concrete wall. They walked along the path leading to the house and stopped at the arched metal gate. The entry to the house was visible though the vertical iron fence posts.

"Demitrius!" Valerie shouted. "Demitrius!"

Two large, black guard dogs charged toward the gate. The barking sounds were deafening. Their sharpened canines were visible, and strings of thick drool fell onto the ground. Giselle and Valerie stopped in their tracks, paralyzed with fear.

"Who's there?" a man's voice called with strict authority. Demitrius materialized in front of them with a rifle in his hand pointed in their direction. Giselle felt her heart racing. Her palms were sweaty, and her breathing was rapid and shallow.

"What are you two doing here?" Demitrius said angrily. He lowered his rifle and stared at them with piercing eyes. Demitrius was not recognizable, Giselle thought. He was not the welcoming person they had met who had kind eyes and a warm spirit. His whole demeanor was different, and the look on his face was menacing and downright terrifying. He patted one of his guard dogs on the head. Giselle's eyes fell onto Demitrius's right shoulder. *It couldn't be*, Giselle thought. It was a tattoo of a pentagram with an eye in the center.

Demitrius directed his gaze toward her. She knew that he sensed a different look in her eyes. It was not only a look of fear but disbelief. He gave her a devious smirk that sent shivers up and down her spine.

CHAPTER 29

"Walk straight ahead, and don't look back," Demetrius sternly ordered. He directed them toward the house. Giselle knew that the gun was pointed at their backs. Her PTSD had returned, bringing her back to that moment about a year ago where she'd had a deadly object pointed at her, but instead of a sharp knife that came close to piercing her skin, it was a gun that could send a bullet through her body. The intense emotions she'd felt returned. Her heart was racing, and she felt beads of sweat forming on her forehead.

Valerie was breathing hard. She sounded choked up, as though she were trying to suppress her tears.

They approached the front entrance. "Now open the door and walk in," Demitrius demanded.

Giselle knew that once they walked into the house, their fate was sealed. She remembered watching an episode of *Oprah* that warned the viewers to never let an attacker take you to a second location. *What do I do?* Giselle thought. *I can't scream. There's likely no one else in this secluded area.* Valerie had opened the door, and following Demitrius's instructions, she'd walked into the house. Giselle followed closely behind. They were in his territory, and he had full control.

The foyer led to a spacious area impeccably furnished with expensive taste. The living room had all-white furniture with an opulent crystal chandelier hanging from the ceiling. There were gold ornaments that decorated the space. Beyond the living room was a half-turn majestic staircase. The kitchen, on the other side of the space, had a large island made of marble with stainless steel appliances.

"Now turn to me," Demitrius ordered.

Giselle and Valerie slowly turned. His eyes were dark and ominous. A devious smirk was etched onto his face. He was almost unrecognizable.

"What are you doing here?" he asked.

Giselle looked into his eyes. She was aware that he knew the answer to that question. He knew that they were looking for Kate, and she knew that he'd played a role in Kate's disappearance. He was a part of the Bulgarian mafia.

"We were hoping that you could help us," Valerie answered. Her voice quivered as she spoke.

"Help you with what?" he responded mischievously. Demitrius was evidently playing mind games with them.

Giselle spoke, "Demitrius, we shouldn't have come to your property unannounced. We were wrong for that, and we're sorry. We didn't mean to be disrespectful, and we can leave your property immediately. Nothing more will be said."

Demitrius's smirk transformed to laughter. His demeanor was condescending and disdainful. It was a stark contrast to the man who welcomed them into Zeus Zest. He was a version of Dr. Jekyll and Mr. Hyde. His shirtless body was intimidating. The pentagram symbol on his right shoulder was like a bullseye on a dartboard.

"I can't let you go," he replied. "After all, you know my secret." He paused, "So, how do you think that this is going to end?"

The tears that Valerie was holding back came down like a torrential downpour. "Please, Demitrius. Please don't do this. Please, I beg you. I have a two-year-old daughter at home who needs me. Please don't let her grow up without a mother. Please, I beg you."

Valerie's tears did not move him. It was as though he were enjoying the power he held. There was still an empty look in his eyes and a smirk on his face.

"Please, I beg you," she continued. Valerie fell to her knees. She pressed the palms of her hands together and fingers pointed up in a prayer position. "Please Demitrius. I beg you. Please let us go. We won't say anything. You have our word. Please let me get back to my daughter."

"Stand up!" he ordered.

Valerie slowly got up. Her legs felt unsteady to support the weight of her body. She used both hands to wipe her eyes.

"Give me your purses!"

Giselle took off her fanny pack and gave it to Demitrius.

He stared at Valerie. She hesitated to take off her purse, criss-crossed around her neck.

"I said give me your purse!"

Valerie slowly removed the purse from around her neck and handed it to him.

Demitrius threw the purses to a side of the room. He lifted the rifle and pointed it in their direction. "Now turn around and walk ahead." They passed the kitchen, which was on their left, and walked into an area with a large dining table and an equally impressive chandelier hanging from the ceiling. "Continue straight ahead. Now take a right."

They took a right down a hallway. It led to descending stairs. "Now, go down the stairs."

Giselle led the way. She could hear sniffling sounds behind her. *Where is he taking us?* she thought. *Where is Nikita?*

"Make a left at the bottom of the stairs."

Giselle made a left. Valerie grabbed onto her shirt from behind.

"Go straight ahead, and open that door in front of you."

Giselle stopped. *What was behind that door?* she thought. Reluctantly, she turned the knob and opened it. It was an empty room with a small window high up toward the ceiling.

"Now get inside," he ordered.

Valerie turned quickly. "Please don't do this, Demitrius. Please. I beg you."

He lifted the rifle again. They immediately walked into the room.

"Now, you both are going to stay here until I decide what to do with you. Consider yourself lucky. It's better than the alternative."

Demitrius closed the door and locked it. Valerie fell again to her knees and sobbed uncontrollably.

Giselle placed her back against the door and slid to the floor. She buried her face in the palms of her hands. She knew that she needed to be strong for both of them if they were going to come out alive. But, how were they going to get out? They were trapped.

———

Almost three hours had gone by. Nothing. There was no sound of Demitrius or any activity in the house. Sitting on the hard tiles had become uncomfortable. Giselle replayed the last few hours in her head. A vision of the pentagram symbol on Demitrius's shoulder repeatedly entered her mind. Questions circled in her brain. *Where is Kate? What did he do to Kate? Is Kate in this house? Is Kate alive?*

"Giselle, this is my fault," Valerie said, interrupting Giselle's thoughts. "All of it is my fault. If I didn't get angry at Kate, she would've never left that hotel room, and she would not have been kidnapped. We are in this room because of me. You told me not to seek after Demitrius. You said that we didn't know him, and you were right. You warned me not to get out of that cab, but I didn't listen to you. Now I've dragged you into this."

"Let's not focus on that. We need to figure out a way to get out."

"How are we possibly going to get out? We're locked in a room with a small window that we can't reach. We don't have our phones. If we even tried to escape, Demitrius would kill us." Valerie lowered her head and cried.

The hours passed, and it was getting dark. Giselle flipped a switch, but the lights did not come on. Soon, the room would be in complete darkness. At that moment, Demitrius opened the door.

He had two trays of food in his hands. He placed them on the floor then closed the door behind him and locked it.

Hesitantly, they each grabbed a tray. They were famished. On the plates were meatloaf, mashed potatoes, and a role. There was plastic cutlery and a bottle of water. They ate in silence.

Valerie drank the last bit of her water in the bottle. "Giselle, I need to pee."

"Me too."

"What do we do?"

"I don't know. Pee in the bottle, I guess."

"How am I supposed to pee in this bottle?"

"Valerie, I have no idea."

Demitrius opened the door again. He placed four blankets and two pillows onto the floor.

"Demitrius, I really, really need to go to the bathroom," Valerie stated.

"One at a time. Come with me."

Valerie exited, and Demitrius locked the door behind them. After a few minutes, the door opened again. Giselle was relieved that Valerie had returned.

"Come with me."

He locked the door with Valerie inside, and Demitrius led Giselle to the bathroom. She pictured Demitrius standing guard outside while she relieved herself. She left the water from the sink running as she searched the bathroom. The medicine cabinet above the sink was empty. The entire bathroom was virtually empty.

She heard a knock at the door. She immediately turned off the water, dried her hands, and opened the bathroom door. Demitrius led her back to the room and locked the door.

There was barely any light coming through the window. Valerie was now a faint silhouette in the still of the darkness. They laid one of the blankets on the floor and covered their bodies with the other. The floor was hard and uncomfortable, the cold from the concrete flooring seeping through the material.

"Giselle, do you think we're going to get out of here alive?"

"Yes, we will. We have to believe it and not lose hope."

"What do you think he plans to do with us?"

"I don't know."

They lay in silence. She could intermittently hear Valerie's sniffles. Her thoughts were swirling in her head, and she had difficulty focusing. It all felt like a dream—a dreadful, frightful dream. It was a nightmare, but it was real. She replayed the entire trip in her mind, from the moment Kate left the hotel room, never to be seen again, to her lying on a cold, hard floor with her friend, held against their will. Who would come looking for them? Would Detective Christou give a thought to their whereabouts? He might assume that they went back to New York and close the case. Even if he considered their whereabouts and conducted an investigation, no one would know their location. No one would know where they were —no one except Demitrius.

Valerie's sniffles were no longer audible. She must have fallen asleep. Thoughts were still racing through Giselle's mind. She had no idea how many hours had gone by. How were they going to get out of this room alive? The window was too small and high above their reach. Could Valerie prop her up on her shoulders? And even if that were possible, the window appeared too small for her to wiggle herself out. Even if that was successful, how would Valerie get out? And there were the guard dogs. She pictured their wide-open mouths with sharpened canine teeth. The idea seemed implausible and dangerous. But then again, who knew what Demitrius had planned? Maybe death was the inevitable alternative.

The light of dawn seeped through the window. The appearance of the room was taking shape.

"Giselle, are you awake?" Valerie's voice was a whisper.

"Yes. I'm awake. I'm not sure if I even slept."

"How are we going to get out of here?"

"I don't know. I thought about it all night. I don't know how we're going to get out of here."

Moments went by, and there was a knock on the door. After a few seconds, Demitrius opened it. Giselle was surprised that Demitrius had the courtesy to knock. He had two trays of food. He laid them on the floor, and without a word, he closed the door behind him and locked it.

The trays each had a plate of scrambled eggs, two slices of toast, tomatoes, and olives. There was a small bowl with yogurt, topped with fruits, a small glass of orange juice, a spoon, a fork and a napkin. A few minutes passed, and there was another knock on the door. After it opened, Demitrius handed them each a bottle of water and left without saying a word. They heard a click as he locked the door.

About an hour went by when Demitrius returned.

"I have come to collect your trays." Those were the first words that had escaped his mouth. They each handed him their tray. He searched both trays. He looked at them with his dark, piercing eyes. "Where is the other fork?"

Giselle and Valerie looked at each other with bewilderment.

"Where is the other fork?" he asked with a deep, stern voice. Without moving his head, his penetrating eyes moved back and forth, studying their facial expressions. He set down the trays. As he slowly approached them, they inched toward the wall until there was nowhere for them to go.

He abruptly patted Valerie down. Giselle reached her right hand behind her back for the fork lodged between her pants and her lower back, covered by her shirt. As soon as she gripped the fork, Demitrius grabbed her right wrist and pushed it firmly against the wall. He flew into a rage, grabbing her neck with his other hand. He pressed her tightly against the wall, and she found herself standing on her toes, hoping to relieve some of the pressure around her neck. His eyes were bulging, almost as if his eyeballs would pop out of their sockets.

Valerie pleaded with Demitrius to stop. She hit his back with both of her hands. Demitrius released his grip around Giselle's neck and backhanded Valerie, sending her body to the floor like a limp rag doll.

Demitrius's breathing was heavy. He looked back and forth from Valerie, who was lying on the floor, with one hand covering her face, to Giselle, who was also breathing heavily, with her hand sheltering her neck.

He picked up the trays and headed to the door. He looked back at them, his face completely transformed from an angry monster to a calm, gentle lamb. The lines of his face had smoothed out, and his eyes were gleaming.

"I'm sorry. I didn't mean to hurt you. I'll be back later with your lunch."

Demitrius closed the door behind him and locked it. Giselle fell to the ground, and for the first time, she sobbed. She was supposed to be the strong one, but her emotions had gotten the best of her. She did not feel optimistic anymore. Valerie depended on her. Kate depended on her. She felt weak and was losing control. The pain in her throat was intense as she wept. Valerie slid next to her and wrapped her arms around her friend. They both sat and wept.

CHAPTER 30

T he next days mirrored the previous days. Demitrius brought them breakfast, lunch, and dinner. It was clockwork. He escorted them individually to the bathroom three times a day. The room began to smell musty, and he allowed them to take showers, once a day, five minutes each. He handed them a clean shirt and shorts, deodorant, and soap when they went into the bathroom to shower. He banged on the door to indicate when they had exceeded the allotted time.

They sat in the corner of the room, contemplating their next move. Ideas were limited and led to dead ends. There was nothing in the bathroom that could assist with an escape plan. Demitrius made sure of that. Also, Giselle shuddered at the thought of Demitrius's hand wrapped around her throat. Next time, he might not be so forgiving.

A familiar knock led to Demitrius opening the door.

Is it already time for lunch? Giselle thought.

Demitrius handed them their original clothes. They were cleaned, ironed, and folded, with two pieces of chocolate on top. "Lunch will be from the restaurant. I'll bring you lamb and beef gyros, your favorite, with baklava." He closed and locked the door.

What are his plans with us? When is this cycle going to end? Giselle thought. *What are these mind games he's playing?*

As promised, Demitrius brought them lamb and beef gyros and baklava. He brought a can of Coke for Giselle, a diet Coke for Valerie and each a bottle of water. He set the trays in front of them. Instead of leaving, as he typically would do, he stood and did not budge. "Go ahead. Eat."

Giselle and Valerie slowly ate their food. It was awkward having Demitrius in the room as they ate.

"Do you not like the food?" he asked quizzically.

"No, we love the food," Giselle quickly answered. "The gyros from Zeus Zest are one of a kind. It's the best food that we've eaten since being in Greece. I can't wait to eat the baklava."

Demitrius gave her a half-hearted smile. She could not tell if he thought that she was buttering him up.

"What are your plans with us?" Giselle asked.

"I don't know yet. We'll see."

"Demitrius, we know this isn't you. This is not the Demitrius we met, and deep down, you know this isn't you," Giselle stated.

His lips curled into another half-hearted smile. "You know nothing about me," he snarled.

"You're right, but deep down, I know this isn't you."

His eyes narrowed, and the coloring of his eyes was almost gone. "How are you so sure?"

"Who hurt you?" Giselle pried. "Someone in your life has hurt you deeply."

The moment of silence felt like an eternity. Giselle did not know whether he would let down his guard or burst into an animalistic rage. She could not read his body language.

A few more moments went by, and Demitrius appeared pensive.

"We come into this world like a blank canvas," he began. "Clean and pure. Unblemished. Every experience in life adds a stroke to that canvas, good or bad. The people we encounter add their own strokes to our canvas, whether we want them to or not. Most importantly, the guardians of our existence, the ones who brought us into this world, have the master brush. That master brush has created an outline, and that outline has been filled with dark color. What would happen if that master brush painted a dark, ugly, evil picture?"

"We can create our own canvas," Giselle said softly. "The paint-brush is in our hand."

"What if there's no more room?" he replied. Demitrius's eyes appeared glassy, and he seemed lost in his thoughts. He momentarily let down his guard as he walked toward the wall and stared up at the window. "Sometimes we feel trapped in our existence. If people saw the real painting, they would run away. We have to show the world a different painting, selling it off as the real thing."

Giselle looked at Valerie. She knew that Valerie was thinking the same thing. The door was wide open. They had to run like their lives depended on it. Who knew if they would get another opportunity? Giselle lifted her right hand and did a countdown on her fingers. On three, they bolted out of the door. Demitrius raced behind them, screaming and cussing. They ran through the living room, and Valerie threw a vase at him, hitting him in the face. Demitrius tripped over his feet and fell to the floor. He slowly picked himself up. Giselle unlocked the front door, and the friends ran to the gate.

"Oh my goodness, Val. The gate is locked. There's a padlock on it."

Two large, black guard dogs charged at them with loud barks. The dogs stood in front of them, growling, daring them to make a move.

Demitrius gave a command through the doorway, and the dogs stayed back, although still on guard. Demitrius emerged, walking slowly, with his hand covering the left side of his face. There was blood trickling as a result of the direct impact of the vase.

Giselle felt her body become weak as she watched Demitrius approach them. It took every bit of strength for her to remain standing. She felt Valerie's body trembling. This was it. They were going to die.

Demitrius's face took on the appearance of that monster that had gone into hiding. The mask was off, and the monster was released. He grabbed Giselle's neck with his bloodied hand and grabbed Valerie's neck with the other. They both flailed their arms toward him. If he had maintained his grip for a second longer, Giselle felt as though she would have passed out. He ordered them back into the house, grabbing their necks from behind. He screamed profanities as he led them back into the small space.

"Give me one good reason that I should not kill you both right now." He spat a bloody wad onto the floor. "Humans cannot be trusted. That's why you can never let your guard down or they will hurt you." Demitrius slammed the door and locked it.

"Giselle, what have we done? We blew our only opportunity. He's going to kill us. I'll never see Donald and Bridget again."

"Val, I promise you that you'll see Donald and Bridget." Deep down, she wasn't so sure. How were they going to get out? Demitrius would never trust them again. They took advantage of his vulnerability. Valerie was right. They blew it. She felt that she had made the wrong decision. They should not have run. She was in the moment with the only window of opportunity, and she hadn't considered the potential obstacles.

They sat in silence, shaken by the events that had happened earlier. There didn't seem to be a light at the end of the tunnel. They were at the mercy of Demitrius. He was free to do with them as he pleased without the interference of the outside world. What did he plan to do with them? How long would they remain locked up? Would he punish them further for what they had done? Or worse, would he kill them? The light streaming through the window faded. Night was approaching, and Demitrius had not brought them dinner. There was nowhere to relieve themselves, except for the water bottles left in the room.

The next morning, Demitrius did not bring them breakfast. Was he going to starve them to death? Was that his plan? The emptiness of their stomachs was perceptible. Giselle was losing hope, but she wanted to remain strong for her friend. She had been praying silently multiple times a day, hoping for a miracle. The hope was dimmed but not extinguished.

Valerie interrupted her thoughts, "Giselle, if we never get out of here alive, I want you to know that I love you, and I've been blessed to have you as a friend. We may not be blood related, but you are my sister. You're one of the kindest, most compassionate, most generous people I've ever met."

"Val, I love you too, and I feel the same way about you, but I need for you to believe that we're going to get out somehow."

Valerie sighed, "I know that you always look for that ray of light. Your optimism is something that I've always admired about you."

"No matter what, we can never lose hope. And right now, hope is all we have."

"Do you think Bridget knows that I love her?"

"Val, I know it's hard to believe right now, but you will see Bridget again."

Valerie placed her pillow behind her head and closed her eyes.

They were uncertain how much time had passed when they heard a knock. Did Demitrius come to bring them food, or did he come to punish them?

The door opened. Giselle was surprised at what she saw.

"Nikita," Giselle stated in shock. She'd wondered at Nikita's whereabouts since they'd been holed up in the room. There were no signs of Nikita throughout the house. She'd often listened intently to see if she heard a female's voice. She'd also wondered if Nikita was in on the plot to keep them hostage. Nikita now stood before them, and Giselle had no idea what to expect.

They waited for Nikita to speak. They didn't know if Nikita had come to rescue them or torture them.

"Demetrius may think that I'm oblivious to his actions, but I know what's going on. I've known what's been going on for years.

I can't turn a blind eye any longer. To do nothing is to be a part of the problem."

Giselle breathed a sigh of relief. She felt as though she were holding her breath. "Nikita, it's never too late to right our wrongs. Please help us get out. Where's Demitrius?"

"He's at the restaurant."

"We'll make sure that you don't get in trouble for this," Valerie interjected. "We'll vouch for you. You have our word."

"Come with us," Giselle stated. "We'll protect you."

"I can't. He's all I've ever known." Her eyes glassed over; her vulnerability was exposed. "I don't know who I am without him. My identity has been wrapped up in him, and frankly, I'm nothing without him."

"You deserve better than this, better than him," Giselle replied as she reached out to hold Nikita's hand. "Look at me, Nikita. Demitrius is not you. You are separate from him. Your identity is not gone. You just have to find it again. Nikita, please look at me. You are strong, and you don't need him. You've shown us your strength by risking your life to save ours. That takes so much courage and strength, and I admire you for that. Val and I will never forget this. I want you to rebuild yourself. Start over afresh. Please come with us."

"I can't. I don't know where to start."

"What time do you expect Demitrius back?" Giselle asked.

"Not for a few hours."

"It's not too late to change your mind," Giselle pleaded. "We'll help you. Trust us."

"I have something that will help your case when you go to the authorities."

Nikita left, leaving the door wide open. She returned a few minutes later. She had a manila folder and a black, wooden container that looked like a jewelry box.

She handed Giselle the folder. "What's in the box?" Giselle asked.

Nikita slowly opened it. Giselle and Valerie gasped in unison.

"Holy mother of God!" Valerie blurted out. "Whose finger is that?" The finger had a ring on it.

"I think it was that of Demitrius's father. It's preserved in formaldehyde. The last I knew, his father was on a train from Athens to Sofia, but he never made it. Demitrius did not seem saddened at all; neither did he make any attempts to find out what happened. He seemed irritated every time I brought it up, and then it became something we never spoke about. Then one day, I was home alone cleaning. The mattress seemed a little uneven. When I lifted it up, there were many files, and there was this box. I almost dropped it when I opened it. It has to be his father's finger. I recognize that ring. His father always wore that ring."

"And what's in the files?" Giselle asked.

"These files will give you information you'll need, but there are many more. It would be too much for you to carry. It's all about the Bulgarian mafia—top people in the organization and crimes that they've committed."

"Oh my goodness," Valerie exclaimed. Her eyes were wide open.

"This organization is dangerous. This is serious, and this information could bring this entire organization down. Right now, I have a target on my back. They'll kill me if they find out what I've done."

"Come with us," Giselle pleaded again. "The authorities will get you into a witness protection program."

"You don't know what you're getting into. This organization is bigger than all of us. You don't know what these people are capable of, the influence they have, the magnitude of their crimes."

"That's why we need to stop them, Nikita," Giselle urged. "We can stop this organization."

"I'm sorry. I can't go with you. But I do have something that belongs to you."

Nikita left again and returned a few minutes after. She had Valerie's purse and Giselle's fanny pack in her hands. "Here you go. Demitrius had them hidden. I'll lead you both out of the gate."

They followed Nikita. She opened the front door, and the dogs sprinted around the corner, barking loudly. Giselle and Valerie stopped dead in their tracks, afraid to even breathe. Nikita gave the dogs a command, and they sat. They had transformed into docile creatures. "You're safe. Follow me."

Hesitantly, they inched toward Nikita, afraid the dogs would transform back into their ferocious state. Nikita used a key to open the lock. The click was the sound of freedom. "Good luck and please be safe."

They walked out, and Nikita closed the gate behind them. Giselle looked into Nikita's eyes through the barrier separating them. There was fear and despair. "Nikita, please come with us."

"Please go," she said softly. "I'll be fine. May God be with you."

Valerie lightly tugged at Giselle's shirt. "We have to go, Giselle. Thank you for helping us, Nikita. Please be safe."

Giselle and Valerie walked away, then they took off running. Valerie held the files, and Giselle had the small box securely tucked underneath her arm, like she was running with a football. She prayed that she wouldn't drop it. They were both out of breath when they reached the road where the taxi had dropped them off.

"Let's go, Val." They ran as quickly as their legs would take them. Giselle was afraid that Demitrius would unexpectedly drive around the corner or one of his workers would appear and recognize them. Her heart was racing, both from running and the fear traveling throughout her body. They finally reached a main street and stopped to catch their breath. Giselle bent over and felt her body trembling. She'd never run that fast in her life, not even when she was on the track team. She was surprised that she hadn't dropped the box. She looked at Valerie, who was gasping for air. Valerie was bent over with her hands on her knees, as her body shook up and down.

Giselle was relieved to see activity around them. There were people walking along the sidewalks and businesses nearby. "Val, are you okay?" Valerie was still trying to catch her breath.

"I think I'm okay," she said, with choppy words. "I didn't know I could run that fast."

She gave Valerie some time to recover. She reached into her fanny pack. As expected, her phone was dead. Her ID and wallet were there. Nothing appeared missing. An empty taxi drove toward them. Giselle flagged him down. "Hi, can you give us a ride?"

"Yes, please get in."

Giselle and Valerie filed into the back seat.

"Where to?"

"The police station," Giselle answered.

"Very well."

Giselle observed the driver periodically looking at them in the rearview mirror. He must have been wondering why they were going to the police station. They drove in silence. She looked out the window, taking in the view. She wasn't sure that she and Valerie would ever escape the confinement of those walls.

They were free, but they were not free. Their lives were in danger, and they still hadn't found Kate. It was imperative that they be aware of their surroundings at all times.

The taxi driver pulled up to the police station. Giselle took some Euros out of her wallet and paid him. They made their way inside."

Giselle quickly approached the receptionist. "Good afternoon, we need to speak to Detective Christou. Is he in? It's urgent."

"Everything is urgent around here. And you are?"

"Giselle Bellamy and this is Valerie Brooks. We have an extremely urgent matter to discuss with Detective Christou, and we need to do so right away."

She dialed a number and spoke in Greek. "Have a seat. He'll be with you shortly."

They sat on the plastic blue chairs next to the water fountain, which was still humming. A few minutes later, Detective Christou appeared through the door.

"Giselle, Valerie, where have you been? It's like you both fell off the grid."

"You can say that," Giselle replied. They followed him into his office.

"Please have a seat. Tell me what's going on."

"We were held hostage," Giselle responded.

"What?" His demeanor changed. He sat back in his chair, and his brow furrowed. "You were held hostage? By who?"

Giselle took a deep breath. "I don't even know where to begin." She told the detective how they'd met Demitrius and the events that led to them finding out that he was a part of the Bulgarian mafia. She recounted how they'd been held captive, their unsuccessful attempts to escape, and the abuse they'd suffered. Then she described Nikita's actions to save them.

Valerie placed the manila files on the desk, and Giselle placed the small box next to the files.

"What's this?"

"There's information about the members of the organization," Giselle answered. "We haven't gone through it. We wanted to do so in a safe space. Nikita said that Demitrius has many documents hidden underneath the mattress—documents of crimes, information that could bring the entire organization down."

Detective Christou took out the documents in the file. "And what's in the box?"

"Open it," Valerie replied.

He looked at the box suspiciously and carefully opened it. He was startled and almost dropped it. "Who the hell's finger is that?"

"Nikita thinks it belongs to Demitrius's father," Giselle answered. "She said he always wore that ring. His father went missing one day and was never found."

Detective Christou's mouth was open, and the color had drained from his body. In his entire twenty-year career, he had never dealt with anything like this. He went page by page through the documents. He showed Giselle and Valerie some of the pictures in the file.

"Giselle, that's the guy who was spying on us in his car."

"Val, you're right." The man had a square-shaped face with straight, shoulder-length, black hair. "That must have been the man Ajax saw in the alleyway who abducted Kate."

Giselle carefully studied the documents. "Oh my goodness. Val, look at this guy. He's the man we met in Athens at the Church of Panagia Kapnikarea. He introduced himself as Deacon Kastellanos." The man's skin was pale, and he had a pink raised scar on his right cheek. "His accent was unfamiliar. I knew he wasn't Greek. He must have been Bulgarian."

"You know this man?"

"We were touring the church, and this man approached us," Valerie replied. "He invited us to Bible study. We couldn't go because we were leaving for Mykonos the following morning. He seemed disappointed, and he left. I'm shaken to think that he could've done something bad to us."

Giselle and Valerie searched through the documents for more clues.

"Okay. You two have been through enough. I don't want you getting more involved. You're deep enough in it as it is."

"But Detective—" Giselle started before being cut off.

"I don't want to hear any buts. This is highly dangerous. This is now out of my hands. This is international criminal activity. I'm escalating this to the Greek national police and Interpol's National Central Bureau. We're going to get you to a secure location, and you will have twenty-four-hour security."

CHAPTER 31

Armed policemen filed into Zeus Zest and arrested Demitrius. He was transported to Athens via helicopter under heavy security. A police car transported him to police headquarters.

The police investigator spoke in Greek. *"Demitrius Borislavov. Yes, I know exactly who you are. Our men have uncovered many files in your home. Your computer has been seized, and our hackers are working on the encrypted data. So what do you have to say for yourself?"*

Demitrius's eyes narrowed, and he stared at the investigator with contempt. After a few moments of intense eye contact, he tilted his head to the right and spat on the floor. *"You think you could intimidate me,"* Demitrius said in Greek. *"You might want to proceed with caution."*

"Are you threatening me?" the investigator responded. He leaned forward and challenged Demitrius with his stare. *"You might want to proceed with caution. I do not respond to threats well."*

Demitrius grunted and sat back in his chair. He clasped his hands together and cracked his knuckles.

"The crimes against you and your organization are enormous. We've uncovered files linking you and the Bulgarian mafia to crimes against humanity: people smuggling, human trafficking, torture and murder, drug trafficking, financial crimes, theft on a grand scale, art heists. This is the tip of the iceberg, but believe me, we will uncover it all, and those involved will pay the price." The investigator leaned in even closer,

staring at him intensely. Demitrius did not flinch. *"When we're done, you will never see the light of day again and wish you were never born."*

———————

Giselle and Valerie were hidden in a small unit in an apartment complex. A police car was parked in one of the spaces to provide twenty-four-hour security. The officer would be relieved by another officer in a few hours.

Giselle peeked through the blinds. The police car was directly in view. "Val, this does not feel real."

"I know. It's like I'm living through a nightmare that I can't wake up from."

"Let's not lose hope. I believe that we're going to find Kate, and we're all going to make it home safely."

"Oh great, my phone is charged." Valerie quickly dialed a number and waited. "Oh my goodness, honey, it's so great to finally hear your voice." There was a pause. "I know." Another pause. "Honey, honey, please listen to me for a moment." Another pause. "I didn't mean to have you scared out of your mind. I didn't have a way to call you." Another pause. "Honey, please listen to me. I know you were worried, but I need you to listen and trust me. I can't go into details." Another pause. "I get it. I understand why you feel that way. I do owe you an explanation, but I can't right now. Please listen to me. Yes, Giselle is fine. She's here with me." Another pause. "No, we haven't found Kate. We're working with law enforcement to find her." Another pause. "We're in an apartment unit. We're under police protection." Another pause. "I know, I know, honey. This is a lot that I'm throwing at you, and I understand that it doesn't make sense. I can't go more into detail because it's classified information. But what I can tell you is that we're okay, and we'll be home soon. Just trust me. Please trust me." There was a long pause. Giselle was imagining what Donald was saying on the other end of the line. "I know, honey. I understand how you feel. How's Bridget?"

Another long pause ensued. Tears welled up in Valerie's eyes. "Please give her a kiss, and tell her that Mommy loves her and Mommy will be home soon." Another pause. "Donald, please do not come. Please don't book a flight." Another pause. "Yes, I know your sister can take care of Bridget, but you can't come. I told you I'm here under police protection. There's an investigation going on." Another pause. "I know you're worried, but I'm okay. I love you, and I'll be home soon."

Valerie stayed on the phone for a few more minutes before disconnecting. It was a relief for her to have heard Donald's voice. Although it was filled with impatience and worry, it was still music to her ears. She'd thought she would never hear his voice again. She'd desperately wanted to hear Bridget's voice, but her baby girl was napping, and she did not want Donald to wake her. She would speak to Bridget the next time she called.

They heated up TV dinners in the microwave and sat on the couch. Their minds had been in overdrive for the past few days, and they needed a moment to decompress. Giselle turned on the television. The news was too heavy to digest. She switched channels until she found a lighthearted station that broadcasted in English.

CHAPTER 32

Deacon Kastellanos was talking to two young women outside of the Church of Panagia Kapnikarea. Two police officers approached and apprehended him. The women were shocked and confused. They appeared to be Americans. Onlookers were baffled as they observed the man, who portrayed himself to be a deacon, being escorted away in handcuffs.

The deacon was brought to police headquarters and placed in the interrogation room.

The police investigator spoke in Greek, *"I'll get straight to it. We know who you are. You are not a deacon, and your name is Igor Yankov. You are a member of the Bulgarian mafia. You've been engaged in people smuggling and conducting human trafficking. This organization is going down, so I strongly recommend that you cooperate with us."*

The police investigator studied the man sitting across the table, thinking he was rather unattractive. His pale skin made him appear ghostlike. The investigator wondered how he got the raised scar on his cheek, which looked like a pink centipede.

Igor was impassive and stoic. He did not respond to the threat.

The investigator continued, *"As I stated, this organization is going down, so I strongly recommend that you cooperate with us. There are some codes we've uncovered that appear to be a language of the organization. We need help decoding them."*

Igor responded in Greek, *"I'm not saying anything."*

"*Let me assure you, we're going to figure it out. You'll just help us figure it out quicker.*"

Igor remained calm and did not display any emotion.

"*Do you think for one second that they would protect you? It's not a brotherhood. You mean nothing to them. You're a means to carry out their operation.*"

Igor again did not respond. He rubbed his index finger back and forth along the length of his scar.

The police investigator reached into his arsenal of threats. "*We've captured your boss. Demitrius Borislavov.*" The investigator paused as he observed Igor flinch. It was the first reaction he'd spotted, and Igor appeared a little uneasy. "*That's right. Demitrius Borislavov is in police custody. He is trying to work out a deal. He was investigated by my partner, and trust me when I tell you that he has no problem seeing you locked away for life.*"

Igor looked down at the table momentarily before making eye contact with the investigator.

The investigator continued. "*Imagine spending the rest of your life in a dark, dingy, dilapidated prison cell. A toilet in your cell that won't flush, filled with excrement. Probably seeing daylight for a few minutes a day, if you're lucky. The food, barely edible. The maggots brushed off of the meat before it's cooked. And to be honest, you have the face only a mother could love. You look like a perfect target for the inmates.*"

The investigator allowed his words to sink in. "*So back to what I was saying, we need you to decode the information for us.*"

After a long pause, Igor asked, "*What deal are you going to get me?*"

"*We'll see what we can do.*"

CHAPTER 33

One of the Italian officers knocked on the door of an exquisite two-story villa. He was accompanied by three other officers. It was a beautiful day in Como, and the sunlight was hitting the lake at a perfect angle, causing the water to sparkle like jewels. The mountains were the perfect backdrop. The lawn of the Italian villa was lush and well manicured.

The officer knocked again and the housekeeper answered the door. She was startled to see them and stumbled with her words. The officer inquired about the homeowner's whereabouts to which she responded that he was not home. He pulled out his warrant and pushed himself past her into the foyer. The other officers followed.

The interior was grand and luxurious. Expensive artwork was skillfully placed on the walls. An ornate crystal chandelier hung from the ceiling of the foyer.

The housekeeper pleaded with the lead officer not to go upstairs. She appeared terrified. The lead officer ascended the steps, and one of his partners followed closely behind. They went from room to room until they approached the room at the opposite end of the enormous villa. There were faint sounds coming from the other side of the door.

The main officer turned the knob, but the door was locked. He knocked repeatedly with a heavy fist, calling for the occupant to open the door. A tall, handsome man opened the door. He was wearing a long, red, satin robe.

In a heavy Italian accent, the lead officer said, "Rorey Wood, you're under arrest."

"Are you all crazy?" Rorey replied in an aggravated voice. "Do you know who I am?"

The lead officer turned him around and placed his hands in handcuffs behind his back.

"Why am I being arrested?" Rorey asked.

"Your name came up in documents linked to the Bulgarian mafia," the lead officer said. Before he could finish his statement, Rorey interrupted him.

"Do I look like I'm a part of a mafia? The Bulgarian mafia?" Rorey shook his head in annoyance, then he let out a big sigh. "I'm an American. I'm an actor, a famous actor. I was in a movie two years ago. *Omen*, one of the highest grossing films. I was a main character on the soap opera *The Young and the Beautiful* for ten years. Look me up. You have me confused with someone else."

The lead officer continued, "Do you know Demitrius Borislavov?"

"Who? I don't know anyone by that name."

"That's interesting because we've uncovered documents linking you to him. Time spent at resorts in the Swiss Alps. Monaco. Saint-Tropez. Sailing on yachts. Meetings in Paris. You two have spent a lot of time together. I'll not only say that you know him, but you know him very well."

"I don't know that person. Maybe the person that you're talking about told me a different name. But what does that have to do with me being arrested? I didn't know that sailing on a yacht or meeting up with someone was a crime."

"I'm going to get straight to it," the lead officer stated. "Demitrius Borislavov has been linked to human trafficking, and we have strong evidence to believe that you are one of his clients."

"What! Are you accusing Rorey Wood of engaging in human trafficking? Do you understand the media attention that this will generate over a big, fat lie? Are you trying to ruin me? I'll make sure you all lose your jobs and never work again."

The lead investigator ignored the threats. "Is there someone else in the room with you?"

"No. I'm in here by myself."

"Then I'm sure you wouldn't mind us looking around."

"Actually, I do mind."

"We have a warrant, and we're at liberty to search your home," the lead officer noted. He sent his partner to look in the bathroom.

The lead officer continued his interrogation but was interrupted by his partner, who yelled something in Italian. The officer directed Rorey into the bathroom. There was a young lady sitting on the marble floor. Her blonde hair partially covered her face. She appeared terrified.

"What's your name?" the lead officer asked.

The young woman slowly lifted her head and made eye contact with the officer. "Kate. My name is Kate Davenport."

CHAPTER 34

The media coverage surrounding the capture of members of the Bulgarian mafia was extensive. News outlets around the world broadcasted the takedown of the corrupt organization. The infiltration of the seemingly untouchable organization was monumental, and the revelation of the crimes committed were unfathomable.

Rorey Wood's connection to the organization created a sensational storm. A clip showing Rorey in handcuffs being escorted by police to the police station circulated throughout the media. His head hung in shame, trying desperately to avoid the flashes of the cameras.

Kate had been flown back to Athens, and she was now on a helicopter being transported to a helipad where she would be reunited with her friends. Kate's story was astounding given her link to Rorey Wood, and the news outlets were in position, awaiting her arrival.

Giselle and Valerie stood there in eager anticipation. A flood of emotions flowed through their bodies. Any moment, they would be seeing their friend in the flesh. It almost seemed unreal. There were feelings of nervousness, suspense, and excitement.

The helicopter was seen in the distance, making its way toward them. As it drew closer, the sound of the spinning blades was audible and grew louder. The helicopter touched down on the helipad, the rotor blades spinning, creating a wind effect. The news media captured every moment. News reporters were stationed in front of the cameras, detailing the events. Giselle and Valerie stood there, eyes fixed to the door of the helicopter. The moment of anticipation had come to an end.

The door of the helicopter opened and Kate appeared. She made her way out and stood on the step, her hair blowing in the wind. She made eye contact with her friends, her eyes welling up with tears. She ran toward her friends and threw her arms around them. Giselle held onto her tightly, and the tears streamed down her cheeks. She looked at Valerie, who was crying too. Time appeared to have stood still. It was almost as though the cameras were not around. It was only the three of them, in their own world, until the sounds of the reporters around them could not be ignored any longer. Kate did not take any questions but gave a general statement, "I'm blessed to be alive and well."

Kate's arms were interlocked with her friends as they were escorted by security. She held on tightly to her two friends, scared that she would be separated from them again. She felt as though she were in a dream, walking in slow motion. But it was not a dream. She was free. She never thought that she would see her friends again. She never thought that she would see her family again or get her life back. Hope was dwindling and freedom seemed elusive until the Italian police showed up unexpectedly and rescued her.

Someone in the police department must have pulled some strings. They were given a complimentary suite at the Four Seasons and provided first-class tickets to New York City the next morning.

The three of them sat on one of the queen-sized beds. There were hugs and tears of joy. They had not yet discussed the events that transpired following Kate's disappearance.

"Where did you go after you left the hotel room?" Valerie asked. It was a question she'd been waiting to ask since their reunion.

"First of all, Val, I want to apologize to you from the bottom of my heart. I want to apologize to both of you. My actions were not fair to you. I was acting selfishly."

"It's okay," Valerie replied, reaching out to touch her friend's hand.

"No, it's not okay. I put you both in second place, and my selfish desires took first place. Although it was not my intention, that's what happened, and for that, I'm extremely sorry. I love you both. Even though we're not blood related, I think of you both as sisters."

"We love you too," Giselle replied. "Val and I weren't going to stop looking for you until we found you." There was a pause. "So what happened after you left the hotel room? Where did you go?"

"After our argument, I honestly didn't want to meet up with Austin anymore. I knew you all were upset, as you should've been. I was too embarrassed to face you. I felt as though I had let you both down and ruined the trip. I finally decided to meet with Austin at the bar. I wanted to have a drink to relax me but more so to give you all some space. Well, Austin was supposed to have sent a taxi to pick me up, but it wasn't scheduled to arrive for an hour, so I decided to catch one at the station off the main road. I took a shortcut along an alley. The sun hadn't quite set yet. There was still a little light in the sky, so I thought it would be okay, but in hindsight, it was foolish of me to have walked down an alleyway by myself. I heard some rustling behind a large trash bag, which frightened me. I thought it might have been a cat or some animal. As I turned around, there was a man behind me with long, dark hair. It's like he appeared out of nowhere. I thought I was paying attention to my surroundings, but I guess I was too distraught. My mind was elsewhere. He cupped his hand over my mouth, and I couldn't scream for help. I tried to fight him off as much as I could, and I ripped his shirt. There was no one else in sight until that rustling behind the trash bag turned out not to be an animal. It was a homeless man. It was like he had no idea that I needed help. He had this wide grin on his face, and he sat there, clapping. The man who abducted me did not pay him any mind, as though he knew the guy was crazy and wasn't a threat."

"That homeless man played a part in saving you," Giselle stated. "Val and I ran into him in that alleyway. He had your scarf. We knew it was yours. It looked like the one you bought in Athens, and it had a gold pin of the letter K."

Giselle told Kate how the man ripped Valerie's bag off her shoulder and how they went running after him. Giselle continued, "The man's name is Ajax. He was certainly delusional and exhibiting hallucinations, but the information he provided, although out of touch with reality, linked the man who abducted you to the Bulgarian mafia."

Kate's mouth dropped. She was shocked at that revelation. "How did he know that man was a part of the mafia?"

"He was able to describe the guy," Giselle answered. "The torn shirt revealed his tattoo. Ajax was able to draw the tattoo on a piece of paper. That image linked the man to the Bulgarian mafia."

"So what happened after the man attacked you?" Valerie asked.

"I lost consciousness. He must have struck me over the head. I woke up, groggy, with a pounding headache. I had no idea where I was. There were two other women in the small cell with me. One did not speak English. I think she was Eastern European. The other woman was an American. She was from Oklahoma. She was as terrified as I was, and she was scared to speak, thinking that someone was listening to our conversations. We were treated like subhumans. Then one day, the American woman was taken away. I had no idea where they took her, and I was scared I was next. The following morning, I was dragged out of the cell and blindfolded. The men around me were speaking in another language. They transported me blindfolded. I had no idea where they were taking me. I don't know how long we traveled, but it felt like an eternity. When we reached the destination, I was instructed to take a shower and brush my teeth. I was given a dress to wear. I was blindfolded again and taken somewhere else. The blindfold was removed, and standing in front of me was Rorey Wood. I couldn't believe it. I grew up watching him on *The Young and the Beautiful*. But I was confused as to what I was doing in his home. It turned out that I was sold to him, and I was now his property."

Kate went on to describe her experience living in Rorey Wood's home. She was treated as a possession with no rights.

Giselle and Valerie cried as they listened to Kate, who also was crying as she relived the experience. The tissues in the box were almost used up.

Giselle detailed the events leading up to Kate's capture. She went on to describe how Demitrius had captured them and held them hostage in a room. They'd tried to escape, but he'd recaptured them and threatened to kill them. Nikita had come to their rescue and freed them. She'd given them documents revealing information about the mafia, which they'd given to the police. Nikita had also given them a small box containing a finger believed to be that of Demitrius's father. All of the evidence was escalated to the Greek national police and Interpol's National Central Bureau.

Kate cried uncontrollably. Her face was red, and her eyelids were puffy. She blew her nose into a tissue. "I'm so sorry that I put you all in harm's way. Because of me, you all could have been killed. I'm so, so sorry."

"We're so relieved that you're alive," Valerie remarked. "I have to admit, there were many times that I lost hope, thinking that you might be dead somewhere or we would not find you. I blamed myself. If I hadn't been so hard on you, you would've never left the hotel room. You would've never been captured. All of this would've never happened. We would've caught our flight back to New York the next day."

"Val, this is not your fault," Kate said, as she reached for her friend's hand. "You had every right to have felt the way you did. This all started because of me. My selfishness. You didn't force me to leave the hotel room. I was the one who made the decision to meet up with Austin. I was the one who made the decision to walk down that alley. None of this is your fault."

"I know we all have guilt, but we can't focus on blaming ourselves," Giselle interjected. "I know that's easier said than done, but blaming ourselves will not serve us. Because of this, an entire organization has been disintegrated. Women held in captivity have been freed and returned to their families. This organization is responsible for so many crimes against humanity, it's sickening. Our lives were at risk, but in turn, it saved so many lives. Let's be grateful that we're all alive and focus on moving forward. It's going to take a lot of work to deal with what we went through, but let's start taking steps forward."

The friends decided to dress up and enjoy their last dinner in Greece. Their reservation time was perfect to catch the sunset while dining on the terrace.

The server poured each of them a glass of champagne. Giselle gave the toast. "To life, to friendship, to family, to freedom. Cheers!"

In unison, they clinked their champagne glasses, "Cheers!"

CHAPTER 35

The flight touched down at JFK airport. Giselle, Kate, and Valerie were the first passengers to disembark, and they were escorted through the airport. The media had already been notified, and they were swarming around them like bees, shouting questions and hoping to get a statement.

At the baggage claim terminal, there was Donald, holding Bridget. Valerie ran to them and wrapped her arms around them. She gave Donald an endearing kiss and took Bridget in her arms. She lay her head on Bridget's head and rotated her body from side to side, cradling her daughter. Tears rolled down her face as she kissed the top of her daughter's head.

It was a long day, and it was now nighttime. Giselle opened the door to her apartment. She was exhausted, physically and mentally. Her family from Louisiana were calling nonstop to ensure that she was okay and to convey how relieved and grateful they were to know that she was back home safely. Her parents wanted to take a flight out the next day to stay with her for a while, but she insisted that she was okay and needed some time to herself to decompress. She assured them that she would take them up on their request the moment she needed their presence for support.

She took a quick, warm shower, brushed her teeth, then fell onto the bed. She had just enough energy to pull the covers over her body. Her body was drained. She was surprised that she slept through the night, given what she'd been through. She didn't know what other nights would bring, but she hoped that she would not be burdened with nightmares. She thought about Kate and Valerie and hoped they were able to sleep well. She would be making an appointment to see her therapist as soon as the office opened.

She rolled out of bed and walked to the kitchen. The last time she was in her kitchen seemed like such a long time ago. So much had occurred since she'd left her apartment. It felt good to be home. She made a pot of coffee. The smell permeated the room, and it was invigorating. It was a warm and comforting smell that made her feel safe. She sat on the couch in her living room and reached for the remote. She flipped through the stations. The first news station reported the demise of the Bulgarian mafia and Rorey Wood's link to the organization. Then there was that infamous clip of Rorey Wood being escorted by police, head hung low as he tried to avoid the cameras. The screen changed to the image of a helicopter touching down, Kate exiting the craft, and the reunion where the friends were engaged in a long hug. It was hard to believe that that moment was less than forty-eight hours ago.

She flipped through the channels again, settling on a station broadcasting *Spill the Tea*, a gossip program. Rorey Wood was the topic of discussion but more in a lighthearted fashion. There were two hosts. One was a flamboyant male, whose name was Manny, wearing a tight pink suit and a fedora. He claimed that Rorey Wood was his ultimate crush. He'd stopped watching *The Young and the Beautiful* when Danny Love, Rorey's character, was killed off in a motorcycle accident. He had even written to production, pleading with them to rewrite the script. Maybe it wasn't Danny Love in the motorcycle accident but his doppelganger or somehow, through a miracle, Danny survived the horrific accident. The other host was a young female whose name was Ginger. She had green streaks in her blonde hair and a nose ring. She had on a green sweater with ripped jeans and combat boots. She echoed Manny's sentiments. She was distraught when Danny Love was killed off, and she and her grandmother had a hard time watching the soap opera after his death. It wasn't the same without Danny Love.

The hosts then spoke about their shock when they found out that Rorey Wood was involved in human trafficking. They debated about how Rorey could have been caught up in such nefarious activity.

Giselle reached for the remote and turned off the TV. Her therapist was out of town, so she made an appointment for the following week. She had no other plans and relaxed the rest of the day. She spoke to Kate and Valerie, who both appeared to be holding up well. She spoke to her parents twice. She ordered a Margherita pizza from her favorite Italian restaurant, Migliore Pizza Italiana.

Two days later, she returned to work despite her boss recommending that she take more time off. She knew that work would be a blessing, and it would allow her to channel her focus and energy into something constructive. She loved her job in forensics. She detested the crimes that had been committed resulting in the cases being brought across her desk, but she loved putting the pieces of the puzzle together and giving the victims and their families justice.

All of her coworkers were happy to see her. There was a banner that read "Welcome Home Giselle." One by one or in groups, her coworkers approached her and expressed how happy they were to see her. Some wanted details and even pushed the boundaries, whereas others respected her privacy and allowed her the opportunity to divulge information on her own time.

Lunch was catered, and the cake had the words "Welcome Home Giselle" inscribed in cursive. There was also a pile of cards carefully stacked at the end of the table. The thoughtful gestures were very much appreciated.

The first case on her desk was that of an eighteen-year-old female who had gone missing after going for a run in her neighborhood in the early hours of the morning. Her roommate stated that she'd left the house around 5:30 am, which was her usual exercise time, and she'd never returned. One of the victim's shoes was found in a wooded area, close to her running route, and Giselle was examining it for trace evidence.

After a full day at work, she called Valerie while she prepared dinner. Valerie and Donald were playing hide and seek with Bridget. Valerie was spending every waking moment with her family, almost as though she were making up for lost time. The thought that they could be taken away from her scared her. She'd even allowed Bridget to sleep between them, which was a habit that she'd tried to break for a month before her trip to Greece. Deep down, she knew that she had to be realistic and not live in fear, but at this time, she wanted her family as close to her as possible. Within that short period of time that she was away, Bridget seemed to have grown. She appreciated every hug, every kiss, every smile. The tantrums were not as frustrating, and Bridget's laughter was music to her ears.

After she hung up from her call with Valerie, she decided to call Kate. She covered the pot, turned the heat down, and allowed the shrimp creole to continue cooking. The aroma reminded her of her childhood in New Orleans. Her mother, Genevieve, made the best crawfish étouffée and gumbo that she'd ever tasted. Her mother took her culinary skills to the business side and opened up her own restaurant, Cecile's Kitchen, which she named after her grandmother. The restaurant was located in the French Quarter and had been featured last year on the Food Network. The restaurant had been awarded three Michelin stars, and in tourists' guides, it was listed as one of the recommended restaurants to dine at in New Orleans.

Kate answered after the third ring. Kate was doing the best she could. She'd started seeing a therapist and had had her first session earlier that morning. Her therapist had given her written exercises to help her process what she went through. Kate's objective was to channel her experience into something positive, something that could be used to help others, to uplift others, to make a positive change in some way. She wanted to reach others who'd experienced similar situations and to convey to them that they were not alone and they mattered. After much research, she joined the organization End Human Trafficking. The director was excited that she'd contacted them. The organization was having a fundraiser luncheon in four weeks, and on the spot, the director asked her to be the guest of honor and to deliver the opening speech. When Giselle had called Kate, she was jotting down points for her speech. She was already nervous, although it was almost a month away. She had always been nervous about public speaking, and for a brief moment, she thought about declining the invitation. She'd quickly silenced that self-doubt. This was something important and something she had to do.

CHAPTER 36

D r. Redd's office looked the same. A large painting on the wall depicted a beach with clear turquoise waters, bordered by powdery white sand. A faint smell of lavender emanated from the air freshener plugged into the wall. The décor consisted of plants meticulously placed throughout the room; the greenery was subtle and created an impression of oneness with nature. The navy-blue sofa pillows were reminiscent of the deep blue waters of the ocean. Strangely, the room comforted Giselle. It was like hot chocolate on a cold winter day or the vibrant leaves of autumn intermingled with the aromas of pumpkin spice and cinnamon. The room created a feeling of tranquility, peace, and safety.

Giselle had developed a good rapport with her psychotherapist. Despite the patient–therapist boundary, Dr. Redd felt like her friend, her confidant, someone who she could be completely open and vulnerable with. She did not feel judged. If she were honest, Dr. Redd's office was the only place that she felt completely safe, aside from her apartment.

"Giselle, how are you doing?"

"As good as I could be."

Giselle observed Dr. Redd's demeanor. She was strong, intelligent, and compelling, but she also came across as compassionate, empathetic, candid, and forthright. But the look in her eyes was different today. A glassy film obscured them, as if she was attempting to suppress tears. Giselle had never seen this side of Dr. Redd, and she had spent countless hours on the couch.

"I've seen the news, and I have to say that I'm relieved and thankful that you're here," Dr. Redd began. "The fact that your heart is still beating and there's air in your lungs means that you're alive, and there is still work for you to do in this world. Giselle, you're a brave person, and you're a fighter."

Giselle let out a deep sigh. "I don't feel brave. I feel like I've lost every bit of fight left in me."

"You've just endured a traumatic experience that has added to the trauma you were already dealing with. I want you to remember the progress you've made, so you can continue to move forward. Progress is not a sprint; it's a journey. It doesn't matter how fast you move; what matters is that you take the steps, one at a time."

"I know. I'm just feeling sad right now," Giselle replied. She leaned over to grab a tissue from the side table. Her eyes were probably red and puffy after hours of crying. Since she'd returned from Greece, she'd remained in a dreamlike state. The nightmare she'd endured did not seem real. The people around her did not seem real. She thought that at any moment, she would awaken from her endless slumber, and her life would rewind to the moment before she'd boarded that flight. Then, this morning, reality hit her like a ton of bricks. The emotions that she had been suppressing were so strong that they physically overpowered her. She'd cried until her body shook, and at one point, she felt as though she could not breathe.

A vision of herself and Valerie locked in that bare room entered her mind, and she started crying again. She tried her best to push those thoughts to the deepest recesses of her mind, hidden away for good.

"I want you to acknowledge your feelings," Dr. Redd said gently. She reached over and handed Giselle another tissue. "Not dealing with your negative thoughts and emotions and not confronting your fears will only keep you captive. These negative feelings will always control you and rob you of your joy. They will rob you of peace. They will rob you of a fulfilled life. Feel your feelings without judgement. Be patient with yourself, and be kind to yourself."

Giselle let out another deep sigh. She knew Dr. Redd was right; she had to deal with the negative thoughts. She had to chip away at their power until they had none. She had to confront her fears until they no longer terrified her. It was going to require consistent work, but she was ready to take that next step. She had done it before. Despite this setback, she could still move in the direction she needed to go.

Dr. Redd continued, "Giselle, this process is going to be painful, but it is a necessary pain. Therapy is not easy. It requires you to be honest with yourself and go to dark, hurtful places. It requires going to the source of the pain and digging it out. It's like an infected wound. If you cover it up, it's still there. The infection will continue to spread unless we clean out the pus and remove the infected tissue. But most importantly, we have to get to the source of the infection so that we can remove all the dead tissue until only healthy tissue remains. But even the healing process hurts. Recovery may still be painful, but it's the necessary pain that you have to go through to heal."

This time, Giselle consciously and deliberately took a deep breath in through her nose. She filled her lungs with air and slowly exhaled through pursed lips. She repeated the action two more times and felt a calmness spread over her body.

"Giselle, I want you to use the tools you've learned. Thoughts are powerful. Your thoughts can build you, and your thoughts can destroy you. Your thoughts can bring you joy, and your thoughts can cause you pain. Your thoughts dictate your feelings."

Dr. Redd paused for a moment, then continued. "Are you journaling?"

"I have to admit, I've slacked off."

"I want you to resume your journaling. Be an observer of your thoughts. Remember that you are not your thoughts. I want you to write down your negative thoughts and dissect them. Ask yourself if the thought is true or if it's false. Ask yourself if the thought serves you or does you a disservice," Dr. Redd looked thoughtful. "You work in forensics; you search for truth. Is that correct?"

"Yes."

"Then search for the truth among your thoughts. After you write down the negative thought, modify the thought to one that serves you positively."

"Okay. I'll try," Giselle replied.

"I'm here to help you through it," Dr. Redd said with a warm smile. "We'll walk through the experience. As frightening as it is to relive, it's important that we confront it so you can release it. If you avoid it, the energy of the emotions will be trapped in you and haunt you. We have to fully feel emotions in order to release them. One of our goals is that you no longer see yourself as a victim, but as a survivor."

Giselle reached for another tissue and dabbed her eyes.

"What is it that you're feeling right now?" Dr. Redd asked.

"I feel like I'm locked in that room," Giselle replied, bursting into tears. "Me and Val. There's no way to escape. It's small and stuffy, and we sleep on the hard floor. There's a tiny window high above, but I can't reach it. We can't escape. And he has a gun. And there are dogs." Giselle had begun to ramble and was no longer making sense.

Dr. Redd allowed Giselle to cry and release her emotions. She pulled her chair closer to Giselle and rubbed her hand back and forth over her client's shoulder. Giselle's body shook as she released the tears. It was rare that Dr. Redd would hug a client, but this was one instance in which she was compelled to do so. She wrapped her arms around Giselle, who in turn laid her head on Dr. Redd's shoulder.

Several minutes elapsed before Giselle regained her composure. She again recounted the experience of being locked in a room with Valerie, but this time, she conveyed the information more clearly and concisely.

"Look around. Where are you?" Dr. Redd asked.

"I'm in your office," Giselle replied softly.

"That's right. You're in my office. You're not locked in that small room on a Greek island. And when you go to bed tonight, it will not be on a hard floor. You'll be on your bed in the safety of your apartment. When you go home, I want you to go through every room and be present. Be mindful and use your senses. See, hear, smell, touch, and taste. Feel your sheets. Feel your comforter. Rub your hands across your sofa. Smell the familiar smells: your laundry detergent, your clothes in the closet. Take it all in. You're in the safety of your home."

Giselle wiped her eyes with a tissue. "Okay. I will."

"What did you learn about yourself during that experience?" Dr. Redd asked.

Giselle was taken aback by the question. "What did I learn about myself?"

"Yes. What have you learned about yourself? What positive qualities did you recognize in yourself? Maybe qualities that you didn't even know you had."

Giselle was lost for words.

"Well, for starters, you are strong. You're a fighter. You're a survivor. You're resilient."

Giselle smiled self-consciously. "Thanks."

"It was not meant to be a compliment," Dr. Redd replied. "Those are qualities that I see in you."

"You're right. I am those things."

"It doesn't matter that I'm right," Dr. Redd responded. "What matters is that you believe it. What do you believe about yourself?"

"I believe that I'm strong. I'm a fighter. I'm resilient. I'm a survivor."

"I want you to journal these thoughts. Write a list of all your positive traits."

"I can't help but feel guilty, even though I tried to encourage Kate and Valerie not to feel guilty," Giselle said quietly.

"Why are you feeling guilty?" Dr. Redd asked.

"I never should've let Kate walk out of that hotel room. I knew something bad was going to happen; I felt it in my gut. If only I had stopped her from walking out that door, none of this would've happened."

Giselle told Dr. Redd about the night Kate had disappeared. She recalled their argument, leading to Kate leaving the hotel room and disappearing.

"Why do you think you're responsible for Kate's actions? Why are you putting that responsibility on yourself?"

"I feel like I wasn't a good friend to her. She could've died."

"Do you really think you're not a good friend to Kate? Is that statement true?"

Giselle was silent for several seconds. "No, it's not true. I love Kate as a sister. I care deeply about her."

"What happened to Kate was out of your control. You are not responsible."

"But what if I had pleaded more with Kate? What if I had prevented her from leaving that room?"

"Those are 'what if' questions. You're making assumptions about the outcome," Dr. Redd said. She pointed to a wall painting that included the Serenity Prayer: "God, grant me the serenity to accept the things I cannot change, courage to change the things I can, and wisdom to know the difference."

Giselle allowed the words of the Serenity Prayer to sink in. Mentally, she acknowledged that she could not change what happened in Greece. She would have to accept and move past the experience in a healthy and positive manner. She began to realize that she felt an unhealthy level of responsibility for others.

Giselle was lost in her thoughts, which were interrupted by the sound of Dr. Redd's voice.

"Giselle, what are you thinking?" Dr. Redd asked.

"I think I've always felt like I needed to be the strong one. I need to be the dependable friend. I need to be the one who holds it together for other people. I have to fix things."

"We'll need to further explore why you have these thoughts and feelings," Dr. Redd replied. "What you're doing, consciously or subconsciously, is trying to control how others see you. You've been pretending that everything is okay. As humans, we all experience insecurities and self-doubt. We all have fears. What's important is how we deal with those insecurities and fears. Being vulnerable does not mean you're weak. It means you're more relatable and authentic. Embrace your vulnerability."

"You're right," Giselle replied. She paused for a few seconds. "I don't want to be seen as weak and, because of that, I've held in my emotions, which have tormented me. I want to be seen as a strong person, but you're right—being vulnerable does not make we weak. It makes me human. When I was dealing with my traumatic experience with Jerry, I pretended that everything was okay. When I couldn't wear the mask any longer, my family and friends urged me to seek help. I was resistant at first; it made me feel weak. But I have to say, I don't know what I would have done without therapy. I was hurting, and I was at a breaking point. Dr. Redd, you have been instrumental in my recovery."

"Giselle, it's okay to ask for help."

"I realize that now."

"You are blessed to have people in your life who genuinely love and care about you."

"Yes, I know."

"I have homework for you. I want you to assess what's happening in your mind without judgement. There are some questions that I want you to journal about," Dr. Redd said. She listed three questions, and Giselle jotted them down on a sheet of paper. "Remember, negative thoughts will enter your mind, but don't give them power. Don't add fuel to a negative thought. Let it run out of energy and lose power. Think of your mind as a highway with cars driving up and down the lanes. The cars represent your thoughts. Sometimes you pay attention to the cars driving by, and sometimes you're oblivious to them. We are aware of only a small fraction of the thoughts that travel around in our minds. If you are aware of a negative thought, don't keep adding fuel to it; let it lose its energy and break down on the side of the road. Let the tow truck haul it away. Or let it take the next exit off the highway of your mind. Think to yourself, 'This thought does not serve me; therefore, it is going to get off at the next exit.' You can say it out loud or write it down."

Dr. Redd continued, "A negative thought is like a drunk driver on the highway of your mind. It can only cause harm. It puts other cars in danger. It's important that the drunk driver gets off the road before it causes injury and destruction. Your positive thoughts are at risk if you allow the negative ones to run rampant. The more negative thoughts, the more risk. The more drunk drivers on the road, the more risk for the safe and responsible drivers. So, get the drunk drivers off the road. Direct them to the exit."

"I love that analogy," Giselle said with a smile.

"I also want you to keep a gratitude journal. Every morning, I want you to write down at least three things you're grateful for. You can write down as many as you like. There is so much to be grateful for; try to focus on what you have rather than what you don't have."

"I will," Giselle replied. "Thank you, Dr. Redd. This session has been very helpful. I'll begin my journaling tonight, and I'll utilize the tools that you've given me. I look forward to our next session. Thanks again for your help."

"You're welcome. And don't forget to practice self-care: eating healthy, exercising regularly, getting enough sleep, and continuing to do activities you enjoy."

"I will. Thank you."

Giselle scheduled an appointment to see Dr. Redd the next week. She walked out of the air-conditioned office building into the warm air. The bustling sounds of the city surrounding her as she walked three blocks to Morrison's Deli, where she had lunch at least once a week since moving to New York City.

Mr. Morrison was behind the counter as usual. He looked surprised to see her. "Giselle, I'm so happy to see you. I've been following the news, and I'm so relieved that you're okay. How are you doing?"

"It's been difficult, but I'm taking steps to allow myself to heal."

"That's great to hear. My wife and I have been praying for you."

"Thank you; I appreciate that."

"What can I get for you today? The usual?"

"Yes, please."

"You got it."

Mr. Morrison prepared a turkey sandwich on whole wheat bread with mayonnaise, lettuce, tomato, and extra pickles sprinkled with black pepper. Giselle grabbed a water bottle and reached into her bag for her wallet, but Mr. Morrison shook his head.

"No charge. This one's on me."

"That's kind of you, Mr. Morrison, but it's okay. I'll pay for my meal."

"Giselle, please, I insist."

"Alright. Thank you very much Mr. Morrison. And please give my warmest regards to your wife."

Giselle sat down at a table next to the window. It was her preferred spot, if it wasn't taken by another customer. She liked to people watch. She imagined what pedestrians' lives and personalities were like based on what they were wearing and how they carried themselves. What jobs did they have? Where were they going?

She finished her meal and waved goodbye to Mr. Morrison before walking two blocks to the subway station. As she descended the steps, the dank, musty smell of the dim underground station greeted her. She passed a young man playing Ed Sheeran's "Thinking Out Loud" on his guitar, adding his own spin to it. She swiped her ticket at the turnstile and stood on the platform, awaiting the eastbound train. It was packed, but fortunately she found a seat. Her mind wandered as she reflected on her therapy session. She could hear Dr. Redd's voice as she replayed their discussion in her mind. She was going to heed Dr. Redd's advice and commit to the process. She wondered how Kate and Valerie were doing; she would give them a call later to check up on them.

Instinctively, Giselle knew that the train had arrived at her stop, and she drifted out of her reverie. She made her way to the exit and ascended the steps into daylight. Her phone rang as she walked to her apartment. It was her mother checking in on her again. She allowed her vulnerability to come through and shared her feelings with her mother. As she talked, it felt as though the extra weight that she had been carrying was gradually being lifted. She accepted her mother's request to visit, admitting to herself that she needed her mother and would delight in the comfort of her warm embrace.

Once they'd worked out the details, Giselle made meal requests. It was imperative that her mother prepare her famous gumbo. Giselle also asked for crawfish étouffée, shrimp and grits, and, of course, her mother's famous bread pudding topped with rich, velvety bourbon sauce. Her mouth watered as she talked about the food, even though she was still full from lunch.

Giselle took the elevator up to her floor and walked to her unit. She stood outside the door for a few seconds and took three deep breaths, in through her nose and out through her mouth. Her body relaxed. She opened the door and stepped into her apartment. It was home. She was not in a small, stuffy room, held against her will; she was in the safety of her own home, free to come and go as she pleased.

Giselle walked into the kitchen, where the smell of bacon grease lingered from breakfast. She smelled the fruits in the fruit basket. She chose an apple and bit into it, the sweet, slightly tangy juices squirting into her mouth. She walked through every room of her apartment, using her senses. The faux fur throw on her bed was so soft, and she gently rubbed it against her cheek, repeating to herself, "I am home. I am safe."

Giselle decided to take an early shower. She allowed the warm water to run over her body from the crown of her head and imagined it washing away her hurts and her fears, her sorrows and her pain. She decided that for the rest of the day, she would reflect and journal.

She slipped into her pajamas and found a comfortable position on the couch. Her last journal entry was four months ago, reminding her how she had been inconsistent with her journaling.

Giselle examined the homework assignment Dr. Redd had given her. She took a deep breath and started writing.

July 24

What am I grateful for today?
I'm grateful that my friends and I are alive and safely back home. I'm grateful for our friendship and the genuine love and strong bond that we share. I'm grateful for my family and their love and support. I'm grateful for Dr. Redd, who has been a rock in my life and in my healing journey. I'm grateful for my job, which allows me to do good in the world by bringing justice to victims and families. I'm grateful that I have a roof over my head and food in my fridge. I'm grateful that I have my physical health, and I'm grateful for the positive changes that I will continue to make with my mental health. I'm grateful

for the warm water that cleansed my body. I'm grateful for life and all the wonderful things it has to offer.

What have I learned from my experience?

I have learned that I'm a strong and resilient person. Like grapes being crushed, I will emerge as fine wine. Like carbon deposits deep in the earth, subjected to extreme pressures and temperature, I will emerge a diamond. Through my strength, I can still be vulnerable. I will live I am living an authentic life; being authentic is powerful.

There are bad people in this world, but there are also a lot of good people. It is important to be cautious but not live in fear.

My failures are not failures, but lessons learned. They are opportunities to do better the next time. God, help me to find the lessons in my negative experiences. Help me to transform my negative experiences into something positive and use them to better my life and help others.

I'm a responsible person. I'm a dependable person. I'm a good friend. I'm a loving and caring person, but I can't be everything to everyone. I'm not responsible for others' thoughts, feelings, and actions. I'm only responsible for my thoughts, my feelings, and my actions.

What am I looking forward to in the future?

I'm looking forward to living my life uninhibited by doubts and fears. I'm looking forward to exploring new hobbies and passions. I'm looking forward to my mother's visit and her famous gumbo. I'm looking forward to my Pilates class on Saturday. I'm looking forward to hearing Kate's speech at the End Human Trafficking luncheon. I'm looking forward to wearing my new Coach boots in the fall. I'm excited to be working toward being the best version of myself.

Giselle paused for a moment. *What biblical verses can I memorize?* She performed an internet search for biblical quotes.

1 Peter 5:7
Cast all your anxiety on him because he cares for you.

Psalm 56:3
When I am afraid, I put my trust in you.

25 Days Later

CHAPTER 37

It was the morning of the End Human Trafficking luncheon, and Kate had her speech in her hand. She was nervous and pacing in the bathroom next to the banquet hall. Giselle and Valerie tried to calm her fears.

"Kate. You'll do great," Giselle said with an encouraging smile. She held Kate's hands, which were a little sweaty. "Take a slow deep breath in and out."

Kate followed the instructions and took slow, deep breaths. She felt her heart slow down. It no longer felt as though it would beat out of her chest.

"Now speak from your heart," Giselle continued. "You got this."

"You got this, Kate," Valerie concurred. "Giselle and I are here for you. Look at us if you get nervous. Pretend that you're speaking to your girlfriends."

"Okay, I got this," Kate replied. "I'm not doing this for myself. I'm doing this to help others."

"That's the spirit," Giselle said with a big smile. "Now let's head in. It'll be starting soon."

The banquet hall was quite large, and circular tables, covered with white tablecloths, were equally spaced throughout the room. The centerpieces were an arrangement of white and pink carnations. Each seating had a booklet that not only detailed the sequence of the event but also had pictures of victims, who were now survivors, and their stories. At the front of the room was a long, rectangular table to seat the host and the guest speakers. The mayor and the deputy mayor were also in attendance.

Kate took her seat up front at the rectangular table, two seats down from the mayor. Giselle and Valerie were seated at one of the circular tables in the front of the room. The luncheon was well attended, and the event was being video recorded. There were three videographers stationed, one in the back and one on the far left and far right of the room. A photographer walked among the tables taking snapshots.

"We'll be starting in five minutes," the director of the organization stated through the microphone. "Could everyone please take their seats?"

The director allowed some time for everyone to get situated. He began, "Ladies and gentlemen, good afternoon. I would like to welcome you all to our first annual fundraiser luncheon, dedicated to raising awareness and stopping human trafficking. It has been my honor to serve as the director of this organization for almost two years, working with other organizations and police forces to end human trafficking. All proceeds from this fundraiser will be used to fight human trafficking. Listed in your booklet on page five specifies how the donations will be used."

The director looked at the panel of guest speakers at the table. "It is my honor to introduce the mayor and deputy mayor of our great New York City." The audience cheered and gave the government officials a standing ovation. "The mayor has pledged that his office will work tirelessly with organizations to end human trafficking." Another roaring round of applause ensued. "We have an influential guest panel here today, all of whom have been instrumental in some way in fighting this cancer in society. We have a special guest with us, whom you all may be familiar with from watching the news. Kate Davenport had the horrid reality of experiencing human trafficking firsthand. She is a survivor, and she's here to tell her story." The audience again gave a standing ovation with resounding applause. The mayor also stood, facing Kate with a smile, and clapped with enthusiasm.

The director introduced all of the other guests on the panel and listed their credentials. "So without further ado, I would like to introduce again our first speaker, Kate Davenport." The audience and those on the panel clapped as Kate made her way to the podium.

Kate took a deep breath and smiled. She saw Giselle and Valerie in the audience, each giving her an encouraging smile. Valerie mouthed the words, "You got this."

"Ladies and gentlemen, good afternoon. My name is Kate Davenport, and I'm a survivor of human trafficking. It is my honor today to be your guest speaker. It is a privilege to be a voice for those who do not have a voice, and for that, I embark on this journey with great responsibility. The sad and unfortunate truth is that every year, there are millions of children, women, and even men who are trafficked worldwide, whether to engage in labor or sex acts. Human trafficking does not discriminate. Victims come from every walk of life. All races, age groups, and nationalities can be affected by this tragic humanitarian crisis. I never thought that I would be a victim. Honestly, it was never something that crossed my mind. Human trafficking seemed like another world that was separate from my life. Never in a million years would I have imagined standing in front of you all today, giving a speech about my experience as a victim of human trafficking. But the reality is that I was brought into that world unknowingly, uncon-scionably, and unscrupulously. My basic rights as a human being were stripped from me."

Giselle looked at Kate with admiration as she was delivering her speech. Kate had delved into detail about her experience of being captured and forced into modern-day slavery. The nervous Kate who was fidgeting and pacing the bathroom floor less than an hour ago was gone. She appeared brave and self-assured. Giselle was proud of her friend and proud of what she was doing. The Kate who had gone on the trip to Greece came back with purpose. She looked around, and everyone appeared engaged.

"Although this was a tragedy, I'm going to channel this into a purpose. I am dedicated to fight human trafficking, and each and every one of you can play a role too. It's important to be able to identify the signs. Not all victims are kept hidden behind closed doors. Sometimes victims may be hidden in plain sight, but they are afraid to reach out for help due to threats of harm to themselves by their captors or threats toward their family members. It may even be a threat of deportation for those who are undocumented. There are millions driven into forced labor. From the outside, it may appear to be a normal job, but in fact, the individual may have been forced into labor with threats of violence. Many of these individuals are lured as they try to escape poverty, support their families, or simply try to find a better life, but instead, they are taken advantage of and abused. Others are essentially kidnapped, solely for the purpose of personal and commercial gain. Like myself, I was living my life, oblivious to the world of human trafficking, when unexpectedly, I was kidnapped and forced into a life of modern-day slavery. In a mere matter of moments, my life drastically changed. The life I once knew was a memory, and my rights as a human being were stripped away. I know the intense pain of physical, emotional, mental and sexual abuse. I know the pain of being controlled and held against my will, the worth of being a human being taken away from me. I know the pain of feeling hopeless and feeling forgotten. I reached such a dark emotional state that I felt that no one cared. I felt like the world was moving along as usual, and I was no longer a thought. The sun rose and set to start another day. Those who knew me would have thought that I was dead and moved on with their lives. Sometimes, I thought that that would have been best, if my eyes never opened again to see the dawn of a new day and those who knew me would move on with their lives. After all, I had convinced myself that my life had no worth. The one time I was able to walk out of the walls of my confinement, though for a short period of time, I was terrified of seeking help out of immense fear. My captor was a powerful man, a well-known man. He was well aware of the enormous power and control that he had over me, and he knew I was not going anywhere. I thought that if I somehow manifested the courage to escape, where would I go? What would happen to me if I were recaptured? Surely intense harm or even death."

"With that being said, I want to thank my dear friends for holding out hope and never giving up on me. I wouldn't be standing here today without their dedication, perseverance, and determination. I would like to take a moment to acknowledge Giselle Bellamy and Valerie Brooks, my dearest friends, my sisters. Giselle and Valerie, could you please stand?"

Giselle and Valerie stood, and they were greeted with loud, deafening applause. The cameras were focused on them. Two attendees at their table stood, and others followed suit until the entire room gave them a standing ovation, even the mayor. Giselle and Valerie sat, and the thundering applause settled and ceased. The attendees took their seats.

Kate continued, "They kept hope when I lost hope. They continued to fight when I had lost every bit of fight in me. They kept the light shining when all around me was dim. To you both, I am thankful and eternally grateful."

Short applause ensued.

"I speak to you today as a person who has been forever changed by this experience. Although the darkness had surrounded me, there is light. There is hope. And that's why it is important for us all to help shine a light on this depravity and give hope to those who have lost hope. Every human life has worth. It does not matter your race, your ethnicity, your gender, your faith, your sexual orientation, what you look like, what disabilities you may have, or any stigma that society has placed on you. Every human life is important, and every human life has worth. Everyone deserves to be treated with respect."

Giselle looked at her friend at the podium and beamed with pride. Although Kate would be considered an extrovert, she always shied away from public speaking, and there she was, commanding the attention of the audience with such eloquence, confidence, and grace. She listened intently and hung onto every word from Kate's mouth.

"It's important for us to familiarize ourselves with signs of physical, mental, and emotional abuse. In your booklet, I've put together red flags that may indicate that someone is being abused. I've also put together some example questions you can ask if you are able to speak privately to a potential victim without putting them in harm's way. If you trust that you've identified a person being trafficked, it's imperative that you alert law enforcement immediately. You can contact 911 in emergency situations. You can also contact the National Human Trafficking Hotline. I've also provided that number in your booklet.

"There are other ways that we can get involved. I have included the Bureau of International Labor Affairs website. Their mission is to strengthen global labor standards, enforce labor commitments among trading partners, promote racial and gender equity, and combat international child labor, forced labor, and human trafficking.

"Again, I would like to thank each and every one of you for allowing me this privilege to speak to you. I have dedicated myself to being a voice to those who do not have a voice and to fight and protect the liberties of others. We all possess the power to make this world a better and safer place; a more just and fairer place, a place where everyone belongs. Thank you again for allowing me to speak at this event, and thank you for this immense privilege. May God bless you all."

Those in the room again stood and erupted in resounding applause.

ABOUT THE
AUTHOR

Juelle Christie is the author of *The Obscure Truth*, the prequel to *Aegean Fate*. She is a board certified Internist, working in hospital medicine. Her profound love for writing led her to explore other passions outside of medicine. She is fond of suspense thrillers that generate excitement and take the reader on an adventure. Dr. Juelle Christie enjoys traveling, and gradually, she is checking off countries off her bucket list. She resides in metro Atlanta.

CPSIA information can be obtained
at www.ICGtesting.com
Printed in the USA
BVHW042137240323
661143BV00005B/114